From the Land of Fear

---

11 side trips to the dark edge of imagination

BOOKS BY HARLAN ELLISON

NOVELS

The Sound of a Scythe [1960]
Web of the City [1958]
Spider Kiss [1961]

SHORT NOVELS

Doomsman [1967]
Run for the Stars [1991]
All the Lies That Are My Life [1980]
Mefisto in Onyx [1993]

GRAPHIC NOVELS

Demon with a Glass Hand
(adaptation with Marshall Rogers) [1986]
Night and the Enemy
(adaptation with Ken Steacy) [1987]
Vic and Blood:
The Chronicles of a Boy and His Dog
(adaptation with Richard Corben) [1989]
Harlan Ellison's Dream Corridor [1996]
Vic and Blood: The Continuing
Adventures of a Boy and His Dog
(adaptation with Richard Corben) [2003]
Harlan Ellison's Dream
Corridor Volume Two [2007]

SHORT STORY COLLECTIONS

The Deadly Streets [1958]
Sex Gang (as Paul Merchant) [1959]
A Touch of Infinity [1960]
Children of the Streets [1961]
Gentleman Junkie and Other Stories
of the Hung-Up Generation [1961]
Ellison Wonderland [1962]
Paingod and Other Delusions [1965]
I Have No Mouth & I
Must Scream [1967]
From the Land of Fear [1967]
Love Ain't Nothing But
Sex Misspelled [1968]
The Beast That Shouted Love at
the Heart of the World [1969]
Over the Edge [1970]
De Helden Van De Highway
(Dutch publication only) [1973]
All the Sounds of Fear
(British publication only) [1973]
The Time of the Eye
(British publication only) [1974]
Approaching Oblivion [1974]
Deathbird Stories [1975]
No Doors, No Windows [1975]
Hoe Kan Ik Schreeuwen
Zonder Mond
(Dutch publication only) [1977]
Strange Wine [1978]
Shatterday [1980]
Stalking the Nightmare [1982]
Angry Candy [1988]
Ensamvärk
(Swedish publication only) [1992]
Jokes Without Punchlines [1995]
Bce 3bykn Ctpaxa (All
Fearful Sounds)
(unauthorized Russian publication only) [1997]
The Worlds of Harlan Ellison
(authorized Russian publication only) [1997]
Slippage [1997]
Koletis, Kes Kuulutas
Armastust Maalima Siidames
(Estonian publication only) [1999]
La Machine aux Yeux Bleus
(French publication only) [2001]
Troublemakers [2001]
Ptak Smierci (The Best
of Harlan Ellison)
(Polish publication only) [2003]

OMNIBUS VOLUMES

The Fantasies of Harlan Ellison [1979]
Dreams with Sharp Teeth [1991]

COLLABORATIONS

Partners in Wonder: Collaborations
with 14 Other Wild Talents [1971]
The Starlost: Phoenix Without Ashes
(with Edward Bryant) [1975]
Mind Fields: 33 Stories inspired
by the art of Jacek Yerka [1994]
I Have No Mouth, and
I Must Scream:
The Interactive CD-ROM
(co-designed with David Mullich
and David Sears) [1995]
2000ˣ
(host and creative consultant of National
Public Radio episodic series) [2000-2001]

NON-FICTION & ESSAYS

Memos from Purgatory [1961]
The Glass Teat: Essays of
Opinion on Television [1970]
The Other Glass Teat: Further Essays
of Opinion on Television [1975]
The Book of Ellison
(edited by Andrew Porter) [1978]
Sleepless Nights in the
Procrustean Bed Essays
(edited by Marty Clark) [1984]
An Edge in My Voice [1985]
Harlan Ellison's Watching [1989]
The Harlan Ellison Hornbook [1990]

SCREENPLAYS, ETC

The Illustrated Harlan Ellison
(edited by Byron Preiss) [1978]
Harlan Ellison's Movie [1990]
I, Robot: The Illustrated Screenplay
(based on Isaac Asimov's story-
cycle) [1994, 2004]
The City on the Edge of Forever [1996]
"Repent, Harlequin!" Said
the Ticktockman
(rendered with paintings by Rick Berry) [1996]

RETROSPECTIVES

Alone Again Tomorrow:
A 10-year Survey [1971]
The Essential Ellison:
A 35-year Retrospective [1987]
(edited by Terry Dowling with
Richard Delap and Gil Lamont)
The Essential Ellison:
A 50-year Retrospective [2001]
(edited by Terry Dowling)

AS EDITOR

Dangerous Visions [1967]
Dangerous Visions:
35th Anniversary Edition [2002]
Nightshade & Damnations:
The Finest Stories of
Gerald Kersh [1968]
Again, Dangerous Visions [1975]
Medea: Harlan's World [1985]
Jacques Futrelle's "The Thinking
Machine" Stories [2003]

THE HARLAN ELLISON
DISCOVERY SERIES

Stormtrack by James Sutherland [1975]
Autumn Angels by Arthur Byron Cover [1975]
The Light at the End of the
Universe by Terry Carr [1976]
Islands by Marta Randall [1976]
Involution Ocean by Bruce Sterling [1978]

THE WHITE WOLF SERIES

Edgeworks.1 [1996]
Edgeworks.2 [1996]
Edgeworks.3 [1997]
Edgeworks.4 [1997]

From the Land of Fear

*11 side trips to the dark
edge of imagination*

by Harlan Ellison®

an EDGEWORKS A B B E Y offering

in association with

E-Reads®

FROM THE LAND OF FEAR
11 side trips to the dark edge of imagination
Is an Edgeworks Abbey® Offering in association with E-Reads. Published
by arrangement with the Author and The Kilimanjaro Corporation.

First E-Reads publication 2009
www.ereads.com
Harlan Ellison website: www.harlanellison.com

Contents

Foreword

In Praise of His Spirits Noble and Otherwise

*Here sighs, plaints, and deep wailings resounded
through the starless air: it made me weep at
first.*
*Strange tongues, horrible outcries, words of
pain, tones of anger, voices deep and hoarse,
and sounds of hands amongst them,*
*made a tumult, which turns itself unceasing in
that air for ever dyed, as sand when it eddies in
a whirlwind.*
Inferno (Canto III, 22—31)

PREAMBLE

Harlan Ellison wrote the stories in this book, and they come
from all over that strange thing we call a writing career. When
a man is a writer and writing means as much to him as it does
to some of us, his career and his life are pretty much inseparable
things. He is what he is because of everything he's been up until
the Now that equals the current Is, and the writing is an integral
part of the Now of its composition and the Is of that time's being
for him. I don't know how else to put it without breeding a
Sudden Metaphysic.

Now, many of these stories come from Nows long gone by and
from many an Is which has since become a Was.

In other words, they're from all over that thing we call a

writing career, and because of this they differ from one another—
which is a good thing indeed for those of us who would, in a way,
observe a pilgrim in his progress. They differ, because of a thing
called growth.

About growth: It means getting bigger, one way or another.
Now forget essential biology and switch to the psyche: The
voice you will hear in such things as *Battle Without Banners*
is the voice of a bigger man than *Time of the Eye*. Why? That
man knows more because he's lived more, is more. What's why.
And growth operates on many levels: One, of course, is that of
technical competence. Another, and I think more important one,
is insight/outsight/hindsight/foresight. This capacity increases
as one gets bigger. What would Thomas Mann or Hokusai be
like if they'd lived to be a hundred and fifty and remained
in full possession of this capacity? I wish I knew. I love them
both. After reading Harlan's Introduction to this volume, I hope
that he makes it at least that far, for he made a promise in there,
knowing it or no, and he's a man who keeps his promises.

Harlan is around my age, and he was born in Painesville,
Ohio, like twenty-five miles east of Euclid, Ohio, which is where
I'm from, and we grew up that close to one another without ever
running into each other and saying, "Hi! You want to write, too!
Huh?" I wish I had known him in those early and, I suppose
the word is "formative," days. I wish I had known him then,
because I like him now.

Harlan, I am happy to say, is a man free of influences. He
is his own man, come hell or high water, and that's one of the
things I love about him. He will freely acknowledge a debt to
such an humane and exceedingly capable writer as Lester del
Rey—but this will be in the way of a journeyman's compliment
to the man who taught him how to use certain tools, because
he and Lester del Rey really have very little in common in the
way of style and thematic materials. Harlan is eclectic when it
comes to subject matter, autodidactic when it comes to what he
knows, offensively personal (in a military, not pejorative, sense)
when it comes to telling you about it and, to use a Henry James
term because it applies here, he is possessed of his own "angle
of vision." Whatever he sees, *he* sees. It is never anybody else's

borrowed view of the subject that informs his materials. He is his own camera. Period.

And in all these respects, he has grown, is growing, will—I feel—continue to grow, because he's got something inside him that won't let him rest until he says what he must, at any given moment, say.

Okay, so much for uniqueness. I call him unique and I mean to honor him by it.

End of Preamble

BEGINNING OF AMBLE

What does it take to be a writer and why? The quotation from Dante which I stuck at the head of this piece contains the answer. There are these sounds, this tumult, turning in that air for ever dyed, eddying in a neat simile and beginning with that all important word "Here." Everybody hears the sounds, some people listen and a writer, for some damfool reason, wants to put them down on paper and talk about them—here, right now. So that's the answer to the question: "Some damfool reason." It's why Dante wrote, too. My damfool thing, the thing inside me that makes me say what I have to say, is a thing that I don't understand at all, and sometimes I curse it because it keeps me awake at night. So I can't tell you what Harlan's is, but go look at those nine lines of Dante's once more.

They're filled with spirits making the kinds of sounds you will hear in this book. That's why I put them there. Harlan writes about sighs, plaints, deep wailings, strange tongues, horrible outcries, words of pain, tones of anger, voices deep and hoarse and the sounds of hands moving to do many things. It's been around four years since I last read the *Inferno*, but when I sat down to write this piece, those lines suddenly came into my head. Because of the fact that I trust my personal demon when it comes to matters such as this, they're valid.

Listen to the sigh in *My Brother Paulie*, just there at the end, the plaint in *A Friend to Man*, the deep wailings in *Battle Without Banners*, the strange tongues in *Life Hutch*, the horrible outcry of "*We Mourn For Anyone...*", the words of pain in *Time of the Eye*, the tones of anger in *Back to the Drawing Boards* and the voices deep and hoarse in *The Sky Is Burning.* And there are hands moving everywhere, slapping, poking, gesturing hands.

I think Harlan Ellison is a pilgrim, and in this book we have a chance to observe his progress. These stories are culled from Nows as far back as 1957 and as current as Our Now, ten years later. What does it take to be a writer and why? Maybe a pilgrim instinct, a thing akin to the sentiments of all those dead lemmings, is a part of it. Any writer from Daphne Du Maurier to Joseph Heller is an idealist. Idealists are always turned-on and hung-up, and if they write, they turn themselves on, wring themselves out, and hang themselves up to dry where everybody can see. I suspect Harlan is a naked pilgrim. He's always turning on, wringing out and hanging up in public, sans clothing. He is a wise guy who insists on telling you the whole story. So, okay. The form he will insist on exhibiting is always interesting. You may disagree like all hell with him, but as with Jacob's Angel, you'll know you've been in a fight. He's that kind of writer. He's busy surviving, so if you get a knee below the belt—well then, the pilgrim profession is kind of rough. That pacifist he thinks he might be is quite willing to rabbit punch you to get his point across. I don't see any contradiction in that. I won't hit you with a word like *enantiadromia*, but I will suggest the anecdote of the old Bishop who had taken a vow not to draw blood and so rode off to the Crusades bearing a *smooth* mace.

End of Amble

BEGINNING OF SPRINT

The Circle is drawn, the words will now be spoken and the spirits will then appear, one by one, from out That Dark Land. It remains only for you to learn where some dreams stray and the ones that didn't will pass then before you. Be prepared. Be Prepared. Here's Harlan.

End of Sprint

BEGINNING OF FLIGHT

FASTEN YOUR SEAT BELTS PLEASE
Roger Zelazny
Baltimore, Md.

Introduction

Where the Stray Dreams Go

Andy Porter put together this special issue of his science fiction fan magazine *Algol*, and he called it the "Ellish," which meant it had a transcribed and edited version of a speech I'd made at a convention, and half a dozen articles by and about me. I can't deny I was flattered and even a little embarrassed by the honor. Particularly by the articles Andy had commissioned to be written by Ted White and Lee Hoffman and Robert Silverberg, three friends who have known me both wearily and well for many years. They had remembered things I'd done and things I'd said and places I'd been that I had long since forgotten. And their views of me were more honest than I'd care to admit.

Silverbob, in particular, reminisced about an incident that took place in 1953 in Philadelphia. He recalled the episode in which three rather heavy lads braced me, for some now forgotten insult I'd leveled at one of them. Bob wrote:

> *"Any sensible man would have disappeared at once, or at least yelled for the nearest bell-hop to stop the slaughter. But Harlan stood his ground, snarled back at Semenovich nose-to-nose, and avoided mayhem through a display of sheer bravado. Which demonstrated one Ellison trait: physical courage to the verge of idiocy. Unlike many tough-talking types, Harlan is genuinely fearless."*

Courage, to me, is one of those dormant qualities one never

knows one possesses until the pressure is applied. I have known many television producers, for instance, with weighty claims to courage who, when the screws were put on them by networks or studios, folded instantly. The one time I made an idol of someone—a man who professed to being a pillar of courage—he turned out to be as weak as any other man, when the pressure was laid on him. (More the fool me, for having demanded anything more of him, or of anyone, than that they be merely human, with all the attendant foibles and feet of clay.) To be courageous when all that is at stake is talk—parlor liberals take note—or a few dollars, is not to be courageous at all. Hemingway, I suppose, knew where it was at. He was never satisfied with the shape and substance of the courage he found within himself. He continually tested it, setting himself in positions of untenability and danger, merely to find out if the courage was still with him, if it still seemed adequate for the life he was compelled to support. I am for larger and more frequent tests of courage.

Not until I was boxed in totally, in situations where there were no other exits than through the mouth of danger with courage the only weapon, did I satisfy myself that I did, indeed, possess what Silverberg calls "courage to the verge of idiocy."

Bob has told of one such instance.

Avram Davidson may recall yet another.

Gay Talese reported on a third.

And so I find at thirty-three, that fear and I mix as well as oil and water. It is not that I am fearless, it is simply that there is nothing I fear. (Let me correct that: I am petrified of wearing contact lenses. My brother-in-law Jerry attempted once, to get me to wear contacts, and when the oculist set a test glass in my eye, the hair went straight up on my head, I wet my pants, the blood drained out of my face, and I was covered with sweat till he got it out Ridiculing myself for this adolescent behavior, I demanded the oculist try again. He was reluctant, but I insisted. It was worse the second time. I still wear my glasses on the front of my head, and I can say with great certainty that I am afraid of things being put into my eyes.)

Yet I do not fear lizards, or drowning, or dark rooms, or rats, or high places, or death, or poverty, or needles, or deep personal involvements, or the wrath of the gods. I choose not to think of this as something deserving of applause. There is no control over it—just as there is no control on my part of an absence of a time sense [see *"Repent, Harlequin!" Said the Ticktockman*]—and so it is as lofty an ability as a good bowel movement. Reflex action (Audie Murphy notwithstanding) is not deserving of the Congressional Medal of Honor.

Ah, but there *is* a fear I fear. A major fear, and one that propels me like a 30.06 slug through life.

I am desperately afraid I will die before I've written all the stories I have in me.

Self-analysis grows chancy, but each man decides at various times in his life who he is, where he's going, what he stands for. Perhaps not in so many words, but in a kind of subconscious codification that enables him to stop the action at any given point and say, "This is good, this is evil; this is right, this is wrong." We call it a sense of morality or ethic. We call it a conscience. We call it maturity or a relation to the universe. But whatever it is—even if it goes by the name of love—it helps a man know what his potentialities may be.

For some time now I have been agonizingly aware that I am a talent of considerable dimensions encased in a man of very limited possibilities. The talent that is Me and the Man that is Harlan Ellison are two very separate and distinct entities. That the Man lugs around the Talent becomes at once a blessing and a curse. Consider: a woman may find me inordinately involving, and an affair begins. Through it all, through all its stately progressions, I wonder: *is it me or is it the talent she is in love with?*

Why must it be me, this puny Ellison, that has to carry the Talent like Quasimodo's hump? Why cannot this Talent be deposited within, say, Cary Grant or Kirk Douglas or even something that looks like Doug McClure. They're beautiful people, they wouldn't have to be jealous of the Talent. Why must it be me that wakes in the early morning because the ideas are fermenting, bubbling up in the mental mire? Why must it be me that has to write television to support the needs of a body that demands comfort and luxury; if it were Steve McQueen, he could write only the great ones, and not have to do the slavey labor.

And because of this jealousy, this rivalry between the Talent that need prove nothing to anyone—and the body that is Harlan Ellison that must prove itself over and over again, the treacherous fifth columnist of the body keeps putting the Talent in jeopardy: risking its neck, taking dangerous stands, getting involved in relationships that promise nothing but flameout, stretching the abilities to the breaking point.

Thus, all the "harlan ellison stories" that are told, all the weird anecdotes, they are the cartoon capers of the pack mule, braying for attention, while the stories merely exist, without side comment or need for defense. They speak for themselves. They are complete and whole and self-contained.

And thus, again, the body that seeks to prove its worth entirely independent of the Talent, is forced to live with the fear. By subjecting the Talent to unnecessary risks, it brings down upon its head the torment and terror of the one big fear: that the body of Harlan Ellison will succeed in destroying itself before the Talent of Harlan Ellison gets said all it has to say.

For the first time I'm beginning to think Geminis may be schizoid, after all.

So...

To get it all said. To wind out all the stories on silver threads. To relate all the relationships of all the people, each with its own tiny death interwoven with the comedy and shadows. So many stories. They now total over six hundred, not counting the novels.

But what of the ones started, and never completed? All the false starts? All the bits and pieces that began well and toured midway through? What of the night flashes that woke me from sleep and toward which I crawled on hands and knees, to the typewriter near the bed, so nothing escapes, even in half-sleep? What of those? What of the vagrant thoughts, the stray dreams, the incomplete fractions of ideas?

Silverbob's reminiscences of me and my courage, and my subsequent analysis of it all—as set down here rather nakedly, I'm ashamed to say—set me to rummaging through the "idea file" I keep, that I suppose *all* writers keep. And I came up with snippets I knew instinctively I would *never ever* manage to get into stories. And I was afraid.

Afraid they would die.

Even as bad stories die.

But at least they deserve a *chance* to live, these stray dreams. So, with your permission, let me offer a few of the ones that seem good even after the long periods since they were written. And if any of them touch you, if any of them seem worthy, perhaps you might drop me a line and let me know, and it might stir me to take them up again, and order the bones and flesh onto them, making stories of them. And if only one or two come from it, then you will have been an important part of the creative act, and we will both be richer for it.

The / One / Word / People

There are some that can be met, strange and twisted ones you know by an aura, a scent, a feel *about them, that if you had one* single word—*like "junkie" or "nympho" or "hooker" or "Bircher"—a key word that labeled their secret bit, you would understand all the inexplicable, off center things about them. Like the girl you meet, and start to date, who can't see you on Thursday nights, but makes weak excuses as to where she goes on Thursday nights. If you had the word "diabetic" you would understand that every Thursday her doctor's appointment keeps her out of circulation, and that's why she doesn't drink, and spends long minutes in bathrooms, shooting insulin. But she's ashamed—don't ask why, people do kookie things—so she just has that one soft foggy spot in her reality, and you wonder what the hell the story is.*

Or your friend who picks fights with Italians, and aside from not telling you what his real name is, couldn't be a better drinking buddy. If you had the word "deportee" you'd understand that he was picked up for anarchist reasons in Italy, and deported, and is in the country illegally.

It's like that. The one word people. One word, and you've got the handle on them, the motivater of this existence.

"Adolescent," "Puritan," "passing," "wino"—they all do it. Granted, it's a dubious sort of categorization...still, it works. And like the old wives poultice of spiderwebs that was laughed at, as a remedy for bruises, cuts and the removal of a mouse under the eye, when a recent medical breakthrough found a cure for these containing many chemical elements found in spiderwebs, it must be concluded that in the final analysis, what works...works.

Bringing me to Nicole Shahin.

Pronounced Shane.
And she's the fastest gun in the East.
Have to be. Shot me down and I didn't even see her draw.

Moth on the Moon

Streiter got so pissed-off arguing, he gave me a shove.

"One more of those, you ignoramus, and I'll put you in the infirmary," I said. It embarrassed me: every time I got in a beef, my voice automatically dropped three octaves. It was my "B" movie villain voice.

The Unit watch-on-duty got between us. A medium-sized apple, neither of us would poke him, he'd crumble like a lunar frog's dust dream. A big ugly piece of furniture like Streiter, a berserker like me when I got hot.

"Come on, back off, both of you!" He pushed us away from the common center, himself. There was enough leverage. I hit one side of the bubble, Streiter the other. Cramped quarters on the Moon can do it, drive you up the curve of the bubble every time.

"I'm tired of him copping out for every mistake he makes," Streiter snarled. "And then dreaming up elves and gnomes to take the blame!"

"Don't blame me for your lack of imagination."

"Moth! You're fulla *shit*, friend!"

"Is Shed number three gone, or isn't it?"

"Yeah...gone, so what! How'd you screw it up. C'mon, it must have been a helluva sweet move to completely destroy a three ton storage shed...what's your story?"

"It was a moth."

Streiter growled and came for me again. The WOD headed him off at the pass between the compUvac and the feeder, and threatened him with the cooler, so he simmered down.

"Now *that* one takes the prize," Streiter rolled his eyes. "A moth, a goddam *moth*, for chrissakes, on the *moon!*"

"Is the shed gone?" I asked, quietly, rationally.

"Yeah, the shed is gone."

"It was a moth. It came swooping down, and chewed it up, the entire shed."

"Oh, Christ, I give up!"

Streiter turned and stumped out of the control bubble. The WOD stared at me a minute. His eyebrows quivered. "Terry," he said, softly, "report to the medic in twenty minutes. I'll get a relief for you."

He left, and I stared out at the lunar surface for a long time. Twenty minutes can be a long time.

It was a moth, dammit!

"They're the Blinds," he said, softly.

"They were created out of an experiment with self-regenerating cell tissue. They lie flaccid and dormant, just flaps of flesh, without eyes or sense organs or souls, until a thought passes them by. Then they fasten on it, litterally pull themselves hand-over-hand up that thought..."

The old Indian rope trick, *Wyckoff thought picturesquely.*

"...until they've established a form for themselves. They have only one drive; survival. *They'll do anything to keep living, such life as it may be. They'll take any form, anything at all—a man, a cockroach, a gull in the sky, anything that has the faintest tinge of thought in it, even a witless thing like a paramecium—and they build from that. But they'll do anything to stay alive."*

"The Blinds," repeated Wyckoff.

"Yes, that's right," the little fat man nodded.

He was perspiring.

"You dirty little weasel," Wyckoff said quietly. "It's both refreshing and discouraging to find out that cowardice hasn't been bred out in this future you're from."

"Why, I—"

"You eat worms! Shut up. Let me think, crud."

Speechless, we stand before Van Gogh's "Starry Night" or

one of the hell images of Bosch, and we find our senses reeling; vanishing into a daydream mist of *what must this man have been like, what must he have suffered*? A passage from Dylan Thomas, about birds singing in the eaves of a lunatic asylum, draws us up short, steals the breath from our mouths and the blood and thoughts stand still in the body as we are confronted with the absolute incredible achievement of what he has done. So imperfect, so faulty, so broken the links in communication between humans, that to pass along one corner of a vision we have had to another creature is an accomplishment that fills us with wonder and pride. How staggering is it then, to *see*, to *know* what Bosch and Van Gogh and Thomas knew and saw. To live for a microsecond what they lived. To look out of their eyes and view the universe from a new angle. This, then is the temporary, fleeting, transient, incredibly valuable priceless gift from the genius to those of us crawling forward moment after moment in time, with nothing to break our routine but death.

How amazed, how stopped like a broken clock we are, when we are in the presence of the genius. When we see what his incredible talents—wrought out of torment—have created; what magnificence, or depravity, or beauty, perhaps in a spare moment, only half-trying; he has brought it forth for the rest of eternity and the world to treasure.

And how awed we are, when caught surprised in the golden web of true genius—so that finally, for the first time we know that all the rest of it was *kitsch*; it is made so terribly, crushingly obvious to us, just how mere, how petty, how mud-condemned we are, and that the only grandeur we will ever know is that which we know second hand from our geniuses. That the closest we will come to our "Heaven," while alive, is through our unfathomable geniuses, however imperfect or bizarre they may be.

And is this, then, why we treat them so shamefully, harm them, drive them inexorably to their personal madhouses, kill them?

Who is it, we wonder, who *really* still the golden voices of the geniuses, who turn their visions to dust?

Who, the question asks itself, unbidden, are the savages and who the princes?

Fortunately, the night comes quickly, and answers can be avoided till the next time, and till the next marvelous singer of strange songs is stilled in the agonies of his rhapsodies.

Snake in the Mind

Shadows lived in that house. A heavy, somnolent madness that pressed against the inner walls and made the very glass of the dark windows bulge outward as though bloated. Carrie had warned me there was a slithering horror in the place, even before either of us had known for certain I would be coming to town, but I had snickered at her, and rummaging on the bookshelves of my own jolly pad in Los Angeles, had tossed the copy of Shirley Jackson's The Haunting of Hill House *at her.*

"Jackson already wrote it up, Punkin'," I laughed. "If you were living in Transylvania or some dark corner of Brittany, I might buy it...but Brooklyn? Come on, kiddo!"

She'd smiled wanly, looking up at me from the sofa, and there had been a wispy, thin, almost timorous smile on her elf face. Brave, and quite frightened. "You'll see," was what she left me with.

And now, here I was in New York, and walking up the steps of the Romaine house in Flatbush (how ridiculous, what a sillyass place for weirdness, in the heart of comfortable mediocrity and middle-class lack of imagination); and I had to admit that what she had promised was true. The house was a typical no-style 1920's monstrosity, with front porch, attic windows and dormers at attention, glass-paneled front doors, mail slot silently pursed as though capable of secrets, if only it would speak.

But there was more: there was the filtered stink of dust long-since gone; of old clothes bundled together; of parchment-skinned hags dead in their apartments with old Life *and* Newsweek *stacks ceiling-high, and forty million dollars in small change under the floorboards; of velour drapes drawn against the sun; of heavy jungle or empty desert. Of non-place, of nontime, of aloneness.*

Poe and Hawthorne and Lovecraft tried to speak of the terrifying desolateness of moors or graveyards or empty stretches of the sea, but for sheer wanton loneliness, there is nothing like a Brooklyn street in late Fall, October, November, when the leaves mat like dark, coagulated blood in the gutters, and the chill wind spins down through the cross-streets, chasing the subway trains like hungry dogs after meat wagons. Empty, chill, helpless, it is the end of the universe, and anyone stupid enough to be caught away from a bubbling TV set or a good nineteen-broad orgy, deserves to stand out there and shiver. Not entirely from the cold.

So I walked up the steps, and turned the old-fashioned door chime in its metal frame, and heard the rasping ringaling of it far inside. The door burst open inward almost immediately, and Carrie, little gnome, was standing there in her Greenwich Village outfit, long hair brushed back in a single braid, her eyes alive, as though I'd come to save her: "Welcome to Dante's Inferno!" she murmured.

Rudy was a prelim fighter. One, two, a right cross just under the heart. The Mob kept him around for laughs, he was a gentle kid. Rudy did twenty-one years with the Mob. Since he'd been seventeen.

But when Rudy was thirty-eight, he was a little too old to be called the kid any more, and he wanted out of the Mob. Not for any specific reasons, there wasn't any heat going, but just because he felt restless, had the feeling there were other things to do.

Rudy had always heard it said: nobody leaves the Mob. Yet, surprisingly, there was no trouble when he told them he wanted out. Why not? He didn't have anything they wanted, or were afraid to turn loose of. Especially knowledge. Rudy had been a hitter, and what he knew was old and unimportant. So they gave a nice buncha twenties, smacked his back, and said so long, Rudy.

In this book everything has been invented except the truth. If there is no truth, there is no book. If there is no invention there is

*no book. Who can be offended by the truth? Who can be offended
by invention?*

                                           —JOHN BERRY
                                           prefatory note to
                                           "Krishna Fluting"

"My fingertips are covered with the scars of people I've touched.
The flesh remembers those touches. Sometimes I feel as though I
am wearing heavy woolen gloves, so thick are the memories of
all those touches. It seems to insulate me, to separate me from
mankind. I very often refrain from washing my hands for days
and days, just to preserve whatever layers of touches might be
washed away by the soap.

"Faces and voices and smells of people I've known have passed
away, but still my hands carry the records with them. Layer
after layer of the laying-on of hands. Is that altogether sane? I
don't know. I'll have to think about it for a very long time, when
I have the time.

"If I ever have the time."

*ACKNOWLEDGMENT: the concept embodied in T—'s speech,
page —, is not original.*

*Nor has it been plagiarized; rather, it is that peculiar melding
of originality and plagiarism that occurs, I am told, in all those
of an artistic bent. It was spurred to life by something someone
else had written. In this case, Salinger. I was reading* Raise High
the Roof Beam, Carpenters *and when I read across the line: "I
have scars on my hands from touching certain people," I stopped
dead, without going further, dashed into the next room and the
typewriter, and wrote T—'s speech, even before that section of the
novel had been drafted. It laid out for me a particularly important
facet of his character; a facet in fact, which planned a direction
I had only vaguely, till then, considered for the book. What that
speech did, in effect, was build the very cornerstone of my book, and
set my thoughts to considering depths I would not otherwise have
attempted in what was originally intended as a straight adventure
novel. When I went back, and found that Salinger had gone on to
say almost precisely what I had said, I felt awkward, small boy*

kicking turf, embarrassed. I have no doubt no one would consider that I had "borrowed" in writing that paragraph, for in the main, readers are barely aware of what a writer tries to do with his mechanics...but I would know there was a debt there, and so, this note. It would be safe to say, then, that this novel was strongly influenced by J.D. Salinger. Though I'm certain he would find such an idea presumptuous, it remains true, in a much murkier sense than merely his works triggering my thoughts. Those words opened doors my mind knew were there, but had never considered looking beyond. At least in this book. And in that degree, I feel Mr. Salinger has helped to make this a worthier effort. My thanks to him.

Harlan Ellison
Hollywood 1963

Pieces of things that will never be written. Where they came from I choose to remember, for the stimulus is often more memorable and important than the shabby fiction it produces. Where they reside, is here, for whatever pleasure or momentary empathy they may cause. Where they are going? Probably no further, for having been set down, they accomplish what they were intended for. A spark gap effect, a bridging of the mind through concepts. By imposing the necessary artificiality of plot and character on them, they become greater than themselves. They become stories.

Which ought to more than satisfactorily answer, for all time (at least as far as I am concerned) the question raised by drunkards and dilettantes at cocktail partties: "Where do you get your ideas?"

About the stories in this book. Each story has its own little prefatory note by the undersigned, but a few words before you attack them (and as a reviewer has noted, *they* attack *you*). For the most part these are old stories. I would not write them this way were I writing them today. Several of them I find painfully amateurish. Most of the stories were written in the late Fifties. When I was learning my craft. This is by way of explanation, not excuse. I still stand behind the stories, even though they were written by quite another Harlan Ellison—or series of Harlan Ellisons.

That they are once again in print is due not only to the Author's continuing need for money and ego-boosting, but to the requests of a large number of readers who have encountered the later works, and have made querulous noises about the ones that came before. Due also to the interest of Belmont's lovely editoress Gail Wendroff, who insisted on including four of the stories from my first collection, *A Touch of Infinity*, among these other, never-before-anthologized pieces. And to the urgings of my literary agent, Mr. Robert P. Mills, a man whose interest in my career has kept me, on numerous occasions, from throwing in the bloodied towel.

It has been a long way from courage and Andy Porter and Silverbob and raw strips of flesh that might (and may yet) some day be stories. A long way, and yet truly a hyperspace jump, for the journey is made through the mind of the creator, by way of lands without signposts; and if those lands *could* be named, if they were not the *Terra Incognita* in which this Author dwells much of the time, it might be seen by the light of revelation that they were Right Here, all the time.

You have been very kind, and I thank you.

HARLAN ELLISON
Hollywood, 1967

Several months ago I bought a pair of very handsome low-modern filing cabinets, in which to store my moldering manuscripts. Until that time, they had been dumped in piles in whatever handy drawer or closet I was not using for clothes or record albums or books. In filing the six hundred-odd manuscripts (with their attendant chipping and falling triangles of yellow-brown page edges—the man who invents a cheap yellow second sheet that doesn't turn doggie-poo brown within five minutes of exposure to the sun will win the undying thanks of professional writers the world over) I found stories I had not reread since I'd written them years before. A heart blow of nostalgia hit me (not to mention a stomach-punch of nausea) as I reread them, sitting there in my Alexander Shields bathrobe on the floor. Many of them were about how itsy-teeny we poor Humans are in the Universe. There was one in which all the saucers were coming here to use us for a parking lot in an overcrowded universe (titled "A Lot Of Saucers," naturally); and there was one where we went to extend the hand of Dominant Homo Sapiens to our poor benighted alien brothers, and were ordered to take our spaceship around back by the service entrance; and one in which we became smorgasbord for a troupe of alien actors; and—well, you get what I mean. Pretty awful. Only once did I really get to it in nitty-gritty terms. That once, a story I still like immensely is

The Sky Is Burning

THEY CAME flaming down out of a blind sky, and the first day ten thousand died. The screams rang in our heads, and the women ran to the hills to escape the sound of it. But there was no escape for them—nor for any of us! The sky was aflame with death, and the terrible, unbelievable part of it was—the death, the dying was not us!

It started late in the evening. The first one appeared as a cosmic spark struck in the night. Then, almost before the first had faded back into the dusk, there was another, and then another, and soon the sky was a jeweler's pad, twinkling with unnameable diamonds.

I looked up from the Observatory roof, and saw them all, tiny pinpoints of brilliance, cascading down like raindrops of fire. And somehow, before any of it was explained, I knew: this was something important. Not important the way five extra inches of plastichrome on the tail-fins of a new copter are important... not important the way a war is important...but important the way the creation of the universe had been important, the way the death of it would be. And I knew it was happening all over Earth.

There could be no doubt of that. All across the horizon, as far as I could see, they were falling and burning and burning. The sky was not brighter appreciably, but it was as though a million new stars had been hurled up there to live for a brief microsecond.

Even as I watched, Portales called to me from below. "Frank! Frank, come down here! This is fantastic!"

I swung down the catwalk into the telescope dome and saw him hunched over the refraction eyepiece. He was pounding his fist against the side of the vernier adjustment box. It was a pounding of futility and strangeness. A pounding without meaning behind it. "Look at this, Frank. Will you take a look at this?" His voice was a rising inflection of disbelief.

I nudged him aside and slid into the bucket. The scope was trained on Mars. The Martian sky was burning, too. The same pinpoints of light, the same intense pyrotechnics spiraling down. We had alloted the evening to a study of the red planet, for it was clear in that direction, and I saw it all very sharply, as brightnesses and darkness again, all across the face of the planet.

"Call Bikel at Wilson," I told Portales. "Ask him about Venus."

Behind me I heard Portales dialing the closed circuit number, and I half-listened to his conversation with Aaron Bikel at Mt.

Wilson. I could see the flickering reflections of the vid-screen on
the phone as they washed across the burnished side of the scope.
But I didn't turn around; I knew what the answer would be.

Finally, he hung up, and the colors died. "The same," he said
sharply, as though defying me to come up with an answer. I
didn't bother snapping back at him. He had been bucking for
my job as Director of the Observatory for nearly three years now,
and I was accustomed to his antagonisms—desperately as I had
to machinate occasionally to keep him in his place.

I watched for a while longer, then left the dome.

I went downstairs and tuned in my short-wave radio, trying
to find out what Tokyo or Heidelburg or Johannesburg had to
say. I wasn't able to catch any mention of the phenomena during
the short time I fiddled with the sweep, but I was certain they
were seeing it the same everywhere else.

Then I went back to the Dome, to change the settings on the
scope.

After an argument with Portales, I beamed the scope down
till it was sharp to just inside the atmospheric blanket. I tipped
in the sweeper and tried a fast scan of the sky, but continued to
miss the bursts of light at the moment of their explosion. So I cut
in the photo mechanism and set a wide angle to it. Then I cut
off the sweep and started clicking them off. I reasoned that the
frequency of the lights would inevitably bring one into photo
focus.

Then I went downstairs, back to the short-wave. I spent two
hours with it and managed to pick up a news broadcast from
Switzerland. I had been right, of course.

Portales rang me after two hours and said we had a full reel of
photos, and should he have them developed. This was too big to
trust to his adolescent whims, and rather than have him fog up a
valuable photo, I told him to leave them in the container, and I'd
be right up, to handle it myself.

When the photos came out of the solution, I had to finger
through thirty or forty of empty space before I caught ten that
had what I wanted.

They were not meteorites.

On the contrary.

Each of the flames in the sky was a creature. A living creature. But not human. Far from it.

The photos told what they looked like, but not till the Project Snatch ship went up and sucked one off the sky did we realize how large they were, that they glowed with an inner light of their own and—that they were telepathic.

From what I can gather, it was no problem catpuring one. The ship opened its cargo hatch and turned on the sucking mechanisms used to drag in flotsam from space. The creature, however, could have stopped itself from being dragged into the ship, merely by placing one of its seven-taloned hands on either side of the hatch, and resisting the sucker. But it was interested, as we learned later; it had been five thousand years, and they had not known we had come so far, and the creature was interested. So it came along.

When they called me in, along with five hundred-odd other scientists (and Portales managed to wangle himself a place in the complement), we went to the Smithsonian, where they had had him installed, and marveled—just stood and marveled.

He—or she, we never knew—resembled the Egyptian god Ra. It had the head of a hawk, or what appeared to be a hawk, with great slitted eyes of green in which flecks of crimson and amber and black danced. Its body was thin to the point of emaciation, but humanoid with two arms and two legs. There were bends and joints on the body where no such bends and joints existed on a human, but there was a definite chest cavity, and obvious buttocks, knees, and chin. The creature was a pale, milky-white, except on the hawk's-crest which was a brilliant blue, fading down into white. It's beak was light blue, also blending into the paleness of its flesh. It had seven toes to the foot, seven talons to the hand.

The God Ra. God of the Sun. God of light.

The creature glowed from within with a pale, but distinct aura that surrounded it like a halo. We stood there, looking up at it in the glass cage. There was nothing to say; there it was, the first creature from another world. We might be going out into space in a few years—farther, that is, than the Moon, which we had reached in 1970, or Mars that we had circumnavigated in

1976—but for now, as far as we knew, the Universe was wide and without end, and out there we would find unbelievable creatures to rival any imagining. But this was the first.

We stared up at it. The Being was thirteen feet tall.

Portales was whispering something to Karl Leus from Caltech. I snorted to myself at the way he never gave up; for sheer guff and grab I had to hand it to him. He was a pusher all right. Leus wasn't impressed. It was apparent he wasn't interested in what Portales had to say, but he had been a Nobel Prize winner in '63 and he felt obligated to be polite to even obnoxious pushers like my assistant.

The army man—whatever his name was—was standing on a platform near the high, huge glass case in which the creature stood, unmoving, but watching us.

They had put food of all sorts through a feeder slot, but it was apparent the creature would not touch it. It merely stared down, silent as though amused, and unmoving as though uncaring.

"Gentlemen, gentlemen, may I have your attention!" the Army man caroled at us. A slow silence, indicative of our disrespect for him and his security measures that had caused us such grief getting into this meeting, fell through the groups of men and women at the foot of the case.

"We have called you here—" pompous ass with his *we*, as if he were the government incarnate, "to try and solve the mystery of who this being is, and what he has come to Earth to find out. We detect in this creature a great menace to—" and he went on and on, bleating and parodying all the previous scare warnings we had had about every nation on Earth. He could not have realized how we scoffed at him, and wanted to hoot him off the platform. This creature was no menace. Had we not captured him, her, it—the being would have burnt to a cinder like its fellows, falling into our atmosphere.

We listened to him to the end. Then we moved in closer and stared at the creature. It opened its beak in what was uncommonly like a smile, and I felt a shiver run through me. The sort of shiver I get when I hear deeply emotional music, or the sort of shiver I get when making love It was a basic trembling in the fibers of my body. I can't explain it, but it was a prelude to something. I paused in my thinking, just ceased my existence if *Cogito Ergo Sum* is the true test of existence. I stopped thinking and allowed myself to sniff of that strangeness; to savor the odor of space and far-away worlds, and one world in particular.

A world where the winds are so strong that the inhabitants have hooks on their feet with which they dig into the firm green soil to maintain their footing. A world where colors riot among the foliage one season, and the next are the pale white of a maggot's flesh. A world where the triple moons swim through azure skies, and sing in their passage, playing on a lute of invisible strings, the seas and the deserts as accompaniests. A world of wonder, older than Man and older than the memory of the Forever.

I realized abruptly, as my mind began to function once more, that I had been listening to the creature. Ithk was the creatures'—name?—denomination?—gender?—something. It was one of five hundred hundred-thousand like itself, who had come to the system of Sol.

Come? No, perhaps that was the wrong word. They had *been*...

Not by rockets, nothing that crude. Nor space-warp, nor even mental power. But a leap from their world—what was that name? Something the human tongue could not form, the human mind could not conceive?—to this world in seconds. Not instantaneous, for that would have involved machinery of some sort, or the expansion of mental power. It was beyond that, and above that. It was an *essence* of travel. But they had come. They had come across the mega-galaxies, hundreds of thousands of light-years...incalculable distances from there to here, and Ithk was one of them.

Then he began to talk to some of us.

Not all of us there, for I could tell some were not receiving him. I don't attribute it to good or bad in any of us, nor intelligence, nor even sensitivity. Perhaps it was whim on Ithk's part, or the way he wanted to do it from necessity. But whatever it was, he spoke to only some of us there. I could see Portales was receiving nothing, though old Karl Leus' face was in a state of rapture, and I knew he had the message himself.

For the creature was speaking in our minds telepathically. It did not amaze me, or confound me, nor even shock me. It seemed right. It seemed to go with Ithk's size and look, its aura and arrival.

And it spoke to us.

And when it was done, some of us crawled up on the platform and released the bolts that held the case of glass shut; though we all knew Ithk could have left it at any second had it desired. But Ithk had been interested in knowing—before it burned itself out as its fellows had done—and it had found out about us little Earth people. It had satisfied its curiosity, on this instant's stopover before it went to hurtling, flaming destruction. It had been curious...for the last time Ithk's people had come here, Earth had been without creatures who went into space. Even as pitifully short a distance into space as we could venture.

But now the stopover was finished, and Ithk had a short journey to complete. It had come an unimaginably long way, for a purpose, and though this had been interesting, Ithk was anxious to join his fellows.

So we unbolted the cage—which had never *really* confined a creature that could be out of it at will—and Ithk was not there! Gone!

The sky was still flaming.

One more pinpoint came into being suddenly, slipped down in a violent rush through the atmosphere, and burned itself out like a wasting torch. Ithk was gone.

Then we left.

Karl Leus leaped from the thirty-second story of a building in Washington that evening. Nine others died that day. And though I was not ready for that, there was a deadness in me. A feeling of waste and futility and hopelessness. I went back to the Observatory, and tried to drive the memory of what Ithk had said from my mind and my soul. If I had been as deeply perceptive as Leus or any of the other nine, I might have gone immediately. But I am not in their category. They realized the full depth of what it had said and, so perceiving, they had taken their lives. I can understand their doing it.

Portales came to me when he heard about it.

"They just—just *killed* themselves!" he babbled.

"Yes, they killed themselves," I answered wearily, staring
at the flaming, burning sky from the Observatory catwalk. It
always seemed to be night now. Always night with light.

"But *why*? Why would they do it?"

I spoke to hear my thoughts. For I knew what was coming.
"Because of what the creature said."

"What it said?"

"What it told us, and what it did not tell us."

"It *spoke* to you?"

"To some of us. To Leus and the nine and others. I heard it."

"But why didn't I hear it? I was right there!"

I shrugged. He had not heard, that was all.

"Well, what did it say? Tell me," he demanded.

I turned to him, and looked at him. Would it affect him? No, I
rather thought not. And that was good. Good for him, and good
for others like him. For without them, Man would cease to exist.
I told him.

"The lemmings," I said. "You know the lemmings. For no
reason, for some deep instinctual surging, they follow each other,
and periodically throw themselves off the cliffs. They follow one
another down to destruction. A racial trait. It was that way with
the creature and his people. They came across the mega-galaxies
to kill themselves here. To commit mass suicide in our solar
system. To burn up in the atmosphere of Mars and Mercury and
Venus and Earth, and to die, that's all. Just to die."

His face was stunned. I could see he comprehended that. But
what did it matter? That was not what had made Leus and the
nine other scientists kill themselves, that was not what filled me
with such a feeling of frustration. The drive of one race was not
the drive of another.

"But—but—I don't underst—"

I cut him off.

"That was what Ithk said."

"But why did they come *here* to die?" he asked, confused.
"Why *here* and not some other solar system or galaxy?"

That was what Ithk had said. That was what we had wondered
in our minds—damn us for asking—and in its simple way, Ithk
had answered.

"Because," I explained slowly, softly, "this is the end of the Universe."

His face did not register comprehension. I could see it was a concept he could not grasp. That the solar system, Earth's system, the backyard of Earth to be precise, was the end of the Universe. Like the flat world over which the Columbus would have sailed, into nothingness. This was the end of it all. Out there, in the other direction, lay a known Universe, with an end to it...but they—Ithk's people—ruled it. It was theirs, and would always be theirs. For they had racial memory burnt into each embryo child born to their race, so they would never stagnate. After every lemming race, a new generation was born, that would live for thousands of years, and advance. They would go on till they came here to flame out in our atmosphere. But they would rule what they had while they had it.

So to us, to the driving, unquenchably curious, seeking and roaming Earthman, whose life was tied up with wanting to know, *needing* to know, there was left nothing. Ashes. The dust of our own system. And after that, nothing.

We were at a dead end. There would be no wandering among the stars. It was not that we couldn't go. We could. But we would be tolerated. It was *their* Universe, and this, our Earth, was the dead end.

Ithk had not known what it was doing when it said that to us. It had meant no evil, but it had doomed some of us. Those of us who dreamed. Those of us who wanted more than what Portales wanted.

I turned away from him and looked up.

The sky was burning.

I held very tightly to the bottle of sleeping tablets in my pocket. So much light up there.

Now we come to an intense little study of paranoia, schiz-ophrenia and psychopathic behavior. And after that long Introduction in the front of this volume, I'm already charting the caroling voices of those who will contend this story is a portrait of the author as a freakout. I assure you this was conceived merely as a "gimmick" story. Aside from the facts that I said in one part of the story that Brad and Paulie were almost-identical twins, and later had Brad reminiscing of a time when he was nine and Paulie was thirteen... and that the story has been made obsolete by the recent Explorer shots...and that Twilight Zone went off the air before I came out to Hollywood and could have adapted it, which would have been the proper medium for this little tripper...aside from all of those...this isn't a bad little suspense yarn, this thing called

My Brother Paulie

IMPOSSIBLE FOOTSTEPS sounded down the catwalk. Impossible, because he was alone with his brother Paulie, sealed up in an experimental rocket two hundred thousand miles from Earth and Paulie was just waiting for an opportunity to kill him.

Impossible because this was the first ship to attempt a circumnavigation of the Moon, and God only knew how rough it was *without* Paulie constantly on the stalk, trying to burn away the top of his skull.

Brad Woodland pressed himself closer to the gigantic hydrazine tank, wedging himself in tighter between the tank and bulkhead of the *Resurrection IX*. Silently, he prayed his brother would drop dead.

The footsteps drew nearer, directly over his head now.

"Brad! Brad Boy! Out, Brad, c'mon out!"

The deep, masculine voice of his brother struck Brad Woodland with the same terror it had held when they were both children, and Paulie had delighted in beating up his brother. "Brad, c'mon out and we'll talk, boy. It's a long pull there and back, Brad. We got to comfort each other—"

He slid his hands up the smooth, cool metal of the tank, clapping them without sound over his ears. It failed to shut out Paulie's insistent, sardonic tones. Paulie, with that damned blaster. He bit his lip, and he could feel his eyes beginning to water.

This was the way it had always been; he could even remember a similar situation when he and Paulie had been nine. He had taken the more brilliant of the two balloons Dad had brought home from the company outing, and Paulie had chased him into the yard, yelling for a trade, and threatening to beat Brad's head in.

Brad had run wildly, and wedged himself under the rear porch. He had laid there, terrified and shaking, seeing Paulie's feet run past the porch—pause—turn—run a few steps back again—stop—and finally go out of sight around the house. Of course, Paulie had taken the balloon later, and had knocked him down with a hard punch in the stomach. But for those few moments he had been safe, and securely hidden, and Paulie had not been able to find him.

He was facing the same danger now. The years had not changed his brother. With the dim light from control country upship filtering down into the fuel tank compartment of this third stage, everything was weird and dusky. Dimly-lit and soft-edged, as in a dream. The way things had been when they had put Brad through his pre-flight mental checkup, at Redstone Tower.

He remembered all the hours before blastoff, when he had lain in the padded troughs of the check-machines getting his brain gouged. The more he thought of the inexhaustible training and checking and priming he had gone through for this most important voyage, the more bewildered he was at the thought of Paulie stowing away.

How his brother had done it, under the very noses of a thousand guards, he could not imagine.

But less than a thousand miles out, he had discovered quickly enough that he was not alone on the *Resurrection IX*, while still strapped into his webbing, he had heard the foot-steps.

And when the compartment door to control country had slammed open, and he had seen Paulie's big, wedge-torsoed body, poised there in the companionway, he had screamed. For there should have been no one else out here with him.

Not only was this a dangerous solo flight! It was a crucial test for him. Eight ships had gone before, and eight ships had exploded in space, or crashed back to Earth, or shot off into the void, or—

Eight ships before, and yet there was no reason why he should not have made it, for he was in great shape, along with the top shape of his ship. He would have made it! Except—

"Brad! Hey, dear brother, where *are* you?"

The footsteps clanked heavily overhead, and Brad prayed again in the cavern of his skull that Paulie would not look down. For, save for the area that was blocked off by the crossbeam of the overhead catwalk, he was plainly visible from above. In the dusking light that was still clear enough to see by, Brad knew that his brother could aim the blaster and char him to ashes before he could extricate himself.

He pressed closer, his breath catching in his throat.

The steps passed by, and Paulie went further toward the "rear" of the rocket. On a lower level, the whine of the spinturbos reminded Brad that without the centrifugal spin of the ship, there would be no gravity. And wouldn't *that* be a help to Paulie....

The steps receded, and Brad breathed easier again. Why had Paulie done this fantastic, incredible thing? Why? Well, he knew the answer to that, too. He knew exactly what had made Paulie think he could get away with the murder of his brother.

He thought back, remembering the first few moments of shock and horror. When the control door compartment door had slammed open, and Brad craned his neck around in chill apprehension, he had found himself staring into a face that was almost identical with his own.

Almost identical for Brad and Paulie Woodland were twins.

But there were differences, too—in eyes and voice and gesture—and when they were together they could easily be told apart. Only when one was absent, did the other seem a replica of both.

"When all those flashbulbs go off, at the landing," Paulie had said softly, smiling at him from the compartment doorway, "everyone'll be so full of hot-juice and hysteria, they won't stop to think you look different. You went up alone, came back alone. Maybe, they'll tell themselves, space *does* that to a man, sort of changes his face a little. No sweat, Brad boy. No sweat at all. You go out the lock, and into the sun, and I go back to glory. How's that, Brad boy?"

Brad had been petrified with horror. The blaster had loomed enormous in his brother's clasp. He had watched the bell-muzzle of it, and felt the roaring blast of its power, deep inside himself. He had waited a split-second for Paulie to pull the trigger, releasing one of the gelatin loads into the reaction chamber, and then he had defended himself. He had fallen forward, and slammed his palm flat onto the light control switch. The compartment had gone instantly black. Only the stars outside the curved viewpoint had cast any light.

Then, as Brad had fumbled with the snaps on the webbing, as he had lunged against the web and fallen free, tumbling to the deck, Paulie had pulled the trigger.

The hissing roar of the blaster had filled the compartment, and in the light of the flash, his face had assumed a gargoyle cast—the eyes wide with hate, the mouth slashed open and hungry, like the mouth of a killer fish, the cheeks strained across in a death-grin.

Brad had rolled, coming up with knees bent, and hitting Paulie low. His brother had cried out in pain and shock, and had gone over backward. Brad had grabbed for the blaster, but Paulie had fought back, stubbornly refusing to release it.

Then Brad had run!

He had been running ever since. Two hundred thousand miles from Earth, he had been dodging and running and trying to escape his brother. The ship could carry itself. The astroplot made the machine almost a robot—until turnover time came— and Brad knew he would not have to worry about getting back up to the control compartment before they rounded the Moon.

Eventually he'd have to go up and slap a few switiches, compute
a few vectors, blast a few bursts. But that could wait. Right now
he had to figure a way to kill Paulie before his brother got to
him.

Far behind him he heard footsteps clanking down the
compartment ladder. When the ship was tail-down, the ladder
ran vertically. But with the ship "horizontal' 'it was a runged
catwalk down the center of the section. Branching off from it,
were several smaller ladders, leading to the compartment floors. It
was down one of these offshoot ladders that Paulie was climbing
now—the ladder into the hydrazine tank compartment. He was
getting closer.

Brad bit his lips again. He was trapped for the moment. If
Paulie examined the compartment thoroughly—and why should
he fail to do so?—he was bound to see Brad wedged in between
the tanks. He had to get out of where he was before his brother
came down to the deck.

He edged out, keeping the round bulk of the tank between
himself and the ladder. He got loose finally, and heard the sound.
Someone jumping, to land heavily. Then the footsteps started
again.

Brad cast an alarmed glance behind hmself. The corridor
stretched back for only a short distance. There was no place to
go. Just more tanks, and water valves to the flow-through ducts,
and tool closets, and—

Abruptly he felt a surge of relief. Had he stumbled on the
solution to his nightmare that had for so long seemed destined to
end only with his death? Was the tool closet his salvation?

He edged down the corridor, keeping close to the tanks. In
a minute he was at the end of the corridor, his back against the
closet, his hand pressed to the opener. He pulled up on it with
one finger, and it slid open easily. He rummaged inside for a
moment, finally coming up with a double-thread wrench. Big
and blocky and steel-jawed, it was not the most powerful weapon
ever invented, but it was better than no weapon at all.

The hand-grip felt reassuring.

Brad melted back against the tanks, the wrench held tightly
in his fist. He saw a shadow floating along the deckplates, in the

cool dusk of the compartment. He saw the shadow's arm extend, saw the blaster clearly. He raised the wrench over his head, and remained poised, waiting.

The shadow drew nearer, and Brad saw the toe of a boot around the tank's bulk.

He drew in his breath sharply, and just at that moment—before he could bring the wrench down—the alarm went off throughout the ship. The sounding button went home, and the red alert screamed, and he knew he must get updecks to turn the ship. The shadow stopped moving and edged backward, and Brad, hardly thinking, knowing he was doomed unless he turned the ship immediately took a quick step forward and *threw* the wrench.

It spanged off the tank beside Paulie's head, and hit the deck with a crash. Brad did not hesitate. He was out and running, crouched low. He hit Paulie low again, and kept right on moving. He was halfway up the ladder before he heard Paulie coming after him. But this time the angle of the tanks and the bulk of the ladder protected him.

He raced down the long corridor, avoiding the tripstops of the ladder that lay along the floor, and hit the control country door with a crash that jarred every bone in his body.

He was inside then, and slamming the door. He braced it closed with a panel chock that fastened magnetically to the floor, and he prayed Paulie could not get in.

Then he was calculating the vectors—putting everything else from his mind for the moment—and slapping home the switches, and blasting the tubes in just the right way.

Beneath the ship, the bloated, cratered white face of the Moon passed by, wheeling and glittering in his eyes as the banks of auto-recorders and telemetering devices probed downward and took readings. Man's first manned jump around the Moon.

Brad Woodland stared fascinated, and speechless. He wanted to yell, "Paulie! Paulie! I've done it! I've made it where the others couldn't! I've passed the Moon, damn it, and here I am!" But he couldn't.

He watched Earth's satellite for a long, long moment, and then he realized the shattering sound he had been hearing for the past few minutes was not in his mind at all but the compartment door being systematically blasted open.

He spun just as it crashed inward, and he got a full-face view of Paulie, his brother, and the blaster…just before Paulie pulled the trigger.

THE DREAM:

Youth in two parts. Split like a pea-pod down the center, with each section possessing a vigorous life of its own. The Alicia party, where Brad had won the girl by his quick wit, and Paulie had lost the girl because of his surly nature and quick temper. The days of wanting to speak, to say something, to get through the wall that stood between brother and brother, but always with silence. The days when Mama and Dad had looked strangely at them and asked themselves, "What's the matter with those two? They've always been such good buddies."

First there had been Alicia, when Paulie was the wiser, and Brad the angrier. Then the hot rod days, and the skin diving days and finally the high school college post-grad Army days. Then the tests for *Resurrection IX*.

Brad

Brad

Brad

No Paulie—just Brad. Paulie left on the outside, a lesser shot with the Redstone missile men. Just Brad into the sky and the night, and the fire with the silvered salmon that was a ship to space dedicated. That had been the way of it, with footsteps that came nearer, nearer, nearer as a face that was *his* face—and all faces—lived there in a ring of flame and fire from the blaster.

Brad Woodland awoke!

Somehow, Paulie had missed. He was still very much alive. He got to his feet, shaking. Silence shimmered through the ship. But Paulie was back there somewhere. It had to be. The ship tilted. The autoplot bleated, and Brad looked at the plot-tank. They were nearly home.

Comm Center Redstone Tower was trying to pin them with location leads; the board was going mad. He was going to make it. Somehow, he had escaped the wrath of his jealous brother, who had always come second to him, always, always, and who would run also-ran this time?

He fell into the webbing, strapped down, and brought the flaming bulk of the *Resurrction IX* in for a perfect pit-landing.

Man had gone around the Moon, and lived to report the event in person. The ship was silent in its pit.

When the elevator brought Brad Woodland down from the ship, he wasted no time with the reporters. He ran instead to the little cluster of Army officers who stood waiting by the ready-pool, and saluted sharply.

They returned the salute, and congratulated him. Brad Woodland did not give them a moment to finish their congratulations.

"Listen, General, I don't know how it happened, but you know my brother Paulie—the one who looks like me? Some- how he managed to smuggle himself on board at blastoff, and he tried to kill me all during the trip. He had a blaster, and he burnt away the control room door, and just missed killing me. Look, General, send someone on board now to get him off. I want to prefer charges."

The General motioned swiftly to the two heavyset med-men and, still talking calmly, still denouncing his brother, Brad was led away.

The General turned to his staff and his face was tight with the crease-lines of strain. "After they remove the suggestion leads in his brain, he'll be back to normal," he said.

One of the reporters, who had been eavesdropping, stepped forward and impudently asked, "Just why did you feel that you had to drive him buggy, General? Statement for the *Globe*."

The General looked for a moment as though he would like to strike the reporter. But then with an effort he controlled himself, and explained in a level voice, "We sent up eight ships. Each trip was a failure simply because all eight pilots went mad. Space does that to the general run of pilots, apparently. So we hypno-conditioned Woodland to think he was in mortal danger, thus keeping his mind off the rigors of space. It worked. He dreamed up a death-brother who was stalking him, and it allowed him to make the turn and get back safely with the ship. That's all I have to say."

The reporter pursed his lips, watching the crews who were bringing down the telemetering devices and autoplot parts from the ship. As they moved past, to the analysis sections, the reporter said, "So there was no brother and no blaster and nothing at all. Just hallucinations, right?"

The General nodded. "Precisely."

The reporter pursed his lips again, and nodded his head in agreement. "I see, General. Then if it was in his mind, and you're sure there was no blaster on that ship—"

The General cut in, "Quite sure. We searched that ship thoroughly before takeoff, to make sure there was no way he could harm himself.

The reporter resumed quickly, "Then if it was all in his mind, General, how do you account for *that*?"

The reporter pointed, and the General's face turned quite white as he watched one of the disassembling crews moving past with a piece of metal.

It was the control compartment door—completely blasted and slagged, with the radiating white lines of glowing destruction that can be made only by a blaster.

Recently, Cosmopolitan Magazine, *for some inexplicable reason, selected me as one of the "most eligible swinging bachelors in Hollywood." They came and took my picture lounging on the steps of my bed, with three attractive young ladies I had been dating draped around me. While it did my ego enormous good, I realized all the while that it was a shuck. I am by no means Baby Pignateli or Porfirio Rubirosa or even Oil Can Harry. I am a poor Jewish kid from Painesville, Ohio and New York City who works exceedingly hard to keep up the house payments and buy himself enough time writing TV so he can take off seven months a year to write books. I am by no means jet set. (Actually, I understood why they selected me. All the other "swinging" candidates were from the same set: loafers and scions of wealthy families who had nothing to do but chase broads. They needed one common day laborer. Since I had been around that set, but was not in or of that set, they felt I was just too-too perfect. Sort of a concession to all the grease monkeys and farm laborers in the audience, showing you too can make it in hotcha society, if you keep your thumbs out of the anchovy dish.) Being officially a swinging bachelor has its responsibilities. One has to make profound and penetrating comments on love and male-female relationships, among other duties. (For my definitive thesis on the subject, see my forthcoming hardcover, "Love Ain't Nothing But Sex Misspelled" from Trident Press.) (In case you weren't paying attention, that was the commercial, friends.) Some years ago, during my first marriage, the lady with whom I was sharing a padded cell made the comment that all my stories were about violence and unhappiness and a world running amuck. She challenged me to write a nice, simple love story; a boy/girl story that would warm the heart, kindofa Frances Parkinson Keyes story. I snorted with laughter. Deprecatingly I replied that nothing could be easier for a diversified genius of my magnitude. So I sat down and wrote this tender, touching love story about a shell-shocked Marine and a blind girl in a madhouse, and I called it*

The Time of the Eye

IN THE THIRD year of my death, I met Piretta. Purely by chance, for she occupied a room on the second floor, while I was given free walk of the first floor and the sunny gardens. And it seemed so strange, that first and most important time, that we met at all, for she had been there since she had gone blind in 1945, while I was one of the old men with young faces who had dissolved after Korea.

The Place wasn't too unpleasant, of course, despite the high, flat-stone walls and the patronizing air of Mrs. Gondy, for I knew one day my fog would pass, and I would feel the need to speak to someone again, and then I could leave the Place.

But that was in the future.

I neither looked forward to that day, nor sought refuge in my stable life at the Place. I was in a limbo life between caring and exertion. I was sick; I had been told that; and no matter what I knew—I was dead. So what sense was there in caring?

But Piretta was something else.

Her delicate little face was porcelain, with eyes the flat blue of shallow waters, and hands that were quick to do nothing important.

I met her—as I say—by chance. She had grown restless, during what she called "the time of the eye," and had managed to give her Miss Hazelet the slip.

I was walking with head bowed and hands locked behind my bathrobe, through the lower corridor, when she came down the great winding stairway.

On many an occasion I had stopped at that stairway, watching the drab-faced women who scrubbed down each level, each riser.

It was like watching them go to hell. They started at the top, and washed their way down. Their hair was always white, always lank, always like old hay. They scrubbed with methodical ferocity, for this was the last occupation for them, before the grave, and they clung to it with soap and suds. And I had watched them go down to hell, step by step.

But this time there were no drudges, on their knees.

I heard her walking close to the wall, her humble fingertips brushing the wainscotting as she descended, and I realized immediately that she was blind.

That blindness deeper than lack of sight.

There was something to her; something ephemeral that struck instantly to the dead heart in me. I watched her come down with stately slowness, as though she tripped to silent music, until I was drawn to her in spirit.

"May I be of service?" I heard myself politely inquiring, from a distance. She paused there and her head came up with field mouse awareness.

"No, thank you," she said, most congenially. "I am quite able to care for myself, thank you. Something that *person*," she twitched her head in the direction of upstairs, "cannot seem to fathom."

She came the remainder of the steps to the napeless wine-colored rug. She stood there and exhaled deeply, as though she had just put a satisfactory finis to an immense project.

"My name is—" I began, but she cut me off with a sharp snort and, "Name's the same." She giggled prettily.

"Names ring of little consequence, don't you agree?" and there was such conviction in her voice, I could hardly disagree.

So I said, "I suppose that's so."

She snickered softly and patted her auburn hair, bed-disarrayed. "Indeed," she said with finality, "that *is* so; very much so."

This was most peculiar to me, for several reasons.

First, she was talking with a rather complicated incoherence that seemed perfectly rational at the time, and second, she was the first person I had spoken to since I had been admitted to the Place, two years and three months before.

I felt an affinity for this woman, and hastened to strengthen our flimsy tie.

"And yet," I ventured, "one must have *some*thing by which to know another person." I became most bold and went on, "Besides—" gulping, "if one *likes* someone."

She considered this for a long second, one hand still on the wall, the other at her white throat. "If you insist," she replied, after deliberation, and added, "you may call me Piretta."

"Is that your name?" I asked.

"No," she answered, so I knew we were to be friends.

"Then you can call me Sidney Carton," I released a secret desire of long sublimation.

"That is a fine name, should any name be considered fine," she admitted, and I nodded. Then, realizing she could not hear a nod, I added a monosyllable to indicate her pleasure was mine also.

"Would you care to see the gardens?" I asked chivalrously.

"That would be most kind of you," she said, adding with a touch of irony, "as you see...I'm quite blind."

Since it was a game we were playing I said, "Oh, truly? I really hadn't noticed."

Then she took my arm, and we went down the corridor toward the garden French doors. I heard someone coming down the staircase, and she stiffened on my arm. "Miss Hazelet," she gasped. "Oh, please!"

I knew what she was trying to say. Her attendant. I knew then that she was not allowed downstairs, that she was now being sought by her nurse. But I could not allow her to be returned to her room, after I had just found her.

"Trust me," I whispered, leading her into a side corridor.

I found the mop closet, and gently ushered her before me, into its cool, dark recess. I closed the door softly, and stood there, very close to her. I could hear her breathing, and it was shallow, quick. It made me remember those hours before dawn in Korea, even when we were full asleep; when we sensed what was coming, with fear and trepidation. She was frightened. I held her close, without meaning to do so, and her one arm went around my waist. We were very near, and for the first time in over two years I felt emotions stirring in me; how foolish of me to consider love. But I waited there with her, adrift in a sargasso of conflicting feelings, while her Miss Hazelet paced outside.

Finally, after what seemed a time too short, we heard those same precise steps mounting the stairs—annoyed, prissy, flustered.

"She's gone. Now we can see the gardens," I said, and wanted to bite my tongue. She could *see* nothing; but I did not rectify my error. Let her think I took her infirmity casually. It was far better that way.

I opened the door cautiously, and peered out. No one but old Bauer, shuffling along down the hall, his back to us. I led her out, and as though nothing had happened, she took my arm once more.

"How sweet of you," she said, and squeezed my bicep.

We walked back to the French doors, and went outside.

The air was musky with the scent of fall, and the crackling of leaves underfoot was a constant thing. It was not too chilly, and yet she clung to me with a soft desperation more need than inclination. I didn't think it was because of her blindness; I was certain she could walk through the garden without any help if she so desired.

We moved down the walk, winding out of sight of the Place in a few seconds, shielded and screened by the high, neatly prunted hedges. Oddly enough, for that time of day, no attendants were slithering through the chinaberry and hedges, no other "guests" were taking their blank-eyed pleasure on the turf or on the bypaths.

I glanced sidewise at her profile, and was pleased by her chiseled features. Her chin was a bit too sharp and thrust forward, but it was offset by high cheekbones and long eyelashes that gave her a rather Asiatic expression. Her lips were full, and her nose was a classic yet short sweep.

I had the strangest feeling I had seen her somewhere before, though that was patently impossible.

Yet the feeling persisted.

I remembered another girl...but that had been before Korea... before the sound of a metallic shriek down the night sky...and someone standing beside my bed at Walter Reed. That had been in another life, before I had died, and been sent to this Place.

"Is the sky dark?" she asked. I guided her to a bench, hidden within a box of hedges.

"Not very," I replied. "There are a few clouds in the north, but they don't look like rainclouds. I think it'll be a nice day."

"It doesn't matter," she said resignedly. "The weather doesn't really matter. Do you know how long it's been since I've seen sunlight through the trees?" Then she sighed, and laid her head back against the bench. "No. The weather doesn't really matter. Not at this Time, anyhow."

I don't know what that meant, but I didn't care, either.

There was a new life surging through me. I was surprised to hear it beating in my ears. I was surprised to find myself thinking minutes into the future. No one who has not experienced it can understand what it is to be dead, and not think of the future, then to have something worthwhile, and begin to live all over again. I don't mean just hope, nothing that simple and uncomplicated. I mean to be dead, and then to be alive. It had come to be like that in just a few minutes since I had met Piretta. I had ignored the very next instant for the past two years and three months, and now suddenly, I was looking to the future. Not much at first, for it had become an atrophied talent in me, but I was expecting from minute to minute, caring, and I could feel my life ranging back to pick me up, to continue its journey.

I was looking ahead, and wasn't that the first step to regaining my lost life?

"Why are you here?" she inquired, placing a cool, slim-fingered hand on my bare arm.

I placed my hand over it, and she started, so I withdrew it self-consciously. Then she searched about, found it, and put it over hers again.

"I was in Korea," I explained. "There was a mortar and I was hit, and they sent me here. I—I didn't want to—maybe I wasn't able to—I don't know—I didn't want to talk to anyone for a long time.

"But I'm all right now," I finished, at peace with myself abruptly.

"Yes," she said, as though that decided it.

Then she went on speaking, in the strangest tone of voice: "Do you sense the Time of the Eye, too, or are you one of *them*?" She asked it with ruthlessness in her voice. I didn't know what to answer.

"Who do you mean by *them*?"

She let her full upper lip snarl, and said, "Those women who bedpan me. Those foul, crepuscular antiseptics!"

"If you mean the nurses and attendants," I caught her line of thought, "no, I'm not one of them. I'm as annoyed by them as you seem to be. Didn't I hide you?"

"Would you find me a stick?" she asked.

I looked around, and seeing none, broke a branch from the box hedge. "This?"

I handed it to her.

"Thank you," she said.

She began stripping it, plucking the leaves and twigs from it. I watched her dextrous hands flitting, and thought *How terrible for such a lovely and clever girl to be thrown in here with these sick people, these madmen.*

"You probably wonder what *I'm* doing here, don't you?" she asked, peeling the thin, green bark from the stick. I didn't answer her, because I didn't want to know; I had found something, someone, and my life had begun again. There was no reason to kill it all at once.

"No, I hadn't thought about it."

"Well, I'm here because *they* know I'm aware of them."

It struck a note of familiarity. There had been a man named Herbman, who had lived on the first floor during my second year at the Place. He had always talked about the great clique of men who were secretly trying to kill him, and how they would go to any extreme to get him, to silence him before he could reveal their dire machinations.

I hoped the same thing had not befallen her. She was so lovely.

"*They*?"

"Yes, of course. You *said* you weren't one of them. Are you

lying to me? Are you making fun of me, trying to confuse me"
Her hand slipped out from under mine.

I hastened to regain ground. "No, no, of course not; but don't
you see, I don't understand? I just don't know. I—I've been here
so long." I tried not to sound pathetic.

Somehow, this seemed to strike her logically. "You must
forgive me. I sometimes forget everyone is not aware of the Time
of the Eye as am I."

She was pulling at the end of the stick, drawing off the bark,
making a sharp little point there. "The Time of the Eye?" I
asked.

She had said it several times. "I don't understand."

Piretta turned to me, her dead blue eyes seeing directly over
my right shoulder, and she put her legs close together. The stick
was laid carelessly by her side, as though a toy it had been, but
now the time for toys was gone. "I'll tell you," she said.

She sat very still for an instant, and I waited. Then:

"Have you ever seen a woman with vermillion hair?"

I was startled. I had expected a story from her, some deep
insight into her past that would enable me to love her the more...
and in its place she asked a nonsense question.

"Why...no...I can't say that I..."

"*Think*!" she commanded me.

So I thought, and oddly enough, a woman with vermillion
hair *did* come to mind. Several years before I had been drafted,
the rage in all the women's fashion magazines had been a woman
named—my God! Was it? Why, yes, now that I looked closely
and my memory prodded, it *was*—Piretta. A fashion model of
exquisite features, lustrous blue eyes, and an affected vermillion-
tint hairdo. She had been so famous her glamour had lapped over
from the fashion magazines, had become one of those household
names everyone bandies about.

"I remember you," I said, startled beyond words of more
meaning.

"No!" she snapped. "No. You don't remember *me*. You
remember a woman named Piretta. A beautiful woman who
cupped her life in her hands and drank deeply of it. That was

someone else. I'm a poor blind thing. You don't know *me*, do you?"

"No," I agreed, "I don't. I'm sorry. For a moment—"

She went on, as though I had never spoken.

"The woman named Piretta was known to everyone. No fashionable salon gathering was fashionable without her; no cocktail party was meaningful with her absence. But she was not a shrinking violet type of woman. She loved experience; she was a nihilist, and more. She would do *any*thing. She climbed K.99 with the Pestroff group, she sailed with two men around the Cape of Good Hope in an outrigger, she taught herself the rudiments of drumming and recorded with Good man.

"That kind of life can jade a person. She grew bored with it. With the charities, with the modeling, with the brief fling at pictures, and with the men. The wealthy men, the talented men, the pretty men who were attracted to her, and who were at the same time held at bay by her beauty. She sought new experience... and eventually found it."

I wondered why she was telling me this. I had decided by now that the life I was anxious to have return was here, in her. I was living again and it had come so quickly, so stealthily, that it could only be a result of her presence.

Whatever indefinable quality she had possessed as a world-renowned mannequin, she still retained, even as a slightly haggard, still lovely, blind-eyed woman of indeterminate age. In her white hospital gown she was shapeless, but the magnetic wonder of her was there, and I was alive.

I was in love.

She was still speaking. "After her experiences with the urban folk singers and the artist's colony on Mohawk Island, she returned to the city, and sought more and different experience.

"Eventually she came upon them. The Men of the Eye. They were a religious sect, unto themselves. They worshiped sight and experience. This was what she had been born for. She fell into their ways at once. Worshiping in the dawn hours at their many-eyed idol and living life to its hilt.

"Their ways were dark ways, and the things they did were not always clean things. Yet she persisted with them.

"Then, one night, during what they called the Time of the Eye, they demanded a sacrifice, and she was the one so chosen.

"They took her eyes."

I sat very still. I wasn't quite sure I'd heard what I'd heard. A weird religious sect, almost devil worship of a sort, there in the heart of New York City; and they had cut out the eyes of the most famous fashion model of all time, in a ceremony? It was too fantastic for belief. Surprising myself, I found old emotions flooding back into me. I could feel disbelief, horror, astonishment. This girl who called herself Piretta, and *was* that Piretta, had brought me to life again, only to fill me with a story so ludicruous I could do nothing but pass it on as dream fantasy and the results of a persecution complex.

After all, didn't she have those shallow blue eyes?

They were unseeing, but they were there. How could they have been stolen? I was confused and dismayed.

I turned to her suddenly, and my arms went about her. I don't know what it was that possessed me, for I had always been shy when women were involved, even before Korea, but now my heart leaped into my throat, and I kissed her full on the mouth.

Her lips opened like two petals before me, and there was ardour returned. My hand found her breast.

We sat that way in passion for several minutes, and finally, when we were satisfied that the moment had lived its existence fully, we separated, and I began to prattle about getting well, and marrying, and moving to the country, where I could care for her.

Then I ran my hands across her face; feeling the beauty of her, letting my fingertips soak up the wonder of her. My smallest finger's tip happened to encounter her eye.

It was not moist.

I paused, and a gleam of a smile broke at the edge of her wondrous mouth. "True," she said, and popped her eyes into the palm of her hand.

My fist went to my mouth, and the sound of a small animal being crushed underfoot came from me.

Then I noticed she had the sharpened stick in her hand, point upward, as though it were a driving spike. "What is that?" I asked, suddenly chilled for no reason.

"You didn't ask if Piretta accepted the religion," she answered softly, as though I was a child who did not understand.

"What do you mean?" I stammered.

"*This* is the Time of the Eye, don't you know?"

And she came at me with the stick. I fell back, but she wound herself around me, and we fell to the ground together, and her blindness did not matter at all.

"But *don't!*" I shrieked, as the stick came up. "I love you. I want to make you mine, to marry you!"

"How foolish," she chided me gently, "I can't marry you: you're sick in the mind."

Then there was the stick, and for so long now, the Time of the Eye has been blindly with me.

Private joke time, friends. "God bless you, little Life Hutch!"
said Robert Silverberg, hauling Randall Garrett into a closet and
locking the door. "Put the robot in the wall!" screamed Garrett,
and Ellison heard, turning to John Campbell who said, "You can't
lecture people, Harlan. Now here's why you can't lecture people..."
and began a seven-hour lecture. Private joke time is over, patient
reader. Now read

Life Hutch

TERRENCE SLID his right hand, the one out of sight of the robot,
up his side. The razoring pain of the three broken ribs caused
his eyes to widen momentarily in pain.

If the eyeballs click, I'm dead, thought Terrence.

The intricate murmurings of the life hutch around him brought
back the immediacy of his situation. His eyes again fastened on
the medicine cabinet clamped to the wall next to the robot's
duty-niche.

Cliche. So near yet so far. It could be all the way back on Antares-
Base for all the good it's doing me, he thought, and a crazy laugh
trembled on his lips. He caught himself just in time. *Easy! Three*
days is a nightmare, but cracking up will only make it end sooner.

He flexed the fingers of his right hand. It was all he *could*
move. Silently he damned the technicain who had passed the
robot through. Or the politician who had let inferior robots get
placed in the life hutches so he could get a rake-off from the
government contract. Or the repairman who hadn't bothered
checking closely his last time around. All of them; he damned
them all.

They deserved it.

He was dying.

He let his eyes close completely, let the sounds of the life hutch fade from around him. Slowly the sound of the coolants hush-hushing through the wall-pipes, the relay machines feeding without pause their messages from all over the Galaxy, the whirr of the antenna's standard turning in its socket atop the bubble, slowly they melted into silence. He had resorted to blocking himself off from reality many times during the past three days. It was either that or existing with the robot watching, and eventually he would have had to move. To move was to die. It was that simple.

He closed his ears to the whisperings of the life hutch; he listened to the whisperings within himself.

To his mind came the sounds of war, across the gulf of space. It was all imagination, yet he could clearly detect the hiss of his scout's blaster as it poured beam after beam into the lead ship of the Kyben fleet.

His sniper-class scout had been near the face of that deadly Terran phalanx, driving like a wedge at the alien ships, converging on them in loose battle-formation. It was then it had happened.

One moment he had been heading into the middle of the battle, the left flank of the giant Kyben dreadnaught turning crimson under the impact of his firepower.

The next moment, he had skittered out of the formation which had slowed to let the Kyben craft come in closer, while the Earthmen decelerated to pick up maneuverability.

He had gone on at the old level and velocity, directly into the forward guns of a toadstool-shaped Kyben destroyer.

The first beam had burned the gun-mounts and directional equipment off the front of the ship, scorching down the aft side in a smear like oxidized chrome plate. He had managed to avoid the second beam.

His radio contact had been brief; he was going to make it back to Antares-Base if he could. If not, the formation would be listening for his homing-beam from a life hutch on whatever planetoid he might find for a crash-landing.

Which was what he had done. The charts had said the pebble spinning there was technically 1-333,2-A M & S, 3804.39#, which would have meant nothing but three-dimensional co-

ordinates, had not the small # after the data indicated a life
hutch somewhere on its surface.

His distaste for being knocked out of the fighting, being
forced onto one of the life hutch planetoids, had been offset only
by his fear of running out of fuel before he could locate himself.
Of eventually drifting off into space somewhere, to finally wind
up as an artificial satellite around some minor sun.

The ship pancaked in under minimal reverse drive, bounced
high and skittered along, tearing out chunks of the rear section;
but had come to rest a scant two miles from the life hutch,
jammed into the rocks.

Terrence had high-leaped the two miles across the empty,
airless planetoid to the hermetically-sealed bubble in the rocks.
His primary wish was to set the hutch's beacon signal so his
returning fleet could track him.

He had let himself into the decompression chamber, palmed
the switch through his thick spacesuit glove, and finally removed
his helmet as he heard the air whistle into the chamber.

He had pulled off his gloves, opened the inner door and
entered the life hutch itself.

Good bless you, little life hutch, Terrence had thought as he
dropped the helmet and gloves. He had glanced around, noting
the relay machines, picking up messages from outside, sorting
them, vectoring them off in other directions. He had seen the
medicine chest clamped onto the wall, the refrigerator he knew
would be well-stocked if a previous tenant hadn't been there
before the stockman could refill it. He had seen the all-purpose
robot, immobile in its duty-niche. And the wall-chronometer, its
face smashed. All of in a second's glance.

*God bless, too, the gentlemen who thought up the idea of
these little rescue stations, stuck all over the place for just such
emergencies as this.* He had started to walk across the room.

It was at this point that the service robot, who kept the place
in repair between tenants and unloaded supplies from the ships,
had moved clankingly across the floor, and with one fearful
smash of a steel arm thrown Terrence across the room.

The spaceman had been brought up short against the steel
bulkhead, pain blossoming in his back, his side, his arms and

legs. The machine's blow had instantly broken three of his ribs. He lay there for a moment, unable to move. For a few seconds he was too stunned to breathe, and it had been that, perhaps, that had saved his life. His pain had immobilized him, and in that short space of time the robot had retreated, with a muted internal clash of gears, to its niche.

He had attempted to sit up straight, and the robot had hummed oddly and begun to move. He had stopped the movement. The robot had settled back.

Twice more had convinced him his position was as bad as he had thought.

The robot had worn down somewhere in its printed circuits. It's commands distorted so that now it was conditioned to smash, to hit, anything that moved.

He had seen the clock. He realized he should have suspected something was wrong when he saw its smashed face. Of course! The hands had moved, the robot had smashed the clock. Terrence had moved, the robot had smashed him.

And would again, if he moved again.

But for the unnoticeable movement of his eyelids, he had not moved in three days.

He had tried moving toward the decompression lock, stopping when the robot advanced and letting it settle back, then moving again. A little nearer. But the idea died with his first movement. The agonizing pain of the crushed ribs made such maneuvering impossible. He was frozen into position, an uncomfortable, twisted positon, and he would be there still the stalemate ended, one way or the other.

He was twelve feet away from the communications panel, twelve feet away from the beacon that would guide his rescuers to him. Before he died of his wounds, before he starved to death, before the robot crushed him. It could have been twelve light-years, for all the difference it made.

What had gone wrong with the robot? Time to think was cheap. The robot could detect movement, but thinking was still possible. not that it would help, but it was possible.

The companies who supplied the life hutch's needs were all government contracted. Somewhere along the line someone had thrown in impure steel or calibrated the circuit-cutting machines for a less expensive job. Somewhere along the line someone had not run the robot through its paces correctly. Somewhere along the line someone had committed murder.

He opened his eyes again. Only the barest fraction of opening. Any more and the robot would sense the movement of his eyelids. That would be fatal.

He looked at the machine.

It was not, strictly speaking, a robot. It was merely a remote-controlled hunk of jointed steel, invaluable for making beds, stacking steel plating, watching culture dishes, unloading spaceships and sucking dirt from the rugs, the robot body, roughly humanoid, but without what would have been a head in a human, was merely an appendage.

The real brain, a complex maze of plastic screens and printed circuits, was behind the wall. It would have been too dangerous to install those delicate parts in a heavy-duty mechanism. It was all too easy for the robot to drop itself from a loading shaft, or be hit by a meteorite, or get caught under a wrecked spaceship. So there were sensitive units in the robot appendage that "saw" and "heard" what was going on, and relayed them to the brain— behind the wall.

And somewhere along the line that brain had worn grooves too deeply into its circuits. It was now mad. Not mad in any way a human being might go mad, for there were an infinite number of ways a machine could go insane. Just mad enough to kill Terrence.

Even if I could hit the robot with something, it wouldn't stop the thing. He could perhaps throw something at the machine before it could get to him, but it would do no good. The robot brain would still be intact, and the appendage would continue to function. It was hopeless.

He stared at the massive hands of the robot. It seemed he could see his own blood on the jointed work-tool fingers of one hand. He knew it must be his imagination, but the idea persisted. He flexed the fingers of his hidden hand.

Three days had left him weak and dizzy from hunger. His head was light and his eyes burned steadily. He had been lying in his own filth till he no longer noticed the discomfort. His side ached and throbbed, the pain like a hot spear thrust into him every time he breathed.

He thanked God his spacesuit was still on, else his breathing would have brought the robot down on him. There was only one solution, and that solution was his death.

Terrence had never been a coward, nor had he been a hero. He was one of the men who fight wars because they must be fought by someone. He was the kind of man who would allow himself to be torn from wife and home and flung into an abyss they called Space because of something else they called Loyalty and another they called Patriotism. To defend what he had been told needed defense. But it was in moments like this that a man like Terrence began to think.

Why here? Why like this? What have I done that I should finish in a filthy spacesuit on a lost rock—and not gloriously but starving or bleeding to death alone with a crazy robot? Why me? Why me? Why?

He knew there could be no answers. He expected no answers.

He was not disappointed.

When he awoke, he instinctively looked at the clock. It's shattered face looked back at him, jarring him, forcing his eyes open in after-sleep terror. The robot hummed and emitted a spark. He kept his eyes open. The humming ceased. His eyes began to burn. He knew he couldn't keep them open too long.

The burning worked its way to the front of his eyes, from the top and bottom, bringing with it tears. It felt as though someone were shoving needles into the soft orbs. The tears ran down over his cheeks.

His eyes snapped shut. The roaring grew in his ears. The robot didn't make a sound.

Could it be inoperative? Could it have worn down to immobility? Could he take the chance of experimenting?

He slid down to a more comfortable position. The robot charged forward the instant he moved. He froze in mid-movement, his heart a lump of snow. The robot stopped, confused, a scant ten inches from his outstretched foot. The machine hummed to itself, the noise of it coming both from the machine before him and from somewhere behind the wall.

He was suddenly alert.

If it had been working correctly, there would have been little or no sound from the appendage, and none whatsoever from the brain. But it was not working properly, and the sound of its thinking was distinct.

The robot rolled backward, its "eyes" still toward Terrence. The sense orbs of the machine were in the torso, giving the machine the look of a squat gargoyle of metal, squared and deadly.

The humming was growing louder, every now and then a sharp *pffft*! of sparks mixed with it. Terrence had a moment's horror at the thought of a short-circuit, a fire in the life hutch, and no service robot to put it out.

He listened carefully to figure out where the robot's brain was built into the wall.

Then he thought he had it. Or was it there? It was either in the wall behind a bulkhead next to the refrigerator, or behind a bulkhead near the relay machines. The two possible housings were within a few feet of each other, but it might make a great deal of difference.

The distortion created by the steel plate in front of the brain, and the distracting background noise of the robot broadcasting it made it difficult to tell exactly which was it.

He drew a deep breath.

The ribs slid a fraction of an inch together, their broken ends grinding.

He moaned.

A high-pitched tortured moan that died quickly, but throbbed back and forth inside his head, echoing and building itself into a paen of sheer agony! It forced his tongue out of his mouth, limp in a corner of his lips, moving slightly. The robot rolled forward. He drew his tongue in, clamped his mouth shut, cut off the scream inside his head at its high point!

The robot stopped, rolled back to its duty-niche.

Beads of sweat broke out on his body. He could feel them

trickling inside his spacesuit, inside his jumper, inside the undershirt, on his skin. The pain of the ribs was suddenly heightened by an irresistible itching.

He moved an infinitesimal bit within the suit, his outer appearance giving no indication of the movement. The itching did not subside. The more he tried to make it stop, the more he thought about not thinking about it, the worse it became. His armpits, the bends of his arms, his thighs where the tight service-pants clung—suddenly too tightly—were madness. He had to scratch!

He almost started to make the movement. He stopped before he started. He knew he would never live to enjoy any relief. A laugh bubbled into his head. *God Almighty, and I always laughed at the joes who suffered with the seven-year itch, the ones who always did a little dance when they were at attention during inspection, the ones who could scratch and sigh contentedly. God, how I envy them.*

The prickling did not stop. He twisted faintly. It got worse. He took another deep breath.

The ribs sandpapered again.

This time he fainted from the pain.

"Well, Terrence, how do you like your first look at a Kyben?

Ernie Terrence wrinkled his forehead and ran a finger up the side of his face. He looked at his Commander and shrugged. "Fantastic things, aren't they?

"Why fantastic?" asked Commander Foley.

"Because they're just like us. Except of course the bright yellow pigmentation and the tentacle-fingers. Other than that they're identical to a human being."

The Commander opaqued the examination-casket and drew a cigarette from a silver case, offering the Lieutenant one. He puffed it alight, staring with one eye closed against the smoke, at the younger man beside him. "More than that, I'm afraid. Their insides look like someone had taken them out, liberally mixed them with spare parts from several other species, and thrown them back in any way that fitted conveniently. For the next

twenty years we'll be knocking our heads together trying to
figure out how they exist."

Terrence grunted, rolling his unlit cigarette absently between
two fingers. "That's the least of it."

"You're right," agreed the Commander. "For the next thousand
years we'll be trying to figure out how they think, why they fight,
what it takes to get along with them, what motivates them."

If they let us live that long thought Terrence.

"Why are we at war with the Kyben?" he asked the older man.
"I mean really."

"Because the Kyben want to kill every human being that can
realize he's a human being.

"What have they got against us?"

"Does it matter? Perhaps it's because our skin isn't bright
yellow; perhaps it's because our fingers aren't silken and flexible;
perhaps it's because our cities are too noisy for them. Perhaps a
lot of perhaps. But it doesn't matter. Survival never matters until
you have to survive."

Terrence nodded. He understood. So did the Kyben. It grinned
at him and drew its blaster. It fired point-blank, crimsoning the
hull of the Kyben ship.

He swerved to avoid running into his gun's own backlash.
The movement of the bucket seat sliding in its tracks to keep his
vision steady while maneuvering made him dizzy.

The abyss was nearer, and he teetered, his lips whitening as
they pressed together under his effort to steady himself. With a
headlong gasp he fell sighing into the stomach. His long, silken
fingers jointed steely humming clankingly toward the medicine
chest over the plate behind the bulkhead.

The robot advanced on him grindingly. Small bits of metal
rubbed together, ashing away into a breeze that came from
nowhere as the machine raised lead boots toward his face.

Onward and onward till he had no room to move.

The light came on, bright, brighter than any star Terrence
had ever seen, glowing, broiling, flickering, shining, bobbing a
ball of light on the chest of the robot, who staggered, stumbled,
stopped.

The robot hissed, hummed and exploded into a million flying, racing, fragments, shooting beams of light all over the abyss over which Terrence teetered. He flailed his arms back trying to escape at the last moment, before the fall.

He saved himself only by his subconscious. Even in the hell of a nightmare he was aware of the situation. He had not moaned and writhed in his delirum. He had kept motionless and silent.

He knew this was true, because he was still alive.

Only his surprised jerking, as he came back to consciousness started the monster rolling from its niche. He came fully awake and sat silent, slumped against the wall. The robot retreated.

Thin breath came through his nostrils. Another moment and he would have put an end to the past three days—three days or more now? how long had he been asleep?—of torture.

He was hungry. Lord how hungry he was. The pain in his side was worse now, a steady throbbing that made even shallow breathing tortuous. He itched maddeningly. He was uncomfortably slouched against a cold steel bulkhead, every rivet having made a burrow for itself in his skin. He wished he were dead.

He didn't wish he was dead. It was all too easy to get his wish.

If he could only disable that robot brain. A total impossibility. If he could only wear Phobos and Dimos for watch-fobs. If he could only shack up with a silicon deb from Penares. If he could use his large colon for a lasso.

It would take a total wrecking of the brain to do it enough damage to stop the appendage before it could roll over and smash Terrence again.

With a steel bulkhead between him and the brain, his chances of success totaled minus zero every time.

He considered which part of his body the robot would smash first. One blow of that tool-hand would kill him if it were used a second time. On top of the ribs, even a strong breath might finish him.

Perhaps he could make a break and get into the air chamber...

Worthless. A) The robot would catch him before he had gotten to his feet, in his present condition. B) Even allowing for a miracle, if he did get in there, the robot would smash the lock doors, letting in air, ruining the mechanism. C) Even allowing for a double miracle what the hell good would it do him? His helmet and gloves were in the hutch itself, and there was no place to go on the plantoid. The ship was ruined, so no signal could be sent from there.

Doom suddenly compounded itself.

The more he thought about it, the more certain he was that soon the light would flicker out for him.

The light would flicker out.

The light would flicker...

The light...

...light...?

His God, if he had had anything to do with it, had heard him. Terrence was by no means a religious man, but this was miracle enough to make even him a disciple. It wasn't over yet, but the answer was there—and it *was* an answer.

He began to save himself.

Slowly, achingly slowly, he moved his right hand, the hand away from the robot's sight, to his belt. On the belt hung the assorted implements a spaceman needs at any moment in his ship. A wrench. A packet of sleep-stavers. A compass. A geiger counter. A flashlight.

The last was the miracle. Miracle in a tube.

He fingered it almost reverently, then unclipped it in a moment's frenzy, still immobile to the robot's "eyes."

He held it at his side, away from his body a fraction of an inch, pointing up over the bulge of his spacesuited leg.

If the robot looked at him, all it would see would be the motionless bulk of his leg, blocking off any movement on his part. To the machine, he was inert. Motionless.

Now he thought wildly, *where is the brain?*

If it is behind the relay machines, I'm still dead. If it is near the refrigerator, I'm saved. He could afford to take no chances. He would have to move.

He lifted one leg.

The robot moved toward him. The humming and sparking was distinct this time. He dropped the leg.

Behind the refrigerator!

The robot stopped, nearly at his side. Seconds had decided. The robot hummed, sparked, and returned to its niche.

Now he knew!

He pressed the button. The invisible beam of the flashlight leaped out, speared at the bulkhead above the refrigerator. He pressed the button again and again, the flat circle of light appearing, disappearing, appearing, disappearing on the faceless metal of the life hutch's wall.

The robot sparked and rolled from its niche. It looked once at Terrence. Then its rollers changed direction and the machine ground toward the refrigerator.

The steel fist swung in a vicious arch, smashing with a deafening clang at the spot where the light bubble flickered on and off.

It swung again and again. Again and again till the bulk-head had been gouged and crushed and opened, and the coils and plates and wires and tubes behind it were refuse and rubble. Until the robot froze, with arm half-ready to strike again. Dead. Immobile. Brain and appendage.

Even then Terrence did not stop pressing the flashlight button. Wildly he thumbed it down and down.

Suddenly he realized it was all over.

The robot was dead. He was alive. He could be saved. He had no doubts about that. Now he could cry.

The medicine chest grew large through the shimmering in his eyes. The relay machines smiled at him.

God bless you, little life hutch, he thought, before he fainted.

A smartass once accused me of being subtle. I decked him with a short right over the heart and an elbow in the trachea. The prison is the structure of bigotry, the prisoners mouth sentences of machinegun polemic, and the story is about as subtle as a turd in a punchbowl. You'll pardon all the hair-chested masculine talk, incidentally, but I bought Mailer's new collection today, and as he puts it, it is as full of shit as a Yule-tide turkey, yet the references to life being one big prizefight arena, and all the studied vulgarity, they're catching. And since I want to truly become a Writer of Stature, like Algren and Mailer and Steinbeck and Hemingway and Irwin Shaw, it looks as though I'll have to cultivate all them crudities of sweaty body-contact sports that prove my credentials for writing ballsy stories are the size of my genitalia. It ain't easy, troops. I find fooball a drag, basketball is dumb, baseball lost me around 1948 after the Indians copped the Series, two pithe-canthropoids in a ring getting their snouts turned to Smucker's jelly and their cerebrums mixmastered into Mrs. Grass' noodle soup turn me off, and I am not presumptuous enough to think I'm in competition with Jimmy Baldwin or even Mr. Mailer, whom I think I can cut, most of the time. Even so, even taking this shocking inadequacy into account, the question of "race" boils my blood. So I'll let Norman work it out his way and I'll talk about a

Battle Without Banners

WHEN THEY FIRST broke out of the machine shop, holding the guards before them, screwdrivers sharp and deadly against white-cloth backs covering streaks of yellow, they made for the South Tower, and took it without death. One of the hostage guards tried to break free, however, in the subsequent scuffle to liberate the machine gun from its gimbals and tracks, and Simon Rubin was forced to use the screwdriver on the man. They threw the body from the Tower as an example to the remaining three hostages, and had no further difficulties. In fact, the object lesson was so successful that it was the guards themselves that carried the cumbersome machine gun, with all its belts of ammunition, back down into the yard. The Tower was an insecure defensive position, interlocked as it was with the other three Towers and the sniping positions on the roofs of the main buildings. They had decided in advance to make it back down into the yard and there, with backs to the wall itself, to take their stand for as long as it took the second group to blow the gate.

Construction on the new drainage system had been underway for only two days, and the great sheets of corrugated sheet metal, the sandbags, the picks and shovels, all were stacked under guard near the wall. They were forced to gun down the man on duty to get into the shelter of the piles of materiel, but it didn't matter either way—if he lived or died—because they were going to take as many with them as they could, breakout or not.

Nigger Joe and Don Karpinsky set up the big-barreled machine gun and braced it sides as well as fore and aft with sandbags, digging it in so the recoil would not affect its efficiency.

Gyp Williams, who had engineered the break, took up a solid rifleman's position, flat out on his belly with legs spread and toes pointed out, the machine rifle braced against right shoulder and left elbow dug deep into the brown earth of the yard, supporting the tripod grip. His brown eyes set deep into his black face were roaming things as he covered the wide expanse of the yard, waiting for the first assault; it had to come; he was the readiest ever.

Lew Steiner and the kid they called Chocolate made up the rest of the skirmish team, and they were busily unloading the home-made grenades and black powder bombs from the cotton-batting of the insulated box…when the first assault broke out of cover around the far wall of the Administration Building.

They came as a wave of white-winged doves, the ivory of their uniforms blazing against the hard cold light of the early morning. First came the sprayers, pocking the ground with little upbursts of dirt, and shredding the morning silence with the noise of their grease guns. Then a row of riflemen and behind them half a dozen longarms with grenades, if needed.

"Away, they comin'!" Gyp Williams snapped over his shoulder. "Dig, babies!" and he got off the first burst of the defense, into their middle. Three of the grease gunners went down, legs every whichaway and guns tossed off like refuse clattering and still chattering on automatic fire, pelting the wall with wasted lead. The second wave faltered an instant, and in that snatch of time Nigger Joe fed the belts to Karpinsky, who swung the big weapon back and forth, in even arcs, cutting them down right across the bellies. None of the riflemen made it a fifth of the distance across the empty yard. One of them went down kicking, and Karpinsky took him out on the next, lowered, arc.

"I am," Lew Steiner screamed, arching high to toss a black powder bomb, "home free!" It hit and exploded fifteen yards too short, but the effect was marvelous. The longarms caught up short and tried to turn.

"Bang

"Bang

"And bang," Gyp Williams grinned and murmured as he snapped off three sharp, short bursts, ending it for a trio of grenade carriers. And it was over that quickly, as the remaining grease-gunners and three longarms fell, clambered, tripped, sprinted, raced back around the building.

"We done that thing," Gyp Williams rolled over on his back, aiming a thumb and finger pistol at his troops. "We sure enough, we done that thing."

"Send those guards outta here," Chocolate nodded his head at the hostages. Gyp agreed with a small movement of his massive head, and the three white-jacketed guards were shoved around the side of the enclosure, out into the open. For a moment they tensed, as though they expected to be shot down by the men in the tiny fort, but when no movement was made, they broke into a dead run, across the yard, arms waving, yelling to their compatriots that they were coming through.

The first burst of machine gun fire came from the North Tower and took one of them in mid-stride, making him miss his footing, leap and plunge in a half-somersault to crash finally onto the ground, sliding a foot and a half on the side of his face. The second burst cut down his partners. They tumbled almost into a loving embrace, piled atop one another.

Chocolate expelled breath through dry lips and asked, "Who's got the cigarettes?" Simon Rubin tossed him the pack and for a while they just lay there, smoking, alert, watching the bodies of the dead white guards who had been shot by their own men.

"Well," Gyp Williams commented philosophically, after a time, "*everybody* knows a white cat gets around niggers is gonna get contaminated. They just couldn't be trust, man. Dirty. Dirty."

"And kikes," Lew Steiner added. "Ding ding."

They settled down for the long wait, till the second group could blow the wall. They watched the shadows of the sun slither across the yard. Nothing moved. Warm, and nice, waiting. Quiet, too.

"How long you been in this prison?" Chocolate asked Simon Rubin. There was no answer for the space of time it took Rubin to draw in on the butt and expell smoke through his nostrils; then his long, horsey face drew down, character lines in the bony cheeks and around the deep-set eyes mapping new expressions. "As far back as I can remember," he replied carefully, thinking about it, "I suppose all of my life." Chocolate nodded lightly, turning back to the empty yards with a thin whistle of nervousness.

Something should happen. They all wanted it.

"When the hell they gonna blow that gate?" Nigger Joe murmured. He had been biting the inside of his full lower lip, chewing, biting again. "I thought they was gonna blow it soon's we got a position here? What the hell they doin' back in there?"

Gyp Williams motioned him to silence. "Quiet, willya. They'll get on it, you take it easy."

"I'm really scared," Don Karpinsky added a footnote. "It's like waiting for them to come and kill you. My old man told me about that at Belsen, how they came around and just looked at you, didn't say a word, just walked up and down, gauging you, looking to see if there was meat on you, and then later, boy oh boy, later they came back and didn't have any trouble picking you out, just walked up and down again, pointing, that one and that one and…"

"Can it," Gyp Williams hushed him. "Boy, you sure can *talk*!" He was silent a second, scrutinizing the young man, too young to need a shave every day, but old enough to be here behind the wall with them. Then, "What you in for, boy?"

Don Karpinsky looked startled, his face rearranging itself to make explanations, excuses, reading itself for extenuating circumstances, amelioration. "I, I, uh, I hurt some people."

Gyp Williams turned toward him more completely (yet kept a corner of his eyes on the empty yard, where the bodies remained crumpled). "You *what*, you did *what*?"

"I just, uh, I *hurt* some people, with a, uh, with a bomb, see I made this bomb and when I tossed it I din't know there was any—"

"Whoa back, boy!" Gyp Williams pulled the young man's racethrough dialogue to a halt. "Go on back a bit. You made *a what? A bomb*?" Karpinsky nodded dumbly: It was obvious he had never thought he would be censured here.

"Now what'n the hell you do *that* for, boy?"

Don Karpinsky turned to the belts of long slugs, neatly folded over themselves, ready for the maw of the machine gun. He would not, or could not, answer.

Simon Rubin spoke up. He had been listening to the interchange but had decided to let the young Karpinsky handle his own explanations. But now it needed ending, and since the young man had confided in him one rainy night in their cell, he felt the privileged communication might best be put to use here. "Gyp," he called the big black man's attention away from Karpinsky. It served to halt the next words from Gyp Williams' mouth.

"He bombed a church, Gyp. Some little town in Iowa. The minister was apparently some kind of a monster, got the local Male White Protestants convinced Jews ate *goyishe* children for Passover. They made it hell on the kid and his family. He was a chemistry bug, made a bomb, and tossed it. Killed six people. They threw him in here."

Gyp Williams seemed about to say something, merely clucked

his tongue, and rolled over once more into a firing position. The only sound in the enclosure was the metallic sliding of the machine rifle's bolt as Gyp Williams made unnecessary checks.

Lew Steiner was asleep against the wall, his back propped outward by a sandbag, a black powder bomb in each hand, as though in that instant of snapping awake, he might reflexively hurl one of the spheroids more accurately, more powerfully than he had in combat.

"Waddaya think, Gyp?" Chocolate asked. "You think they gonna try an' take us in daylight, or wait till t'night?" He was as young as Don Karpinsky, somewhere under twenty, but a reddish ragged scar that split down his left cheek to the corner of his mouth made him seem—somehow—older, more experienced, more capable of violence than the boy who had bombed the small Iowa church.

Gyp Williams rose up on an elbow, gaining a better field of vision across the yard. He talked as much to himself as to Chocolate. "I don't know. Might be they'd be careful about waiting till dark. That's a good time for us as much as them. And when the other boys make the move to blow the gate, the dark'll be on our side, we can shoot out them search-lights..."

He chuckled, lightly, almost naively.

"What's so funny?" Nigger Joe asked, then turned as Simon Rubin asked, "Hey, Joe, I got a crick in my back, here, want to rub it out for me?" Nigger Joe acknowledged the request and slid across the dirt to Rubin, who turned his back, indicating the sore area. The Negro began thumbing it smooth with practiced hands, repeating, "Gyp, what's so funny?"

Gyp Williams' ruggedly handsome face went into a softer stage. "I remember the night they came for us, the caravan, about fifteen twenty cars, came on down to Littletown, all of them with the hoods, lookin' for the one who'd grabbed a feel off the druggist's wife. Man, they were sure pretty, all of them real black against the sky, just them white hoods showing them off like perfect targets.

"They's about ten of us, see, about ten, all laid out like I am now, out there on a little hill in the tall grass, watching them cars move on down. Showoffs, that's what they was. Showoffs, or they wouldn't've sat up on the backs of them convertibles, where we could see 'em so plain. No lights on the cars, all silent, but the white hoods, as plain as moonlight.

"We got about thirteen or fourteen of them cats before they figured they'd been ruined. I was just thinkin' 'bout it now, thinkin' 'bout them searchlights when they come on. Those white uniforms gonna be might fine to shoot at, soon's it gets dark." Then, without a break in meter, his tone became frenzied, annoyed, "When the hell they gonna blow that goddam *gate*?"

As if in reply, a long, strident burst from a grease gun sprayed from the roof of the Administration building, pocked the wall behind them, chewing out irregular niches in the brick. They were spattered with brick chips and mortar, dirt and whizzing bits of stone. Lew Steiner came rigidly awake, grasped the situation and ducked in a dummy-up cover, imitating the other five defenders.

They were huddled over that way, when they heard the whispering, choking whirr of helicopter roters chewing the air. "They're coming over the wall in a 'copter!" Don Karpin-sky shrieked.

Gyp Williams turned over, elevating the machine rifle, bracing it on an upright sheet of corrugated metal. "Lew! Get set, them bombs...they comin' over...Lew!"

But Steiner was lost in fear. It was silence he heard, rather than the commanding voice of Gyp Williams. His buttocks stared out where his face should have been, and Gyp Williams cursed tightly, eyes directed at the wall, scanning, tracking back and forth for the first sight of the guard helicopter, coming with the tear gas or the thermite or a ten-second shrapnel cannister. "Joe, do somethin' about him, you Joe!"

Nigger Joe slid across the ground, grasped Lew Steiner by the hair, and jerked him out of the snail-like foetal position he had assumed. Steiner still clutched the black smoke bombs, one in either fist, like thick, burned rolls, snatched from an oven.

The colored man was unconcerned with niceties. He slapped Steiner heavily, the sound a counterpoint to the copter's rising comments. Lew Steiner did not want to come back from wherever he had gone to find peace and security. But the black man's palm could not be ignored. He bounced the work-pinkened flesh off Steiner's cheeks until the milky-blue of sight unseen had faded, and Steiner was back with them.

"Them bombs, Lew," Nigger Joe said, softly, with great kindness. "They comin' over the wall right'cheer behind us." Steiner's defection was already forgotten.

No more was said as Steiner rolled over, ready to meet the helicopter with his bombs. Chocolate and Don Karpinsky stayed with the fixed machine gun, prepared for a rear guard attack in the face of the aerial threat. Nigger Joe and Simon Rubin lay on their backs, rifles pointed at the sky.

The whirlybird came over the wall fifty feet down the line, and Gyp Williams quickly readjusted himself for its approach. The machine was perhaps twenty feet over their heads, and came churning toward them rapidly, as though intent on low level strafing. Gyp Williams loosed his first burst before the others, and it missed the mark by two feet. The helicopter came on rapidly, steadily. The six men lay staring at it, readying themselves, trying at the same time to find places for their naked bodies in the earth.

When it was almost directly overhead, Lew Steiner rose to a kneeling position and hurled first one black powder bomb, then the other, with tremendous force. The first bomb went straight, directly up into the air, passed over the cockpit of the machine, and tumbled back wobbling, to hit the top of the wall, bounce and explode on the other side. The reverberation could be felt in the wall and the ground, but no rifts appeared in the brick. The second bomb crashed into the side of the machine and a deafening roar split up the even sussuration of the 'copter's rotors. The machine tottered on its course, slipped sidewise and lost minor altitude, but was compensated, began to climb, and just as it hurled itself away in a slanting curve, a projectile tumbled dizzily, end-over-end from the machine.

Then the 'copter was gone, and they watched the projectile falling straight for them. Gyp Williams began screaming, "Fire, fire, hit it hit it hitithitithitit..." and they all poured flame into the sky, missing the tear gas bomb as it fell a few yards from their enclosure, exploded, and sent rolling clouds of tear gas straight toward them.

The vapors struck, and they began to feel the sting of the chemicals, and their eyes went blood-red in a moment, and Don Karpinsky fell on his side, clutching his face, crying like an infant. Lew Steiner grabbed up another bomb from somewhere, and hurled it at the empty yard, a motion of wanton fury and impotence that no one saw, himself most of all. Gyp Williams refused to cry. He dug his broad face deep into the dirt and enjoyed the cool feel of pain from gravel and sod, but the stinging was terrible and his grunts of feeling were strangely intermingled.

The others recoiled, tried to protect themselves, and knew the guards would attack in this moment. They could hear them coming, rebel yells of victory and bloodlust strung out rustily in the air. And over the battle cries, the malicious rattle of the machine gun as Chocolate sprayed the yard in steady, back and forth sweeps. Blind to everything, tears running out of his burning eyes, knowing only that he had the power to cut them down, the young man with the livid scar continued his barrage, building a wall of death the guards in their white uniforms could not penetrate.

And after a while, when the belts were exhausted, and the guards had gone back to cover, when the gas had blown away, stringers of mist on a late afternoon breeze some God had sent to prolong their passion, they they all lay back with eyes crimson and streaming, knowing it had to be over soon, and hoping the second group would finally, please dear Lord, blow that frigging gate!

"Man, how long, how long," Nigger Joe spoke to the advancing dusk. "How long this gotta go on. It seem like I been livin' off misery all my life, you'd think it'd end sometime, not just keep goin' on and on and on."

Simon Rubin sat up and looked at him, and there was compassion in his lean, ascetic face.

"How many lives I gotta lead, steppin' down into the gutter for some 'fay cat? How many times I gotta be called 'Boy', an' when'm I gonna get some memories I wanta put away to think back on, another time?" His eyes were lost in the twilight, set deep under bony eyebrow ridges, but his fierce voice was all around them, very soft but compelling. "Even in here they makin' me be somethin' I ain't. Even in here I'm tryin' to get away, get some life, what's left to me, and they got me down with my face in the dirt; they don't know. Man, they'll *never* know. I can remember every *one* them cats, makin' jokes, pokin' fun, sayin' things, a man's got to have *pride*, that's what matters, just his goddam pride. They can have all the rest of it, just gimme the pride. An' when they come 'round takin' that too, then you gotta raise up and split some sonofabitch's head with a shovel…"

Simon Rubin's voice came sliding in on the semi-darkness, a cool soft fabric covering tiny sounds of crickets and metal clanking on metal from somewhere out there. "I know how you feel, Joe. There are a lot of us in that kind of ghetto."

"Only for some of us it gets worse, even when it gets better. You *knew* your kind of hate, but it was different for me."

Gyp Williams snorted in disgust. "Sheet, man, when you Jewish cats gonna come off that kick? When you gonna stop lyin' on yourself, man, that you been persecuted, so you know how a black man feels? Jeezus, you Jewish own most of the tenements up in Harlem. You as bad as any the rest of them cats." He turned away in suppressed fury, turning his anger on the machine rifle, whose bolt he snapped back twice quickly.

Simon Rubin began speaking again, as though by the continuing stream of words he could negate what Gyp Williams had said. "I wanted to get into dental college, but they had a quota on Jews. I didn't have the money or the name to be in that quota, so I went out for veterinary medicine. I got set back and set back so many times, I finally said to hell with it, and I changed my name, and had my nose fixed, and then I married a gentile.

"It even worked for a while." He smiled thinly, remembering, out of his not-very-Semitic face. "And then one night we had a fight about something, I don't remember what, and we went to bed angry, and in the middle of the night I turned to her and we started to make love, and when she was ready she began saying over and over in my ear, 'Now, you dirty kike, now, you dirty kike...'"

Simon Rubin buried his face in his hands.

Don Karpinsky asked, "Simon...?"

"So...so I know how you feel Joe," Simon finished. "I hated myself more than she could ever hate me; and when they sent me here for her, because of her, what I did to her, I gave them my name the way I came into the world with it. So I know, Joe, believe me, I know."

Nigger Joe started to turn away, his thoughts turned inward. He paused, looked directly at Simon Rubin: "I'm sorry you feel bad, Simon," he lamented, "it's just I been in chains four hundred years, and all that clankin' makes me hear not so good. I'm sorry you got troubles, man."

And their contest of agonies, their cataloguing of misery, their one-up of sorrow was cut short as the loudspekaer blared from across the yard, from the Administration Building.

"Hey! Hey over there!"

It was the main loudspeaker, mounted on the Administration Building, where the guards were waiting to come for them, holding out—it was now obvious—until their nerves were raw.

"Hey, Simon...Lew...all the rest of you...this is David, do you hear me, can you hear me, all of you?"

Gyp Williams fired off a long flaming burst, and they could hear the tinkle and shatter of window glass when he hit. It was an answer, of sorts.

"Listen, we can't blow the gate. We just can't do it, you guys." Chocolate rasped at his companions, "Hey! That's David, the one who was with the second group, what's he doin' in there with them?" Gyp Williams motioned him to silence. They listened.

"They've got the gate staked out, listen you men! They have it fixed so we can't get at it. Simon! Lew Steiner! All of you, Gyp, Gyp Williams, listen! They said they won't punish us if we go back to our cells. They said they wouldn't demand payment, we can go right on like we were before, it's better this way, it isn't so bad, we know what we can do, we know what they won't let us do! Simon, Gyp, come on back, come on back and they won't make any trouble for us, we can go on the way we were before, don't rock the boat, you guys, *don't rock the boat!*"

Gyp Williams rose to both knees, somehow manhandling the heavy machine rifle against his chest, and he screamed at the top of his voice, throwing his head back so his very white teeth stood out like a necklace of sparkling gems in his mouth—*"Sellout bastards!"* and he fired, without taking his finger from the trigger, he fired and the flames and heat and steel and anguish went cascading across the yard, hitting unreceptive stone and gravel and occasionally one of the already dead would leap as a slug tore its cold flesh.

Finally, when he had made it clear what their answer was to be, he fell exhausted behind the sandbags, where he would die.

In that instant of minor silence, Simon Rubin said, "I'm going back." And he got up and walked across the yard, his head down, his hands locked behind his head.

Don Karpinsky began to cry, then, and Chocolate slid across to him, trying by his nearness to stop the fear and the fury of being too brave to live, too cowardly to die without tears. No one behind the barricade moved to shoot Simon Rubin. There was no point to it, no anger at him, only pity and deep revulsion. And the guards in their immaculate white did not shoot him. Back in their world he was infinitely more valuable as a symbol, a broken image, for the others who might try to free themselves another time.

They would point to him and say, "See Simon Rubin, *he* tried to rock the boat, and see what he's like?"

Behind the barricade Nigger Joe turned to Lew Steiner and the crying kid who had not fled with Simon Rubin. "There, that's how much your people understand," he condemned them all.

And Lew Steiner said, "There were half a dozen of your boys in that second group, Joe. My back aches again, you feel like doing that thing?"

Nigger Joe chuckled lackadaisically, slid over and began thumbing Lew Steiner's back.

They were like that, waiting, when the final assault began. The high keening whine of a mortar shell came at them like the doppler of a train passing on a track, and it landed far down at the end, where Chocolate caught it full, and split up like a ripe, dark pod. He was dead even as it struck, and the other four fell in a heap to protect themselves from screaming shrapnel.

When the ground had ceased to tremble, and they could see the world again, they tried not to look toward the end of the barricade, where a brown leg and a torn bit of cloth showed from under the heap of rubble, from under the fallen sheets of metal. They tried not to look, and succeeded, but Gyp Williams's face was now incapable of even that half-bitter, knowing smile he had offered before.

Another whining shell came across, struck the wall above them and exploded violently, with Lew Steiner's howl of pain matching it on a lower level.

The shard of twisted metal had caught him in the neck, ripping through and leaving him with a deep furrow, welling out wetly, black-red down his shirt and over the hand he raised to staunch the flow. Nigger Joe tore his shirt down the front and made a crude bandage. "It ain't bad, Lew, here, hold this on if you can."

The four of them turned back to see the first wave of white-uniformed guards breaking from the cover of the Administration Building and another group from around the end of the Laundry.

They came on like a wide-angled "V" with a longarm grenade hurler at the point. Gyp Williams turned loose with the machine rifle, and swept the first attackers; they fell, but one of them got off a grenade, and it sailed almost gracefully, a balloon of hard stuff, over and over into the enclosure. The earth split up and deafened them, and great chunks of steel and stone cascaded about them. It was enough to ruin the machine gun, and send Don Karpinsky tumbling over backward, his body saturated with tiny bits of steel and sand. He lay sprawled backward, eyes open at the sky of free darkening blue, over the wall he would never climb.

They huddled there, the three of them left—Gyp Williams, Nigger Joe and Lew Steiner, still clutching the bloody rag to his neck.

The guards in their white uniforms would not let them go back to the cells. They knew the ones who were weak enough to keep from rocking the boat, and they knew the ones who had to be destroyed. These three were the last of the ones who had sought their freedom and their pride. They would be killed where they lay, when the ammunition had run out and all the strength was sapped from them, not only by the fighting, but by the ones who had betrayed them, the ones who had said it was better not to make trouble.

And as the waves of faceless, soulless attackers streamed toward them across the dead-piled yard, no more intent on the particular men behind the barricade than they would have been about any other vermin who threatened them, Gyp Williams said it all for all three of them, and for the few strong ones who had found peace, if not pride: "We all of us down in the dark. Some day, maybe...some day."

Then he managed somehow to get the machine rifle steadied, and he fired into the midst of them, screaming and running with their immaculate white uniforms the badges of purity and cleanliness.

But there were just too many of them.

There were *always*, just too many of them.

The story that follows is one of the original group from "A Touch of Infinity." It was written while I was in the Army, and on rereading it seems a pleasant enough little fillip. I doubt seriously whether the story, even when fresh, could have changed the course of Western Civilization; and now that it's almost ten years old. I'm positive it was merely good clean fun. Yes, I know that practically, *the gimmick in this story could never work, that people would never allow it to work, but when you are a paid liar—né Writer—you presuppose people will go along with you. That, Virginia, is called the "suspension of disbelief" and without it Heinlein, Asimov, Vonnegut and myself would be the most imaginative quartet of bricklayers in the world. The story is called*

Back to the Drawing Boards

PERHAPS it was inevitable, and perhaps it was only a natural result of the twisted eugenics that produced Leon Packett. In either case, the invention of the perambulating vid-robot came about, and nothing has been at all the same since.

The inevitability factor was a result of live tri-vid, and the insatiable appetite for novelty of the vid audience. If vid broadcasts came from Bermuda in tri-vid color with feelie and whiff, then they wanted wide-band transmission from the heart of the Sudetenland. If they got that, it wasn't enough; next they wanted programs from the top of Everest. And when they had accomplished that—God only knows how—the voracious idiot mind of the audiences demanded more. They demanded live casts from the Millstone, circling above the Earth; then it was Lunar fantasies with authentic settings...and Mars...and Venus... and the Outer Cold Ones.

Finally, Leon Packett stumbled upon the secret of a perfect, self-contained tri-vid camera, operating off a minute force-bead generator; and in his warped way, he struck instantly to the truth of the problem—that the only camera that could penetrate to those inner niches of the universe that the eyes of a man demanded to glimpse, was a man himself.

How completely simple it was. The only gatherer of facts as seen by the eyes of a man...were the eyes of a man. But since no man would volunteer to have his head sliced open, his brains scooped out, and a tri-vid camera inserted, Leon Packett invented Walkaway.

In all due to the devil, it was coldly logical, and it was a beautiful bit of workmanship. Walkaway had the form of a human being, even to ball-and-socket joints at the knees and elbows. He stood just under seven feet tall, and his hide was a burnished permanodized alumasteel suit. His hands could be screwed off, and in their stead could be inserted any one of three dozen "duty" hands, withdrawn from storage crypts, located in the limbs. His head was the only part of him that was slightly more than human. Brilliantly so, again offering Satan his plaudits.

Where the center of the face on a human would have been, the revolving lens wheel with its five turrets bulked strangely. Beneath the lens wheel a full-range audio grid lay with criss-crossed strangeness. The audio pickups were located on either side, as well as front and rear, of the head.

Two sets of controls were used on Walkaway. One set was imbedded in the right arm (and would snap up at the proper coded pressing of a lock-snit at the wrist) and was chiefly used by Walkaway himself when he was asked to play back what he had heard or seen.

The other console controls were in the back, and to my knowledge, were never employed after Walkaway's initial test runs. He disliked being pawed.

Naturally, the dissenters at Walkaway's birth, who declaimed the sanity of giving a robot volition and "conscience" with as much strength as his metal frame held, were shouted down. The creature—well, wasn't he?—had to have the right of free choice, if he was going to get the story in all its fullness and with a modicum of imagination, which the vid audience demanded.

So Walkaway was made more human.

He was able to disagree, to be surprised, to follow instructions *almost* as they were given, and to select the viewing subjects he wished, when he was filming. Walkaway was a most remarkable... what?

Creature.

"Leon, you've *got* to do it. Don't be obstinate, that's just being foolish. They'll get him somehow, Leon!"

Leon Packett spun in the chair, facing the window. His back was very straight, and his neck held a rigid aloofness. "Get out, McCollum. Get out and tell your pony-soldiers to do the same. Leave me alone!"

Alan McCollum threw up his hands in eloquent frustration. "Lee, I'm trying to get *through* to you, for God's sake! All I ask is you listen to them, and *then* make a decision—"

Packett spun in the chair. His feet hit the floor with a resounding clump and he leaned one elbowed arm at McCollum. His index finger was an unwavering spear, the tip of which aimed between McCollum's sensitive dark brown eyes.

"Now look, McCollum, I spent fifteen years in a cellar lab, working what I could, and experimenting as best I could, soldering old pieces together because I couldn't get a Frericks Grant. Then I happened to think of putting two old gadgets together, and I came up with a miracle. Now I'm big time, and the Frericks Foundation uses me in their institutional advertisements."

His lean, horsey face was becoming ruby-blotched.

"But Walkaway is *mine*, McCollum! Mine! I dreamed him up and I sweated constructing him. I starved for fifteen years, McCollum. Fifteen. You know how long that is? While you and all your MIT buddies were piddling around putting chrome on old discoveries, I was missing all the good things."

McCollum's jaws worked. His eyes dulled with suppressed fury. "That isn't fair, Lee. You almost enjoy your misery, and you *know* it."

Packett stood up. His face was a crimson and milk patchwork. "Get out!" he snarled. His thin lips worked loosely, and his nostrils flared. "Get out and leave me alone. Walkaway is *not* going to Carina. Not Epsilon Carinae, not Miaplacidus, nowhere in Carina. Walkaway is staying here, where I can keep getting my commissions, where I can guarantee my future. It's been too dirty for me to start being patriotic now, McCollum, so you can trot out there and tell your Space Patrol buddies I'm not in the market."

McCollum was about to shout an answer, but he stood up instead. Stood up and stared at the contorted features of Leon Packett.

He turned and took three steps to the slidoor. With his palm—but not fingertips—fitted into the depression, he paused and looked back at Packett. "There are doctors who can help you, Leon."

"Get out, you fool!"

A heavy plastex ashtray crashed into the wall beside McCollum's head. His fingertips touched and the door slid.

Perhaps he knew it was inevitable. The machinery he had always despised, now ground its wishes out in the dust of his ambitions. He had cursed the powers that had suffered by his own hand, and overlooked him. But now they wanted his vid-robot, his Walkaway. He knew they would reimburse him handsomely, but that was not what he sought.

Packett knew, and he moved to preserve his will, despite the loss of his invention. Late into the night he worked, on the smallest, most unnoticeable alterations in the printed circuitry of Walkaway's "mind" and "conscience." Late into the night on a space of plastex no longer than the surface of an eyeball. And when he fell into an exhausted sleep, as the daylight ribboned across the laboratory walls, Walkaway stood as he had stood.

Unchanged.
Apparently.
But changed.
Inwardly.

He managed to salvage his old age. By the simple expedient of refusing to allow ownership to switch from his hands—and after his death the hands of the Frericks Foundation—into the hands of the military, he preserved a hold on Walk-away. The Guard—his terminology "Space Patrol" had long since been

aborted, despite the tabloid's efforts to keep it alive—were forced
to hire Walkaway. They signed him on as a civilian employee,
paid a monthly wage, a per diem remuneration, as well as travel
expenses.

The wages were to be paid on demand, and books were
kept by the Frericks Foundation, whose interest in Packett and
Walkaway were more than merely scientific. With the world-
famous Leon Packett associated with them, there could be no
doubt about doles and grants. The Frericks Foundation had men
at its helm whose interests penetrated into other fields than
scientific: politics, finance, authority. The men were exceedingly
careful to keep books.

The Guard's first enterprise in which Walkaway figured
prominently was the remote from Bounce Point.

Bounce Point was the supersatellite constructed out beyond
Pluto. It had been thrown up as the last outpost of Solar enterprise.
Man's final touch with what was known, before he leaped off
into the unknown.

From Bounce Point, great and silver and ebony in Pluto's sky,
Walkaway was destined to begin the long ride out.

McCollum and his contemporaries had not been idle. While
Leon Packett nursed his hatred of Authority and the Machine of
Empire, they had been hard at work. The warp-drive was ready.
Nuzzling the gleaming inner hull of its drive chamber, the warp-
drive was larger than later models would surely have to be. It
was a giant nest of power units, small inside larger, larger inside
still larger, and finally, resting in a brace-socket at the tip of
the final unit, a force-bead of incalculable power. That was the
random factor. How hard could the warp-drive be pushed by
this force-bead?

What were the effects on a man, sent through not-space?

For the test, what better guinea pig than a metal man with a
camera face? In tri-vid, with audio pick-up, what better record
could be offered for study?

The initial flight of W-1 to Carina, lost in the star heaps
of space, would be accomplished with no human hand at the
controls. The robot would take the bounce.

Leon Packett lay on a dirty bunk in a haven back of the Central Port space pads. The room was a flop, with the tackboard walls only stretching halfway to the ceiling. The other half of the wall was strand-wire, put in to offer a slight deterrent to thieves in the other cubicles, in no way to offer privacy. Packett lay on the bunk, a half-emptied bottle of Paizley's rigid between his side and his arm, held upright by his arm-pit. His long, almost oriental eyes were closed in stupor, and his horsey face was a Madame Toussaud wax reproduction. His breathing was irregular...when McCollum found him.

"Packett!" All civility was gone. There are worse things than insults. The insults had not alienated McCollum. The others had. "Packett! They want you. Get out, Packett!"

He dragged the bottle with its sour smell from Leon Packett's armpit, and threw it to the floor. Where the wrench of the bottle had not disturbed the drunken man, where McCollum's shot-like shouts had not roused him, the soft gurgling emptying of the bottle succeeded.

Packett came straight up on the bunk, hands in his wild hair, and he screamed. With eyes closed, with deep lined areas about the sockets, he shrieked. *"Let me alone!"*

Then he opened his eyes.

After he had sobbed, and dry-heaved, McCollum got him to his feet and out of the filthy wino-odored cubicle. There was a small argument about three days rent, with a ferret-like man behind the cage, but McCollum flashed over a five-note and they went into the street. Where the sounds of traffic overhead on the expressways deafened Packett, rising over him, like the spread, leathery wings of a pterodactyl, and dropped over him with suffocating strength. He tried to bolt back into the building.

McCollum was forced to hit him.

The hack ride was uneventful.

The Frericks Foundation rose alabaster on the third tier of the New Portion. McCollum would have paused to clean Leon Packett's face and innards, had not the Guard representatives spotted them as they left the hack at tier level. The gay uniforms of the Guard were ranked in the hall as McCollum steadied his sodden cargo into the building.

"My God, purulent!" one Guardsman snorted sourly.

"Is that Packett?" a dapper, balding Guardsman asked. His shoulders bore Commander boards. McCollum nodded. He tried to move past with Packett.

The Commander stopped them. McCollum explained, "He was on the Strip. He's not been well."

"Don't cover for him, McCollum. He's a waste, and there should be no glossing. The man is a waste. Can he talk?"

McCollum shrugged, still supporting Packett, whose legs were taffy. "I suppose. I don't know how much coherence you'll get out of him, but I suppose he can talk."

The Commander nudged a thumb toward a conference room. "Bring him along."

They started toward the room, and Packett began to blather. Even as they thrust him into a chair, his words fumbled and roiled. "They with power...laws and can't do, and do, and have this with what they let you do. I know! I've *always* known! The wheels with grinding down and they are afraid, so they rule you...rule..."

He went on ramblingly, almost semi-conscious, his words— more, his accents—tirades against authority and government. They had hampered him, but he would get even.

The Guard listened closely, for after all, this was Packett, the inventor of Walkaway. They listened, and finally, the Commander put his gloved hand, his crimson gloved hand, across Packett's mouth. "That will be enough, man," he deep-throated, with suppressed fury.

"Tell him what we want, McCollum," the esoteric purulent-caller urged the Frericks man.

McCollum's eyebrows went up and his lips thinned with resignation. The military never *could* pull its weight in these matters. "Leon," McCollum said, slipping to one knee beside Packett's chair. "Leon, they want to take Walkaway back to the drawing boards. They think he has too much initiative, Leon? Can you understand—"

"No!

"No, by God, damn their eyes, *no*! Not a touch. Not a wire. Nothing! He stays as he is! If they want to use him, damn them they've robbed me of my fortune, now they'd pick my brainwork apart, no I say!"

They argued and pleaded and cajoled and screeched at him for the better part of five hours. But he was firm. He still owned Walkaway. The Frericks Foundation employed Packett by grant, but Walkaway was still his own, and when it came down to it, not a military personnel at all. Walkaway was a free entity. A bond slave of metal set free. If they wanted him to go to Carina—as Packett had resolved it to himself—he would go as he was now, today, now.

So the Guard had to accept it that way. They had to take Walkaway with individuality...too much for a robot? And they had to send him on the first bounce to the stars, as a metal man with thoughts of his own.

That was as it should have been.

For had not Leon Packett created Walkaway?

Had not Packett re-arranged the circuits to provide a hidden factor the Guard knew nothing about?

Had it not all been planned that way?

To results we know now.

The ship was crazily-shaped. It was a sundial. With a thick trunk, and two clear face-plates at either end. Great face plates of clear substance, through which Walkaway could train his turret eyes, and see the universe as it whirled by in not-space. The drive apertures were set at angles around the thick trunk of the ship, and there were no sleeping compartments, no galley, no chairs, nothing a metal servant would find useless.

The ship W-1 blasted free of Bounce Point on March 24th, 2111, its sole occupant a robot named Walkaway, whose face was a triple-turret tri-vid camera and whose mind was the mind of a metal man with initiative. A certain initiative that only one man knew existed.

The ship left on March 24th. On March 31st, Leon Packett gripped a pair of heavy scissors and thrust them deep into his neck.

His will was a masterpiece of maudlin self-pity; but it released Walkaway from all human obligations, setting him *en toto* free.

He was a singular now. Not an invention, but a civilian employee of the military Guard. He was to receive payment per diem for his work, and his accounts were to be handled by the Frericks Foundation.

Whatever Walkaway earned, remained his own.

The ship went out on March 24th, 2111.

It returned three hundred and sixty-five years later.

And the future began.

Oh, Lord! The records were covered with dust. But valid, that was the rub. The Frericks Foundation had sunk in its own mismanagement, and a pleasure sanctuary had risen on its whited bones. The New Portion was now called the Underside, for tiers had risen high on high to the fiftieth level above that tier. Now there was a planet-wide government, and the ship W-1 had become a legend. The robot Walkaway had become a myth. The ship had never been heard from again, and as will happen, with all cultures, time had passed the concept of star travel by.

There was a broken-nosed statue of Leon Packett on the third tier, many miles from where the Frericks Foundation had stood, a statue that called him one of the great inventors of all time and all Mankind. There were no scissors in the statue.

When the ship came down past the Moon, and its warning gear telemetered out the recog-signals, the Earth Central control tower was lost in disbelief. A sloe-eyed brunette who was in charge of deciphering and matching recog-signals with the call letters of those ships out, called for a checker. Her section chief, a woman who had been on the job for eighteen years, matched the recog-signals, and turned to the younger girl with a word lost on her lips.

The call went in to Guard Central immediately.

They denied landing co-ordinates to the W-1 and held it aspace till they had found the records in the sub-cellar of the pleasure sanctuary on the third level. When they had the files, they knew the story completely, and they sent word to berthin the W-1.

Walkaway looked the same. Huge and graceful, his face

vaguely human, his body a sort of homo sapiens plus, he slid down a nylex rope from the cargo aperture of the sun-dial-shaped ship. He had not bothered to lower the landing ramp. As he came down the single strand, his metallic reflection shone in the smooth landing-jack's surface. The reflection of Walkaway shone down and down and over again down as he slid quickly to the pad.

They watched, as they might watch a legend materialize. This was the fabled robot that had gone out to seek the stars in Carina, and had returned. Three hundred and sixty-five years the W-1 had been away, and now it had returned. What would the vid-cameras of this perambulating robot show? What wonders awaited man, now that his interest was roused in the immensities of space? The Guard watched, ranked around the pad, as Walkaway slid down the nylex rope. The great sundial-shaped ship held high above them—unlike any other of the sleek vessels in the yard—tripod poised on its high-reaching legs.

Then the robot touched Earth, and a shout went up.

Home is the hunter, home from the hill...

Three hundred and sixty-five years. No one was left who remembered this creature of flawless metal. No one who had seen Walkaway go out on the shuttle to Bounce Point.

Bounce Point that was itself two hundred years dust. Gone in the struggle for the Outer Cold Ones.

The robot came across the pad, his shining feet bright against the blackened pad-rock, and his close-up turret ground near-to-silently away, taking in the reception ceremony for posterity.

Before the Guard representative could issue forth with the practiced phrases of a hundred other receptions, the robot said clearly, "It is good to be back. Where is Leon Packett?"

How strange it was—they said later—a legend. Paul Bunyan inquiring after Zeus. What could they say? Few of them even knew of the man named Leon Packett. Those who knew, were vague where he was concerned. After all, three hundred and sixty-five years. The Earth had changed.

"I asked: where is Leon Packett? Which of you is from the Frericks Foundation?"

There were no answers. And then someone in the front ranks

of the Guard, someone who knew his history, said: "You have been gone three hundred years and more, robot."

"Leon Packett...?"

"Is dead," finished the Guardsman. "Long dead. Where have you been so long?"

And a circuit closed as data was fed to Walkaway.

And the future was assured.

Loneliness. Leon Packett had done his work well. The attempts to take Walkaway back to the drawing boards would have shown them what Packett had done. He had freed the robot's soul completely. Not only legally, but in actuality. Walkaway felt great sadness. There had only been one other who knew his inner feelings. That had been Leon Packett. There had been empathy between them. The man a bit mad, the robot a bit man. They had spent evenings together, as two childhood friends might have; the man and the faceless metal creature, product of the man's mind. They had not talked much, but a word had brought understanding of concepts, of emotions:

"All of them."

The robot, immobile, answering metallically, "Power."

"Somebody, someday..."

"Checks."

"Balances."

"Oh, Walkaway. Someday, just someday!"

"I know."

The nights had passed restlessly for Packett, while the sickness within him festered. The robot had been constructed in the image of the man. Seeing everything through its vid-eyes, hearing everything through its pickups, but saying little, working hard. Then Packett had known he would die, and Walkaway would live on. An extension of himself; the sword he would someday wield.

He had worked long into the night, foreseeing where they had the knowledge. For Leon Packett had been gifted. Sick, but gifted, and he had left his curse, left his justice, left his vengeance, to live on after he was gone.

Walkaway learned of Leon Packett's death, and the circuit Packett had tampered with, that he had wanted to close at the knowledge of his death, snapped to with a mental thud that only Walkaway felt, that the universe was soon to know.

The robot turned to the Guardsmen and made the one request no one would have considered, the one request that was his legally to make:

"Pay me my wages."

Three hundred and sixty-five years on Earth. Nine months and fifteen days in space. The warp-drive had been better than ghosts had thought. Memories of McCollum and his fellows from MIT lived within the force-bead, and had given it power. Better, far better, it had been, than their wildest imaginings. But Einstein had been correct. Mass, infinity, time zero. He had been correct, and Walkaway had earned three hundred and sixty-five years worth of wages. Per diem. Plus travel pay according to military regulations. They could not withhold it on grounds that he was using military transportation; Leon Packett had seen to that: Walkaway was a private citizen.

Plus interest accrued.

The sum was staggering. The sum was unbelievable. The sum could, would, *must* bankrupt the Earth government. It was unheard of. The Prelate convened, and the arguments raged, but Walkaway needed no defense. He merely requested: "Pay me my wages." And they had to do it.

Oh, they tried to dodge their way out of it. They tried to ensnare him in legalities, but he was a man of alumasteel, and legalities could not affect him.

The circuit had closed, and his life's plan was set. In the mind of Walkaway burned the conscience and soul of his creator. Leon Packett was not dead. In his creation was reborn the intense, vibrant hatred of power and government and authority. In Walkaway was the perfect weapon; indestructible, uncaring, human as human it need be, inhuman as inhuman it *must* be, to bring about the downfall of that which Packett had despised.

Fifteen years in a cellar laboratory had carried forth for over three hundred years, and the future was molded on printed circuits.

Finally, they acceded. They paid him his wages. The government of Earth was bankrupted. The world belonged to a man of alumasteel. It was no longer Earth. Had he wished, he might have named it Walkaway's World.

For such it was.

Leon Packett had foreseen such. He had applied Einstein's equations, and he had known what would happen. The scientists of the Frericks Foundation had known, also, and they had considered it all. But the job had had to be done, in that era before Man had turned inward once more. They had feared what might happen, but not considered it an inevitability. They had looked on it the way the farmer looks on earthquake. Yes, it might happen, but that would be an act of God, not a thing that must be.

But they had not considered Leon Packett. He had taken steps. He had altered his creation, and made it want its pay, when it knew he was dead. For dead he was dead, and alive he was dead. But in the soul of Walkaway he lived again.

So he had created an act of God.

Twisted in thought, crying in the darkness of his tormented mind, Leon Packett had changed the future. Changed it so irrevocably, evened the score so beautifully, Man would remember and curse and live with his name forever. They had known of the possibility, and they had tried to prevent it.

"Let us take Walkaway back to the drawing boards," McCollum—that shadow lost in the past—had cried. But Leon Packett had overruled him, "No!"

He would not let his name and his future be stolen from him. There was no need for him to go on living out a worthless life. That was bitterness. He had a tool that would drive forward to his ordained destiny. He had Walkaway, and though they suspected what might be, what could be, they never thought it *needed* to be. They figured without the drive and thirst of Walkaway's master. They figured without the hatred of a man for himself and for all other men.

Walkaway wanted his wages.

He got them, by getting the Earth.

There was not that much money in the world. Nor was there

that much property. But there was the government, and soon Walkaway was the government.

That was the future Leon Packett built for himself, as the shrine of his memory.

Walkaway was not vindictive.

But Leon Packett was.

There haven't been many changes. Not many. Not for us. It has been the same for a very long time.

Walkaway was fair, and carried forth Packett's desires in the only way an alumasteel man could.

Changes? No, not many.

But you'll forgive me, of course. I must hurry now. I'm quite overdue.

I should have been at my lubrication hours ago.

Two years is what I served as a trooper. I can't really get all teary and old-grad about my days in the Army. It was hell; as I was a bad college student, I was a bad soldier, but for entirely different reasons. Soldiering is a skill to which I feel no sane man should aspire. It is the professional gunslinging of a world too chickenshit to drive in the knives with individual combat. War becomes a stupidity, a dumb thing, no matter what the rationale, no matter what the color of the banner or the name of the ideology. True, it is the most exclamatory of all points that can be made, but when it settles, the dust covers victor and vanquished alike: that's a cliche already, they've made bad movies about it. But the argument holds. I have no patience with Birchers, MinuteMen, Nazis, violent overthrowers of governments or advocates of clearing out the Vietnam foliage with a little low-yield radiation. There seems to me nothing noble in war, nothing heroic, nothing golden or valuable. I suppose this makes me a pacifist. I never thought of it before, really. But I suppose at some point or other even the PFC whose serial number was US 514 033 52 has to stop and say, "I'd rather not." It's either that, or something I hope is not a self-fulfilling prophecy, a little boomp in the night called

A Friend to Man

TWIN GLOBES, polished surfaces buried in golden sand, still staring at a face-down universe. Molybdenum claws, powered from a groin of metal, futilely stretched in the golden sand. Powerpak dead...counterweights thrown from sockets... rust making the first microscopic smearings on gloss-bright indestructable hide.

Most Unworthy One lay on his face mid the shock-blasted wreckage of His home. Most Unworthy One's right arm was extended, as he had fallen, reaching for the last can of lubricant.

Blessed oil, that could pick him up, start his synapses sparkling, trigger his movements, send him to His aid, where-ever He might be, whatever danger surround Him.

Instead, he lay face down, whirling motes of dust rising shape-into-shape up flues of moist green sunlight. A sky diseased, leprous and shimmering in a world-socket turned to ash.

While Most Unworthy One stretched short of life.

Life gauged in millimetres, ball bearings and closed circuits. Life imparted on a production line in a now-fled time in a now-dead place he had known very well as Detroit. Where cars had been made, and vacuum sweepers, and generators, and robots.

It had never been difficult, the knowing. There was flesh, and there was the way *he* was, not-flesh. It was his honor, his destiny to serve flesh; and when they had sent Most Unworthy One to serve Him, it had been the sun and the warmth and the hunger for work. It had been so very, very good.

He had been an artist. Working with palette and brush and cassein He had often called over His shoulder from the high stool before the easel: "See, friend (He had indulged Himself by calling the servant with friendship) see how the paleness of the eyes attracts before the red of the mouth. Do you see it?"

Or other words that drew Most Unworthy One's attention to something in His work. And oddly, Most Unworthy One *did* see, *did* sense, *did* revel in the wonder there on canvas.

Then He would turn, wiping his fingertips dry on the square of muslin, and stare deeply at Most Unworthy One. "My art," He would say, "is nothing compared to yours. The beauty of you... can you know what I mean?"

And Most Unworthy One's gears would mesh, for he did not completely understand, but he knew that His words held affection, and they had programmed affection, so it had value, it had merit.

"May I serve you forever?" Most Unworthy One would ask at those times, hoping the answer would be the same as it had always been; hoping silently, hoping.

"I'll always take care of you," He would say, which had no meaning, really. For everyone knew that the robots took care of the flesh. That was the way the world was set up. But it was kind of Him to say it, and again, oddly, Most Unworthy One believed it. He would take care when the time came. Though Most Unworthy One watched over Him, if ever the robot needed succor, it would come from Him, or others like Him.

For Man was good and strong and forever. Metal was flawed by the ills of time and rust and climatic caprice. So Most Unworthy One lay and waited, confidently, knowing He would one day come and lift the robot from the sand, and pour the life-bringing oil into the proper feeder channels. Then Most Unworthy One could return to his tasks of seeing after Him.

Minor chores, the looking-afterness? Yes, that was for men of metal. But the *real* chores, the work that could only be done by Him...that must come when He came.

As He would come. Some time soon.

He did not forget His friends.

Across the moor that had once been a borough, nine men huddled inside a shell that had been a lobby. Behind a frosted, melted non-shape that had been a florist's booth, they crouched, rifles only slightly off-ready. One of the men had been a plumber. Another had been a statistical consultant. A third had been a chassis dynamometer technician in a large automobile agency. A fourth had used a stick with a nail at its end in parks.

One had been an artist and had owned his very own robot, who now lay face down in the rubble of the artist's former home. The artist was unaware of the robot's condition or needs.

Right now, he was thirty-five minutes from possible death.

"They came in the Brooklyn-Battery tunnel," the taxidermist murmured, shovel-fingering back his long, grey hair. "I saw a smoke signal about an hour ago from down there." The others nodded their heads knowingly, imperceptibly. "George Adams told me they had a battalion of robots with them," the taxidermist concluded.

"But *dammit* that's against the treaties; no gas, no germs, no fusion bombs, no robots," snarled the plumber. "What the hell are they trying to prove?"

The artist mused ruefully, "They're trying to kill us, man. And they've gotten far enough so they don't have to worry about treaties. If they want to use robots, there isn't really a lot we can do to stop them, is there?"

Agreeing mutters went up.

The old man, the one who had taught comparative philosophy in one of the greater Midwestern universities, thrust, "We should have attacked them before they attacked *us*! It was foolish to have gone on letting them bait us, killing us here and there, and when they were ready...they jumped. We should have attacked them *first*!"

They all knew there was something wrong with his concept, but they could not voice their objections. There was no doubt he had a point.

A tall, emaciated man with pants legs flapping stumped into the lobby. "Hey, y'round?"

The plumber stood up and waved the rifle over his head. "Over here, and *shut up*, you goddam bigmouth!"

The thin man flap-legged to the florist's booth. "I seen 'em. I seen 'em comin' down Fifth Avenue. They got a rank'a robots in the front. Everybody's scatterin'!"

"Well, *we* won't scatter," the philosophy professor made a fist and his shadow did the same. "Come along! Let's get them..."

The artist gripped the rising man's shoulder. "Sit *down*. Don't be imbecilic. They'd cut us into strips if we wandered out there. There's only ten of us, with sporting rifles. They've got flame throwers, robots, tanks, what the hell's the matter with you?"

"I can't stand to see Americans running like—"

"Cut the patriotism," the park attendant chopped.

"Anybody got a suggestion," the garage mechanic ventured, tired of the bickering.

There was silence.

Tehuantepec, thought the artist absently, illogically, *how I'd love to be back in Tehuantepec, doing the mountains with brush strokes like flowing gold or burning in the sun's death.*

But Mexico had long since fallen to the locust-like advance of the Enemy.

The last patriots in America's greatest city huddled and hummed silently, and were without direction or plan.

One of the ten was a bowlegged, withdrawn man who had,

at one time, combed his thinning hair straight back over the bald spot that lay accusingly in the center front of his scalp. His eyes were watery behind corrective lenses. He had been an optometrist.

"I have a suggestion," he offered. Heads turned to him; they looked at him, but received only an image. People saw *at* this man, they did not see *him*. But he had an idea.

"In del Castillo's service under Cortes—" he began, and was cut off by a rueful snort from the professor, which, in turn, was cut off by a slap on the back from the plumber, "—he reports in his book how they defeated an unwary group of hostile Aztecs by rolling boulders down on them from above."

"Yes, very nice," the professor snapped irritatedly. "You, sir, are a monumental ass. How does a book written in the 16th Century help us? Grow up!"

The artist's face lit. He remembered Mexico, the look of it, the smell and sound of it, and the sight of rock basins grew where it had once been. "Shut up, you," he asserted. "I know what he means. Fella, I think you've got something there. I do, I really do..."

The Enemy came down the street rank on rank. There was no need for reluctance, no need for hesitation or skulking. The preparatory seeding of the city had been an eminent example of pre-consolidation softening. There was a light-hearted manner to them. They had paused to camp in the Battery, changing to dry socks, filling their bellies with rice and fish heads, regaining the topness of their morale.

Now they were here, the conquerors.

First came the file of robots, their sleek and shining hides decorated with yellow calligraphy, connoting ferocity, intrepidness, or ancestor honor.

Behind them, in a marsh-wagon adaptable to any terrain, came the coxswain, his electronic megaphones aimed at the rank of robots, ready to order them at an instant's awareness. Then came the troops.

The artist, the plumber, the optometrist, the other seven, they watched from above as the robots passed beneath. "Get the coxswain," the artist directed. "Get him and the robots won't have direction."

The others nodded. The statistician, who had done some bear hunting in the Adirondacks, had been labeled the sharp-shooter of the group, but three others backed him in case of a miss. They weren't expecting one, but safety, you know, fella, just safety.

The last rank of troops—there were only fifteen waves in this group—turned onto the street, and the sharp-shooter raised the 30.06, removed from a gutted sports store, to his shoulder. The cheek welded down tight to the metal behind the sight, and the eye came close to the tiny hole. The polished wood of the stock fit under the shoulder as though it had grown there, and the left hand cupped gently but firmly along the barrel and receiver grouping. The right hand moved without hesitation to the trigger housing and paused on the curved bit of metal before moving on to the trigger itself. The sharp-shooter followed with his eye and the muzzle of the rifle, tracking the marsh-wagon and plotting the course of the coxswain's helmeted forehead.

Then, as the sun rode behind a ridge of cloud, the finger curled around the trigger, the sight came down to a micro-point three feet in front of the marsh-wagon, and as the vehicle slid between the crossed hairs of the sight, the finger lovingly squeezed the tongue of metal.

The rifle leaped, bucking against the statistician's shoulder, a wisp of muzzle gas lifted away on the wind, and the report echoed between the buildings like a steel casting, thrown from a great height.

The coxswain shrieked and slapped a hand to his erupting forehead, tearing away the megaphone control helmet with the other hand. His mouth opened wide in a toothy, wordless scream, and as the dark fluid blinded him, he pitched forward, over the raised-high side of the marsh-wagon. His body sprawled on the street. It was a signal.

The laboriously-handmade fire bombs cascaded from the building-tops. They landed and spattered and napalm blossomed among the ranks. The robots, unguided, milled about an instant, then silently, fluidly gathered into a knot away from the center of destruction.

An attack team—ringed in by fire and weirdly dancing comrades faced with flames—bracketed up their heavy mortar and lobbed a shell at the building. The shell dropped short, smacked the outcropping cornice of the building and plummeted to explode amidst their own men.

In a matter of minutes the fifteen ranks were decimated, all but one atomic artillery piece, manned by three men in heat-suits. They brought the weapon into play, and on the third shot tore away the first two floors of the building, killing the tiny knot of guerillas, and ending the sortie.

Before they could escape, however, the flames enveloped them (for the street itself had been pre-soaked—deadly bathroom mechanics those Americans) and within their heat-suits they blistered, gagged and died.

The street was silent. The line of robots, now a glittering array of metal as the sun broke through once more, milled uncertainly, and finally moved off.

For a long while the city was filled with noise, then as though a cosmic symphony had concluded...silence leaf-dropped and this particular war was ended. The winner had won.

Most Unworthy One could not know death. His was a life easily imbalanced, but never ended. He lay face down, one arm extended in hungry prayer to the cask of oil, and remorselessly waited for total darkout.

Then the sand and rubble clattered and snapped.

Someone was coming, and Most Unworthy One knew it was Him, it could only be Him. The silent promises and the spoken promises He had always made to take care of His servant were coming true. He was coming.

Most Unworthy One felt the footsteps progress past to the can of oil, and heard its bulk being wrenched from the sand and debris. Then the footsteps came back, and someone knelt beside Most Unworthy One. The feeder box was gently opened, the telescoping funnel was extended, and a moment later the golden-crimson-violet stream went gurgling into the proper channels.

"You'll be all right now," a voice said. "The war's over and we've got a lot of work to do." It was colloquial, it was the way

He had talked, it was the master and the protector back from death to help His Most Unworthy One.

"Let me help you," the voice said. And strong arms went under Most Unworthy One's shoulders, lifting him.

Strong arms of metal.

Most Unworthy One looked up as he stood, into multi-faceted eyes that burned with Man-given intelligence. The friend of Man had returned.

Sadly, he felt it would not be difficult to re-form allegiances. Times change, and few things are forever.

The day would be chilly, but it didn't really matter.

Jessica Mitford did all of us a tremendous service with her exposé of the graveyard ghouls, "The American Way Of Death". It showed what a casket and interment worshiping nation we've become, with all the attendant vampirism of money-sucking on the part of those black-suited swine who cajole us when our darkest hours of misery are at hand. For the record, and just so my wonderful middle-class Jewish relatives won't have their way with my poor mortal coil once I've shucked it off, be it herewith known, before all and sundry, that being of sound mind and body, I want the cheapest funeral imaginable. One of those $1.98 jobbies with the card-board casket. Then after the closed-lid ceremony at which I want only my enemies in attendance (I see no need to make my friends suffer the peculiar tortures of watching someone they've loved lying there about ready to become worm-food), kindly sell off my eyeballs and my bones and my skin and anything else medical science can use to help somebody else, and send the proceeds to either the Deacons down South, to buy some guns, or to the St. Labre Indian Mission, to buy those redskin kids some decent clothes. And that, friends and lovers, is the final dispensation of my mortal remains on this Earth. And let Tutankhamen have nothing on me; this be my curse: if any schmuck defies this decree, and my body be laid out in all the grotesque finery of the undertaking cosmetic art, with weepers and wailers and necrophiles surrounding, so that my headstone is finally set to read "Nothing in His Life Became Him as Much as the Leaving of It", then may all those involved in this perfidy be condemned to the deepest strata of Hell, in which they will roast forever, and be compelled to read, over and over and over till Time doubles back on itself and starts again, my condemnation of the Funereal Society,

"We Mourn for Anyone..."

IT HAD BEEN the work of perhaps a minute and a half to kill his wife.

Gordon Vernon stepped back from the edge of the roof, out of the line-of-sight from the building across the way. Deliberately, he began to puddle the weapon.

The weapon was a small knobbed box. It had cost him ten thousand dollars; and the man who had constructed it had "luckily" been outdrawn in a duel the month before. The box's sole function was the emission of a beam which affected the semicircular canals of the inner ear. The canals which govern the balance of the body. The little box can-celled this function. It was ingenious, and Vernon was thankful he had seen to the duel which had killed the inventor. The man might have wanted to patent the device some day, and that would have been fatal. The only person, as a consequence, who knew of the existence of the little box was Gordon Vernon.

And he was destroying it...for it had served its sole purpose. It had foolproofedly murdered his wife.

The little box with its protruding dials and thin wire antenna began to slag away into molten nothingness under the controlled heat of his flamer.

He kept the beam on the box, which lay on the plasteel roof of the building, making certain the heat was enough to melt the weapon—but not enough to char the plasteel.

In a few moments the box had been reduced to a shining, flat wafer of fused metal. The sun's light caught a plane of the surface, and reflected brightly in Vernon's blue eyes.

He holstered the flamer, making certain to set the air-wick in the barrel cleanser to *spray*—cleaning away all evidence that the flamer had been fired.

Then he stooped and picked up the wafer of metal.

He carried it to the opposite side of the building. Scaling it like a plastic plate, he threw it out over the city. He saw it arc down between the towering pastel-tinted buildings and disappear onto a side street. The refusemecks would dispose of it in (he looked at his ring-watch) about three-quarters of an hour. Then all evidence would be gone.

The perfect murder had been tastefully committed.

Vernon walked swiftly to the dropshaft and lowered to the seventieth floor of the building. From there he took the seldom-used escalator down the back way, and seven minutes later was on the street.

A crowd had already gathered across the street, in front of his building.

He looked across at the building he had just left, up to where he had stood, and was reassured that no one in his own building could have seen him.

The crowd was deepening. But he didn't join it. Several uniformed Legalizers were forming an arm-locked circle, trying to keep the crowd away. He already knew what was in the center of that throng.

Lisa. Dead from a ninety-six storey fall. Quite dead, and by his hand. But ostensibly dead from an accidental fall. He had committed the perfect murder simply by jamming the balancing faculty of his wife's inner ear.

When the kill-box had negated her sense of balance, she had left her roof garden luncheon party precipitously. Over the parapet, and down to the street. The giving plastic of the streets was constructed to give ease to walking, but from the height Lisa had fallen, it was as stone hard as steel.

He walked past the crowd disinterestedly. As a man would, who was returning from work, and had no time for idle street-gawking.

As he passed, a woman turned and called to him almost hysterically. He recognized her as one of the women Lisa had invited to the roof luncheon. *The old ghoul must have dropped down that shaft like a greased pig to see the mess*, he thought wryly.

"Mr. Vernon! Mr. Vernon! Your wife, your wife! She's—" The woman's face was pasty-white and she seemed to be clogging on her own tongue, yet there was an unnatural gleam in her eyes. *The old bat enjoys the sight of death, I do believe*, Vernon added mentally. The woman couldn't let the rest of her sentence fall, but she had served her purpose.

Vernon let a look of terror and disbelief course across his square, almost-handsome features.

He ran to the crowd and elbowed through.

There in the center, sprawled crazily, worse than he had thought it could possibly be, was Lisa.

It wasn't a very pleasant way to end your little affair, Liz, darling, he thought with finality, *but I've never much cared for unfaithful wives. They seem so tediously melodramatic.*

"My God, what happened!" Gordon Vernon screamed, falling to his knees in the street, burying his face and hands in the crumpled, bloody shape. Before his view was cut off, he saw the faces of the people.

The crowd breathed tragedy, and condolences for him.

Vernon's flamer clattered in its sheath against the sidewalk as he writhed. No one noticed.

I've got to get that sheath oiled, he thought clearly. *And I'd better hire a Mourner, too.*

It had been a good day. After the brief inquest, and after the coroner had clicked its decision—flashing DEATH BY ACCIDENT on its viewslit—Gordon Vernon had begun his show of sorrow.

It wasn't strictly protocol; he might have already hired himself a Mourner, and left the chore to him, but Vernon was a cautious man, and laying it on a little heavier could do no harm. It was annoying to have to look woeful about Liz's demise, but he knew it wouldn't last long. Just till those surly members of her family that had attended the inquest were appeased. They were duelers, those Sellmans. They would duel on a moment's provocation, and they were all crack shots. It was easier just to look bereaved, than to worry whether one of them had been insulted.

It wasn't a bad day at all, and he left the inquest as soon as possible after making arrangements for the funeral. "I have to hire a Mourner, the very best in the city," he told friends, and caught the icy stare of the Sellman family.

They had never liked him. They were certain he had married Liz for her money (and they would have been right, of course) and that he was no good, but there was nothing they could do. There was no suspicion that Liz had committed suicide out of unhappiness; it seemed to be an accident.

But right now his primary concern was hiring a Mourner. Particularly with those duel-crazy Sellmans around. If they thought there was any slightest breach of etiquette on his part, there would be a stand as sure as he lived. He had to find the very best Mourner available.

A good Mourner was important.

Not only because he was too busy to mourn himself, but just because it wasn't *done* any more. The proper thing to do (and the thing to do if you didn't want the Mourners Guild picketing the funeral) was hire the most expensive one his accounts would allow, and let the black-cloaked Mourner do the job.

It was a sign of being well-to-do, it was the accepted thing to do, and it took the tiresome and time-wasting strain of mourning a lost one from the bereaved.

How in the world they ever got along, getting upset, wasting time, energy and emotion mourning their own dead, before the Guild, is something I'll never understand, Gordon Vernon mused as he flagged a flitcab outside the Courts Building.

"Third level, professional block 88, Building A," he snapped at the flitman, settling back as the cab lifted to its outbound slot in the streams of traffic. *Who should I engage for the funeral?*

It had to be a well-known Mourner, for the Vernons were a well-known family. Both the Vernon and Sellman standards flew in the Titled Family group at the Duelarama. And it had to be one who would do a top-notch job—chest-beating and histrionics if at all possible—because he couldn't take a chance on one of the Sellmans being insulted. If they thought their little Lisa had been slighted at her own funeral, they would cast the glove for a duel surely.

Gordon Vernon had several Mourner friends in his own circle of acquaintances. Should he hire Ralph Moody-Bennoit? Ralph had been one of the Mourners engaged for the big War Rally Funeral Pyre in the Duelarama three months before, to raise funds for the Aldeberan War.

No...Ralph was too slow building. He started out with a perfectly normal speaking voice, and clapping of hands. And while he personally preferred this more restrained type of mourning, Vernon knew the Sellmans would expect something much more flamboyant. No, tears were slow in coming to Ralph. No, he couldn't chance it with Moody-Bennoit.

What about Alistair Chubb? No, too much saccharine for this job. Sincerity, but with high emotional content, and a great deal of semantically charged hysterics...those were the keynotes this time. He *had* to have...

"Flitman, change that. I don't want to go to my office. Instead, second level, residential-office block 14, Building M."

Certainly. Why hadn't he thought of Maurice Silvera before this? Why bother with all the piddlers and three-shot funeral boys when Silvera was a close friend of the family, when he could have the great Silvera mourn at his wife's funeral.

Maurice Silvera, Mo.D. A long-time friend of the Vernons, and acknowledged the top Mourner in the country.

He would draw on their friendship to get Silvera's services. And perhaps lower the rate a bit.

"Is your phone tagged in?" he asked over the partition.

The flitman nodded his head briskly, and Gordon Vernon pulled the receiver from its stikplate, dialed WEchsler 992084K. There were a few moments waiting till the machines hooked their beams in connection, and the viewplate turned reflective during that time.

Vernon stared at his reflection in the mirror of the view-plate, and realized he had a good many years ahead of himself. With Lisa out of the way, and with his good looks and determination, there were no heights to which he could not aspire.

His hair was a sandy brush-cut, with the current stylistic sliver of silver slashing vertically to the widow's peak above his high forehead. His eyes were a deep blue that seemed to pulse when he stared at them too closely. His mouth was firm, and his nose just off-center enough to prevent any hint of femininity. He was, indeed, a good-looking man, and Liz had not been the only woman in the city.

There were eight flashes before Silvera lifted the receiver at his end. The viewplate remained mirrored.

"Good afternoon. I can't see you, would you tag in your view please."

Vernon pressed at the view stud, but the plate remained blank. "Flitman, what's the matter with your view, is it dead?"

The flitman half-turned his head, shrugged his shoulders and replied, "Don't know, mac. This's a replacement flit. Must be bunko. Sorry."

"Maurice, this is Gordon Vernon," he answered brightly, "I'm in a flit, on my way over to your office. The view's out, but it doesn't matter. I just wanted to make certain you were in. Can you spare me a half hour?"

The rich baritone voice of the Mourner came back clearly. "Why certainly Gordon. Any time. I'm free till six. What do you want, a vodkatini or straight hi-Scotch?"

"The hi-Scotch'll be fine, Maurice. Have it warmed for me. Be there in ten."

"Fine. See you."

"Pip-ho."

"Pip." And he blanked off.

Vernon restuck the receiver and slumped back in the flitcab's cushions.

It had started out slowly today, but things were moving rather nicely now. He had had to look sorrowful for a while there, which had been an unaccustomed strain, but soon he could dump all that tedious routine work in Silvera's capable hands.

The whole thing had worked out so beautifully, he wondered why he hadn't done it sooner. *If you can't find the man she's been sleeping around with, then you nip the evil at its very source,* he thought, sucking a cigar alight.

Gordon Vernon had known for some time that Liz was cheating on him. But there hadn't been anything he could do. Nor did he *want* to do anything. He had married Liz for her money and her position, and now that he had them, he was quite willing to let her tramp around to her heart's content. It kept her out of the way effectively, and let him pursue career or other companionship with equal ease.

But then the offers of presidency for Titano-Aluminum had come up, and he knew they would screen much too carefully. Much too carefully to allow his name to be muddied by Liz's ill-timed infidelity. A scandal would puncture any chances for the appointment.

So he had tried to discover them in the act, to let blame fall where it should, and let himself get out from under unbesmirched. He had failed. The man, whoever he was, was being cautious and clever about the clandestine meetings.

When he had confronted Liz with it, she had screamed at him, laughed raucously, thrown things, threatened to give the exposé to the confidentials for publication. That was when he had decided the presidency was more important than the har-pie-tramp he had married.

So he had killed her.

And the presidency of Titano-Aluminum was within his very grasp. Just a Mourner, and the funeral (I won't be able to attend that...a preparatory board meeting of T-A...more important... oh, well, the Mourner usually handles it solo without help from the surviving members of the family, anyhow) and then the screening clearance for the appointment.

He sank into the flitcab's cushions, dragged deeply on his cigar, and smiled at the skyslit of the flitcab.

Somewhere up there, Liz had met her Maker.

There had been a hasty stand on the landing deck when the flitcab landed. One man accusing another of denting his flit's fender, an argument, and a besmirching of character.

Vernon had paid the flitman and watched interestedly for a few minutes. They both seemed to be inept with their flamers, and he always enjoyed watching a pair of fools make bigger fools of themselves.

He stood at cross angles to their line of flame, with the rest of the crowd, and watched the two men go through the ritual. The insulted party "cast the glove" by slapping the insulter's face. A red, four-pronged flush appeared on the insulter's face, and he demanded, "When, where, what weapons?"

The insulted party answered sharply, "Here, now, flamers."

They glared at one another for a moment, backed-to-back, and a Legalizer who had arrived shortly after the beginning of the argument paced them off.

"One. Two. Three. Four. Five..." he counted off, keeping his eyes steadied to make certain none of the crowd had strayed into the line of flame.

"...Eight. Nine. Ten." He paused. "*Turn!*"

Both men spun awkwardly, and the insulted clutched for his sheath. He was an instant too slow, and the insulter's hand slapped fabric, came away with the blued-steel flamer in his palm, and a spray of livid orange flame boiled straight line for the insulted. But the shot was a hasty one. It grazed the insulted, charring his left shoulder, crackling the fabric of his suit, and tossing the man sidewise.

The insulted had his own weapon out, and the next shot—free and clear—was his. He steadied himself, slapping at the sparks on his suit, and a slow grin came over his face.

Clods, Vernon thought. *They'd both be dead were they dueling the Sellmans or myself.* Then at the realization of the ability he had acknowledged on Liz's family's part, he tensed, and watched the duel more closely, trying to get those damned relatives from his mind.

The insulted brought his flamer up, and the insulter quivered slightly as the gun came to rest on a line with his stomach.

At least the fool knows enough to go for the vitals.

The shot roared from the bell-mouth of the gun, and caught the insulter high in the chest. It had been bad aim, and the man's face was washed by a sheet of flame. He screamed high, and pitched over, the flames licking up and around, charring his skin, burning off his hair. He lay there whimpering for a few seconds, then settled quietly. Following the ritual terms, the insulted was over to him quickly, beating out the flames with his own cape. Then he turned the dead man over, carefully avoiding looking at the ruined face, and extracted the man's ident from his ringwatch. He handed the ident, along with several bills from his own pouch, to the Legalizer, adding, "If this doesn't cover the cost of Mourner and funeral, have his surviving members ring me at this num-ber." He handed the Legalizer a slip of printed paper and walked away.

As the insulted's flit took off, Vernon sneered in derision. *The clown. The unmitigated clown. Pompous ass, walks away as though he'd really defended his honor. What would he have done if he'd been forced to face a real gun?*

Then abruptly he dragged himself back to the matter at hand. He walked to the dropshaft banks. The dropshaft lowered him to Silvera's corridor, and he found the apartments without difficulty. The door louvred open at his approach. He let the servomeck take his cloak, and let it unbuckle his gun belt, making certain the flamer was on safety.

Never can be too sure with these servomecks.

Maurice Silvera, professional Mourner, was waiting in the music cubicle. A tape of Delibes *Sylvia* was sending soft harmonies through the room baffles. The music seemed to be emerging from the air next to Vernon's ear.

Silvera rose to greet his guest. The Mourner was a tall man, at least a full head taller than Vernon, with a high-combed mat of silver grey hair. His nose was thin and aquiline and his face held breeding. He was a handsome man by any standards, but not superciliously handsome. There was a certain humanity in his appearance, strange to be found in one of his occupation.

He had been Liz Vernon's lover.

Silvera walked smoothly to the room opening and took Vernon's hand. "Gordon, how nice to see you again. When was the last...oh yes, at the bareskin party Liz threw. Marvelous!"

He smiled at Vernon, and the visitor renewed his liking for the tall Mourner. Silvera had been a family friend for several years, though they got together seldom, and Vernon had always enjoyed the man's company. He wasn't like the other Mourners with their predilection for death and its trappings; there was a certain gaiety to him, and a jocularity of speech that belied his profession.

Abruptly, Vernon remembered this was not a social call. It was a business call, so accordingly, he used the Mourner Ritual:

"Will you mourn in my behalf?" he asked Silvera seriously, using the accepted colloquial form of the ancient Mourner phrases.

Silvera's dark eyes widened momentarily at the words...

He had thought this was a pleasure visit. He responded instantly, however, following the prescribed rune.

"We mourn for anyone."

"Will you convey my heart?"

"We will share your sorrow."

"Will you save my agony?"

"We will shed your tears."

They both sat down, and Vernon continued: "How will you mourn my lost one?"

Silvera answered in tones of utter sincerity, though he must have spoken this formula a thousand times. "With the honor of the dead, with the love and sincerity of the living, with the sorrow of the bereaved, with the glory of the upraised."

He pressed a stud on the tabletop beside his relaxer, and a cigarette came up through a tube, already alight.

He took it, and drew deeply, watching Gordon Vernon carefully, tensing for the answer to his next question.

Vernon asked, "What must I pay for your services?"

"Who has died?" Silvera tensed, hoping.

Vernon licked his lips. "My wife has died."

There was no indication of changing mood on the Mourner's placid face, but he took a sharp stinging drag on the cigarette.

"I'll have to emote you."

Vernon's eyes narrowed...this was a departure from the Ritual. "Is that necessary?"

The Mourner spread his hands. "In cases where there is a close tie to the deceased, the only way we can gauge our rates, provide the very best service, is to emote you."

Vernon knew how the Mourners worked. They used their emotion-counter on the bereaved, and gauged exactly how much sorrow he held. If it was substantially lower than what decorum might demand for a widow or widowers, the Mourner made up in added effort what the bereaved lacked in reality.

And they charged accordingly.

There didn't seem to be any other way, so Vernon agreed.

Silvera led him from the music cubicle, walking stiffly erect, and they went into the office portion of the Mourner's combined office home.

He pressed the stud on his deskonsole, and the emoter slid free from its hidden cubicle in the wall. It was a large ball-shaped chair, with a special sensitive pad covering it. The pad was sticky, and adhered to the body of the subject. It connected itself with the nerve ends in the body, giving a true reading on the dials and meters set into the control panel.

"Strip," Silvera said.

Gordon Vernon hurriedly shucked his clothing, piling it unceremoniously on the deskonsole. His one piece suit unstuck in a second, and he removed his jump boots with equal ease. The insulating layer under his clothing came off next, and he stood naked in the office.

"Sit down, please," Silvera said, adding in a friendly tone, "Gordon."

Vernon slumped into the chair, and instantly he could feel the sticky pad clamp itself to his flesh. It made goose pimples rise on his skin, but he sat very still, while the machine hummed softly beneath him. In a few moments Silvera slapped him on the shoulder.

"That's it. I've gotten a good reading."

Vernon stood up, the pad unsticking sharply with a vague sucking sound, and redressed. He pulled a fresh cigar from his pouch, and drew it to a red coal at its tip.

"Well, what's the reading?" he inquired curiously.

"Let's go back into the music room," Silvera suggested lightly. "We can be more comfortable out of this air of business. After all, we *are* friends."

"But...business *is* business," Vernon reminded with a grin.

Silvera's smile was strained, but Vernon did not notice. "Yes, that's right. Business certainly *is* business."

They returned to the music cubicle, and sank back into their relaxers.

"Well...?" Vernon inquired.

"You must pay me standard Mourner rates, plus two hundred dollars an hour overtime."

Vernon sat up abruptly. "What? That's the most exorbitant price I've ever..."

Silvera leaned forward, stared intently into Vernon's face. "Gordon, my patient and polite manner extends far outside these walls. What happens in here goes no further. But let's be perfectly frank with one another."

"What do you mean?"

"Gordon, I've been reading emotion charts for thirteen years now as a licensed and practicing Mo.D. In all that time, I've never seen an emoter reading lower than yours."

"Well...what—what does *that* signify?" Vernon was nervous now. He twisted the cigar between unsteady fingers.

"It means you aren't sorry Liz is gone."

Vernon's face flushed, and he sputtered. "Why—why that's, that's just ridiculous! Of course I'm sorry Liz is...why, I've never heard anything...you may be a great Mourner, Silvera, but this is..."

Silvera remained calm and steady. "Gordon, I know my business. To handle this funeral, I'd really have to generate, to make up for your total lack of bereavement. That means a considerable drain on my emotion drugs, a great deal of time and preparation, the hiring of a good sorrowwriter, and a lot of incidentals the average man knows nothing about.

"My price is quite fair, Gordon. If you had a bit more sorrow in you, the price would have been lower." He was finished, and it was obvious that arguing would get nowhere. These Mourners were not fish peddlers, to be talked down in price. What they said was what they said. And since they had tied up the field with the Guild, what they said, stuck.

It wasn't the usual procedure, and much more than Vernon had considered putting into the funeral, but since he had decided it was safest to throw a *big* funeral for Liz—those belligerent Sellmans would have to be pacified—the total would come close to four thousand dollars. But it would be worth the outrageous fee, if the mourning was done properly.

Vernon agreed inside himself, and reluctantly fell back into the ritual:

"I agree to your terms, Mourner.

"Then mourn for me."

The ritual was concluded, and they settled back in their relaxers. The conversation lost its echo of authority, and settled into a more relaxed—but still tense—tone.

"Look, Maurice," Vernon began, "perhaps I'd better explain about Liz and myself..."

Silvera tried to stop him with, "That isn't necessary at all, Gordon. My professional standing doesn't demand a thing, and as a friend of the family, you don't have to tell me unless you want to."

"No, no, I *want* to tell you," Vernon resumed hurriedly, "so you'll understand why my emoter reading was low."

Silvera listened intently.

"Liz was keeping time with someone else...she'd been cheating on me for quite a while now."

Silvera asked carefully, "Have you any idea who the man was?" He waited tightly.

"None," Vernon replied, shaking his head. "But that's why Liz and I weren't close at all, why I have no sorrow at her going. We've been like strangers to one another for over a year." He looked sad, but Silvera knew there was no sorrow in the man.

Silvera looked concerned. "How did she die, Gordon?"

Gordon Vernon looked infinitely sad for a moment, then replied, "She was holding a luncheon party for her club on the roof garden. I was out at the time...one of the women at the inquest testified she was carrying a tray past the parapet wall... it's very low and ornamental right around the tables there, you know...and she screamed and fell over."

"How horrible!"

"Yes, yes, yes," he said with weariness. "Even though she wasn't true, and we had our fights, I'm afraid I'll miss Liz a great deal. Basically, Maurice, she was a fine woman." *A dirty tramp cheat is more like it*, he added bitterly.

They talked a while longer, Silvera through his pleasant conversation overcoming Vernon's annoyance at the extra-high tariff on his services. Then Vernon begged leave, paid Silvera by scriptocheck, and allowed the door to louvre open for him.

"Well, pip-ho, Maurice, and do your very best at the funeral."

"Pip, Gordon. And I certainly will."

Vernon dropshafted up to the roof, where he flagged a flitcab, while down Building M, down in apartments 554-559, Maurice Silvera, Mo.D. was sitting with eyes dark and clouded. He bit the flesh of his fist, till the marks were left there in sharp relief.

Then he rose, carefully tore the scriptocheck into a hundred pieces, and systematically fed the shredded bits of paper to his incintray. Cursing Gordon Vernon for the murder of Liz Vernon... the woman he had loved in secret.

And swearing he would even the score with Vernon.

Yes, he would *certainly* do the best he could at the funeral.

No one would tell Gordon Vernon, for it would be a mark of social inelegance to bring a thing like that to a man's attention. No one would tell him that the Mourner—masked and caped—had done a rotten, a *shameful* job of grieving. No one would tell him of the scene Liz's relatives—the duel-crazy Sellmans—had made. No one would tell him how they had raved at the Mourner's show of no sorrow, how they had stamped about, and thrown down the bowers of flowers, calling, "Sacrilege! Sacrilege! Duel!" No one would tell him because it was obvious: the Mourner had no personal interest in the funeral. He was merely doing a job, he was merely reflecting the sorrow—by proportion—of the surviving family. If he had done a rotten job, it was obvious the reason was because Gordon himself had no sorrow at Liz's passing.

It was an accepted thing: *When a Mourner did a bad job* (for weren't they impartial and merely hired to do the job of spewing emotions) *it was evident, there had been no sorrow with which to work, basically. And no Mourner would falsify his emoting. There had to be a point where they emoted truth.*

So the Mourner did a bad, bad job, and the Sellman's guns were out.

No one would tell Gordon Vernon, but he knew something had gone wrong in his scheme. He knew it soon, and suddenly.

"We all knew Liz never shoulda married you, Vernon. All of us knew you were a fortune-hunter. Now she's dead, and you're gonna pay for it!"

The Sellmans had come from Upper Pittsburg, and there was still a Nyork State twang in their voices. They were an unpleasant family, who had gotten rich quickly on ferrami-no-oxides found on otherwise worthless property they owned. Gordon Vernon had never cared for them, for they had bought their family's prestige, while the Vernon standard had been much-respected for decades.

"But I was nowhere *near* her when she fell, so why are you challenging *me*?"

Rance Sellman, the youngest son, stepped forward. His fame with flamer and jag-knife was written up in all the cheap Duelist periodicals, and Gordon Vernon prayed deep inside himself that the boy would not offer the challenge as a personal stand. He had seen too many hasty stands, such as the one the other day on Silvera's roof, and he knew he'd never have a chance in a fast draw contest.

The boy's hand came up and around swiftly, cracking into Vernon's jaw, snapping the man's head around. Tears came to his eyes, and he stared as through a film at the tense-faced Sellman boy. "Vernon, I'm callin' it at you. I'm challengin' you. When, where, what weapons?"

Vernon swallowed, heard himself answering, "The Mall, tomorrow morning at ten . . flamers."

"And by God you *be* there," the boy snapped, turning.

As the Sellmans left, there was the tell-tale hip-movement of the boy that marked an accomplished gunsman, a crack-shot duelist.

Vernon was dead...and he knew it.

"Maurice, what happened at the funeral? What happened,

Maurice? I've been challenged. The Sellmans want to kill me. What happened, Maurice?"

Vernon's face was a motley of sweat, and his hands shook as they wound in Maurice Silvera's velvet collar.

Silvera brought his hands up sharply, knocking Vernon's clutching fingers away.

"I'm afraid I wasn't very convincing, Vernon, old man. They don't think you regret Liz's death enough. They don't think you're sorrowful enough, so they want to increase your sorrow." A faint tinge of smile gleamed on Silvera's handsome face. "I just wasn't very convincing."

"You weren't *what*? You weren't con…you weren't *convincing*? Good God, Silvera, I paid you enough!"

"Yes, but you murdered Liz."

Vernon's mouth slid open, and his eyes suddenly glazed over with huntedness. He stammered something unintelligible.

"Yes. Yes, that's right," Silvera answered in a perfectly normal, conversational tone. "I sentenced you to death. Liz and I talked about it many times. She was certain you'd try to kill her if you found out about us."

"You! Then it was…"

"That's right, Gordon. That's right."

"You planned it all—"

Silvera was nodding his head in assent. He was just a moment in time to knock the flamer from Vernon's hand. He slapped Vernon twice, quickly, back and forth, and the sandy-haired man slumped down to a hassock, his breath beginning to come raggedly, a sob mounting in his chest.

"My God, my God, what will I do…what'll I do…he'll kill me…they'll be watching the areaways, I won't be able to get away…he'll burn me down…what'll I do…"

Silvera smiled down at the murderer, his handsome face washed by unnamed emotions. Then he said something; without waiting for the beginning of the ritual, he said:

"We mourn for anyone…"

This is a recent piece, written strictly as a one-liner at the famous Milford, Pennsylvania Science Fiction Writers Conference, last year about this time. Anything more than this brief word would be gilding inordinately what is, essentially, the final twist on the ultimate version of the end of the world story. And the next voice you hear will be

The Voice in the Garden

AFTER THE BOMB, the last man on Earth wandered through the rubble of Cleveland, Ohio. It had never been a particularly jaunty town, nor even remotely appealing to esthetes. But now, like Detroit and Rangoon and Minsk and Yokohama, it had been reduced to a petulantly shattered tinkertoy of lathe and brickwork, twisted steel girders and melted glass.

As he picked his way around the dust heaps that had been the Soldiers and Sailors Monument in what had been Public Square, his eyes red-rimmed from crying at the loss of mankind, he saw something he had not seen in Beirut or Venice or London. He saw the movement of another human being.

Celestial choruses sang in his head as he broke into a run across the pitted and blasted remnants of Euclid Avenue. It was a woman!

She saw him, and in the very posture of her body, he knew she was filled with the same glory he felt. She knew! She began running toward him, her arms outstretched. They seemed to swim toward one another in a ballet of slow motion. He stumbled once, but got to his feet quickly and went on. They detoured around the crumpled tin of tortured metal that had once been automobiles, and met in front of the shattered carcass that was, in a time seemingly eons before, The May Co.

"I'm the last man!" he blurted. He could not keep the words

inside, they frothed to emerge. "I'm the last, the very last. They're all dead, everyone but us. I'm the last man, and you're the last woman, and we'll have to mate and start the race again, and this time we'll do it right. No war, no hate, no bigotry, nothing but goodness...we'll do it, you'll see, it'll be fine, a bright new shining world from all this death and terror."

Her face lighted with an ethereal beauty, even beneath the soot and deprivation. "Yes, yes," she said. "It'll be just like that. I love you, because we're all there is left to love, one another."

He touched her hand. "I love you. What is your name?"

She flushed slightly. "Eve," she said. "What's yours?"

"George," he said.

Two versions of the same story. One as the printed page, the other as shadow images across a television screen. When I first came out to The Coast in 1962, many of my friends mourned, "That's the last we see of him in print." They had swallowed the cliche myths hook, line and stinker. But as anyone can tell, from the 120,000 words I've written in just short stories alone in the past five years, it is not the town, nor its opulence, nor living well, nor working in a different medium, that ruins a writer. It is his own inability to get a handle on life. It killed Fitzgerald and Horace McCoy out here, but the town had very little to do with it. In fact, Hollywood offers some very special and invaluable assistance for a writer who works in the marketplace. It provides sufficient funds so he can live not merely well, but very well. (I do not think there is anything particularly noble, uplifting or artistically enriching about being dirt-poor past a certain point. At first, it helps, because it brings a writer into close contact with his subject matter, with the world, and with the exigencies of reality. But by the time you hit thirty, you had better damned well be living like a mensch or you cannot in all good conscience call yourself a Bohemian. You are merely a seedy bum. As a corollary, it goes hand in hand: the better a writer gets at his craft, the more he sells; the more he sells, the better-known his name becomes; the better-known he becomes, the more money they give you, and the better you live. It isn't always a yardstick for quality, but it helps.) Hollywood also brings recognition. I co-scripted a dreadful motion picture whose name I will not mention here, and if you saw it and were as nauseated as I was, then I extend my sincerest apologies for having contributed to something as dishonest and cheapjack as the epic in question. But even when the work is bad, the Great Unwashed learns about it, and a writer may find himself confronted—as I was—by the singular spectacle of his name ten feet high in Times Square. It is a heady wine. But the most important benefit Hollywood offers is an association with the visual medium, as exciting and demanding an arena as any open to a writer in our times. Many of my stories in magazines have been translated into scripts. Some of them work very nicely. The one that follows is an example. It was a statement of anti-war sentiments on my part, and when Hans Stefan Santesson originally bought it for Fantastic Universe in 1957, he gave me ninety-one dollars for it. That was a pile of money for me at the time. In 1964 when I rewrote and adapted the story for television,

I received five thousand dollars. Times change, media change, but my beliefs about the senseless stupidity of war remain unchanged. Though I served my two years in the Army, were I to be called up now, I would refuse to serve. I'm afraid I would have to go to jail like Tommy Rodd, a boy I've never met, but for whom I feel great brotherhood. He literally follows the philosophy of Thoreau that "he serves the State best who opposes it the most." Were I in his position, I would try to be as heroic, as brave. But as I am not, the best I can do is sit on my fat ass, write my stories, take their five grand, and hope that out there in Knobtwiddlesville The Great Unwashed who would shriek in horror if two lovely people fornicated with pleasure on their TV screen, but who purr with patriotic delight when their sons are decorated in Viet Nam for miscalculating and dropping "a little defoliation" on US troops or amber-skinned babies in schoolyards, will one day soon come to their senses, rise up in their wrath, and send all the face-saving politicians scuttling to their holes rather than allow them to continue senseless warfare in remote corners of a globe that has come to think of us in terms of atrocities and aggression. Some of this I tried to say in the story and teleplay that follow. But for those who need ready categorizations to ignore the unsettling remarks of others, I am not now nor have I ever been anything Robert Welch and his Birchies would consider subversive. I'm just a guy like many out there, who has come to maturity realizing God ain't necessarily on our side. In point of fact, I don't think he can ever be on the side of the

Soldier

QARLO HUNKERED down further into the firmhole, gathering his cloak about him. Even the triple-lining of the cape could not prevent the seeping cold of the battlefield from reaching him; and even through one of those linings—lead impregnated—he could feel the faint tickle of dropout, all about him, eating at his tissues. He began to shiver again. The Push was going on to the South, and he had to wait, had to listen for the telepathic command of his superior officer.

He fingered an edge of the firmhole, noting he had not steadied it up too well with the firmer. He drew the small molecule-hardening instrument from his pouch, and examined it. The calibrater had slipped a notch, which explained why the dirt of the firmhole had not become as hard as he had desired.

Off to the left the hiss of an eighty-thread beam split the night air, and he shoved the firmer back quickly. The spider-web tracery of the beam lanced across the sky, poked tentatively at an armor center, throwing blood-red shadows across Qarlo's crag-like features.

The armor center backtracked the thread beam, retaliated with a blinding flash of its own batteries. One burst. Two. Three. The eighty-thread reared once more, feebly, then subsided. A moment later the concussion of its power chambers exploding shook the Earth around Qarlo, causing bits of unfirmed dirt and small pebbles to tumble in on him. Another moment, and the shrapnel came through.

Qarlo lay flat to the ground, soundlessly hoping for a bit more life amidst all this death. He knew his chances of coming back were infinitesimal. What was it? Three out of every thousand came back? He had no illusions. He was a common footman, and he knew he would die out here, in the midst of the Great War VII.

As though the detonation of the eighty-thread had been a signal, the weapons of Qarlo's company opened up, full-on. The webbings criss-crossed the blackness overhead with delicate patterns—appearing, disappearing, changing with every second, ranging through the spectrum, washing the bands of colors outside the spectrum Qarlo could catalog. Qarlo slid into a tiny ball in the slush-filled bottom of the firmhole, waiting.

He was a good soldier. He knew his place. When those metal and energy beasts out there were snarling at each other, there was nothing a lone foot soldier could do—but die. He waited, knowing his time would come much too soon. No matter how violent, how involved, how pushbutton-ridden Wars became, it always simmered down to the man on foot. It had to, for men fought men still.

His mind dwelled limply in a state between reflection and alertness. A state all men of war came to know when there was nothing but the thunder of the big guns abroad in the night.

The stars had gone into hiding.

Abruptly, the thread beams cut out, the traceries winked off, silence once again descended. Qarlo snapped to instant attentiveness. This was the moment. His mind was now keyed to one sound, one only. Inside his head the command would form, and he would act; not entirely of his own volition. The strategists and psychmen had worked together on this thing: the tone of command was keyed into each soldier's brain. Printed in, probed in, sunken in. It was there, and when the Regimenter sent his telepathic orders, Qarlo would leap like a puppet, and advance on direction.

Thus, when it came, it was as though he had anticipated it; as though he knew a second before the mental rasping and the *Advance!* erupted within his skull, that the moment had arrived.

A second sooner than he should have been, he was up, out of the firmhole, hugging his Brandelmeier to his chest, the weight of the plastic bandoliers and his pouch reassuring across his stomach, back, and hips. Even before the mental word actually came.

Because of this extra moment's jump on the command, it happened, and it happened just that way. No other chance coincidences could have done it, but done just that way.

When the first blasts of the enemy's zeroed-in batteries met the combined rays of Qarlo's own guns, also pin-pointed, they met at a point that should by all rights have been empty. But Qarlo had jumped too soon, and when they met, the soldier was at the focal point.

Three hundred distinct beams latticed down, joined in a coruscating rainbow, threw negatively charged particles five hundred feet in the air, shorted out...and warped the soldier off the battlefield.

Nathan Schwachter had his heart attack right there on the subway platform.

The soldier materialized in front of him, from nowhere, filthy and ferocious-looking, a strange weapon cradled to his body... just as the old man was about to put a penny in the candy machine.

Qarlo's long cape was still, the dematerialization and subsequent reappearance having left him untouched. He stared in confusion at the sallow face before him, and started violently at the face's piercing shriek.

Qarlo watched with growing bewilderment and terror as the sallow face contorted and sank to the littered floor of the platform. The old man clutched his chest, twitched and gasped several times. His legs jerked spasmodically, and his mouth opened wildly again and again. He died with mouth open, eyes staring at the ceiling.

Qarlo looked at the body disinterestedly for a moment; death... what did one death matter...every day during the War, ten thousand died...more horribly than this...this was as nothing to him.

The sudden universe-filling scream of an incoming express train broke his attention. The black tunnel that his War-filled world had become, was filled with the rusty wail of an unseen monster, bearing down on him out of the darkness.

The fighting man in him made his body arch, sent it into a crouch. He poised on the balls of his feet, his rifle levering horizontal instantly, pointed at the sound.

From the crowds packed on the platform, a voice rose over the thunder of the incoming train:

"*Him*! It was *him*! He shot that old man...he's crazy!" Heads turned; eyes stared; a little man with a dirty vest, his bald head reflecting the glow of the overhead lights, was pointing a shaking finger at Qarlo.

It was as if two currents had been set up simultaneously. The crowd both drew away and advanced on him. Then the train barreled around the curve, drove past, blasting sound into the very fibers of the soldier's body. Qarlo's mouth opened wide in a soundless scream, and more from reflex than intent, the Brandelmeier erupted in his hands.

A triple-thread of cold blue beams sizzled from the small bellmouth of the weapon, streaked across the tunnel, and blasted full into the front of the train.

The front of the train melted down quickly, and the vehicle ground to a stop. The metal had been melted like a coarse grade of plastic on a burner. Where it had fused into a soggy lump, the metal was bright and smeary—more like the gleam of oxidized silver than anything else.

Qarlo regretted having fired the moment he felt the Brandelmeier buck. He was not where he should be—*where* he was, that was still another, more pressing problem—and he knew he was in danger. Every movement had to be watched as carefully as possible...and perhaps he had gotten off to a bad start already. But that noise...

He had suffered the screams of the battlefield, but the reverberations of the train, thundering back and forth in that enclosed space, was a nightmare of indescribable horror.

As he stared dumbly at his handiwork, from behind him, the crowd made a concerted rush.

Three burly, charcoal-suited executives—each carrying an attaché case which he dropped as he made the lunge, looking like unhealthy carbon-copies of each other—grabbed Qarlo above the elbows, around the waist, about the neck.

The soldier roared something unintelligible and flung them from him. One slid across the platform on the seat of his pants, bringing up short, his stomach and face smashing into a tiled wall. The second spun away, arms flailing, into the crowd. The third tried to hang onto Qarlo's neck. The soldier lifted him bodily, arched him over his head—breaking the man's insecure grip—and pitched him against a stanchion. The executive hit the girder, slid down, and lay quite still, his back oddly twisted.

The crowd emitted scream after scream, drew away once more. Terror rippled back through its ranks. Several women, near the front, suddenly became aware of the blood pouring from the face of one of the executives, and keeled onto the dirty platform unnoticed. The screams continued, seeming echoes of the now-dead express train's squealing.

But as an entity, the crowd backed the soldier down the platform. For a moment Qarlo forgot he still held the Brandelmeier. He lifted the gun to a threatening position, and the entity that was the crowd pulsed back.

Nightmare! It was all some sort of vague, formless nightmare to Qarlo. This was not the War, where anyone he saw, he blasted. This was something else, some other situation, in which he was lost, disoriented. What was happening?

Qarlo moved toward the wall, his back prickly with fear sweat. He had expected to die in the War, but something as simple and direct and expected as that had not happened. He was *here*, not *there*—wherever *here* was, and wherever *there* had gone—and these people were unarmed, obviously civilians. Which would not have kept him from mudering them…but what was happening? Where was the battlefield?

His progress toward the wall was halted momentarily as he backed cautiously around a stanchion. He knew there were people behind him, as well as the white-faced knots before him, and he was beginning to suspect there was no way out. Such confusion boiled up in his thoughts, so close to hysteria was he—plain soldier of the fields—that his mind forcibly rejected the impossibility of being somehow transported from the War into this new—and in many ways more terrifying—situation. He concentrated on one thing only, as a good soldie should. *Out!*

He slid along the wall, the crowd flowing before him, opening at his approach, closing in behind. He whirled once, driving them back further with the black hole of the Brandelmeier's bell mouth. Again he hesitated (not knowing why) to fire upon them.

He sensed they were enemies. But still they were unarmed. And yet, that had never stopped him before. The village in TetraOmsk Territory, beyond the Volga somewhere. They had been unarmed there, too, but the square had been filled with civilians he had not hesitated to burn. Why was he hesitating now?

The Brandelmeier continued in its silence.

Qarlo detected a commotion behind the crowd, above the crowd's inherent commotion. And a movement. Something was happening there. He backed tightly against the wall as a blue-suited, brass-buttoned man broke through the crowd.

The man took one look, caught the unwinking black eye of the Brandelmeier, and threw his arms back, indicating to the crowd to clear away. He began screaming at the top of his lungs, veins standing out in his temples, "Geddoudahere! The guy's a cuckaboo! Somebody'll get kilt! Beat it, run!"

The crowd needed no further impetus. It broke in the center and streamed toward the stairs.

Qarlo swung around, looking for another way out, but both accessible stairways were clogged by fighting commuters, shoving each other mercilessly to get out. He was effectively trapped.

The cop fumbled at his holster. Qarlo caught a glimpse of the movement from the corner of his eye. Instinctively he knew the movement for what it was; a weapon was about to be brought into use. He swung about, leveling the Brandelmeier. The cop jumped behind a stanchion just as the soldier pressed the firing stud.

A triple-thread of bright blue energy leaped from the weapon's bell mouth. The beam went over the heads of the crowd, neatly melting away a five foot segment of wall supporting one of the stairways. The stairs creaked, and the sound of tortured metal adjusting to poor support and an overcrowding of people, rang through the tunnel. The cop looked fearfully above himself, saw the beams curving, then settle under the weight, and turned a wide-eyed stare back at the soldier.

The cop fired twice from behind the stanchion, the booming of the explosions catapulting back and forth in the enclosed space.

The second bullet took the soldier above the wrist in his left arm. The Brandelmeier slipped uselessly from his good hand, as blood stained the garment he wore. He stared at his shattered lower arm in amazement. Doubled amazement.

What manner of weapon was this the blue-coated man had used? No beam, that. Nothing like anything he had ever seen before. No beam to fry him in his tracks. It was some sort of power that hurled a projectile . . that had ripped his body. He stared stupidly as blood continued to flow out of his arm.

The cop, less anxious now to attack this man with the weird costume and unbelievable rifle, edged cautiously from behind his cover, skirting the edge of the platform, trying to get near enough to Qarlo to put another bullet into him, should he offer further resistance. But the soldier continued to stand, spraddle-legged, staring at his wound, confused at where he was, what had happened to him, the screams of the trains as they bulleted past, and the barbarian tactics of his blue-coated adversary.

The cop moved slowly, steadily, expecting the soldier to break and run at any moment. The wounded man stood rooted, however. The cop bunched his muscles and leaped the few feet intervening.

Savagely, he brought the barrel of his pistol down on the side of Qarlo's neck, near the ear. The soldier turned slowly, anchored in his tracks, and stared unbelievingly at the policeman for an instant.

Then his eyes glazed, and he collapsed to the platform.

As a grey swelling mist bobbed up around his mind, one final thought impinged incongruously: *he struck me...physical contact? I don't believe it!*

What have I gotten into?

Light filtered through vaguely. Shadows slithered and wavered, sullenly formed into solids.

"Hey, Mac. Got a light?"

Shadows blocked Qarlo's vision, but he knew he was lying on his back, staring up. He turned his head, and a wall oozed into focus, almost at his nose tip. He turned his head the other way. Another wall, about three feet away, blending in his sight, into a shapeless grey blotch. He abruptly realized the back of his head hurt. He moved slowly, swiveling his head, but the soreness remained. Then he realized he was lying on some hard metal surface, and he tried to sit up. The pains throbbed higher, making him feel nauseated, and for an instant his vision receded again.

Then it steadied, and he sat up slowly. He swung his legs over the sharp edge of what appeared to be a shallow, sloping metal trough. It was a mattressless bunk, curved in its bottom, from hundreds of men who had lain there before him.

He was in a cell.

"Hey! I said you got a match there?"

Qarlo turned from the empty rear wall of the cell and looked through the bars. A bulb-nosed face was thrust up close to the metal barrier. The man was short, in filthy rags whose odor reached Qarlo with tremendous offensiveness. The man's eyes were bloodshot, and his nose was criss-crossed with blue and red veins. Acute alcoholism, reeking from every pore; *acne rosacea* that had turned his nose into a hideous, cracked and pocked blob.

Qarlo knew he was in detention, and from the very look, the very smell of this other, he knew he was not in a military prison. The man was staring in at him, oddly.

"Match, Charlie? You got a match?" he puffed his fat, wet lips at Qarlo, forcing the bit of cigarette stub forward with his mouth. Qarlo stared back; he could not understand the man's words. They were so slowly spoken, so sharp and yet unintelligible. But he knew what to answer.

"Marnames Quarlo Clobregnny, pyrt, sizfifwunohtootoonyn," the soldier muttered by rote, surly tones running together.

"Whaddaya mad at *me* for buddy? I didn't putcha in here," argued the match-seeker. "All I wanted was a light for this here butt." He held up two inches of smoked stub. "How come they gotcha inna cell, and not runnin' around loose inna bull pen like us?" he cocked a thumb over his shoulder, and for the first time Qarlo realized others were in this jail.

"Ah, ta hell wit ya," the drunk muttered. He cursed again, softly under his breath, turning away. He walked across the bull pen and sat down with the four other men—all vaguely similar in facial content—who lounged around a rough-hewn table-bench combination. The table and benches, all one piece, like a picnic table, were bolted to the floor.

"A screwloose," the drunk said to the others, nodding his balding head at the soldier in his long cape and metallic skin-tight suit. He picked up the crumpled remnants of an ancient magazine and leafed through it as though he knew every line of type, every girlie illustration, by heart.

Qarlo looked over the cell. It was about ten feet high by eight across, a sink with one thumb-push spigot running cold water, a commode without seat or paper, and metal trough, roughly the dimensions of an average-sized man, fastened to one wall. One enclosed bulb burned feebly in the ceiling. Three walls of solid steel. Ceiling and floor of the same, riveted together at the seams. The fourth wall was the barred door.

The firmer might be able to wilt that steel, he realized, and instinctively reached for his pouch. It was the first moment he had had a chance to think of it, and even as he reached, knew the satisfying weight of it was gone. His bandoliers also. His Brandelmeier, of course. His boots, too, and there seemed to have been some attempt to get his cape off, but it was all part of the skintight suit of metallic-mesh cloth.

The loss of the pouch was too much. Everything that had happened, had happened so quickly, so blurrily, meshed, and the soldier was abruptly overcome by confusion and a deep feeling of hopelessness. He sat down on the bunk, the ledge of metal biting into his thighs. His head still ached from a combination of the blow dealt him by the cop, and the metal bunk where he had lain. He ran a shaking hand over his head, feeling the fractional inch of his brown hair, cut battle-style. Then he noticed that his left hand had been bandaged quite expertly. There was hardly any throbbing from his wound.

That brought back to sharp awareness all that had transpired, and the War leaped into his thoughts. The telepathic command, the rising from the firmhole, the rifle at the ready…

…then a sizzling shusssssss, and the universe had exploded around him in a billion tiny flickering novas of color and color and color. Then suddenly, just as suddenly as he had been standing on the battlefield of Great War VII, advancing on the enemy forces of Ruskie-Chink, he was *not* there.

He was here.

He was in some dark, hard tunnel, with a great beast roaring out of the blackness onto him, and a man in a blue coat had shot him, and clubbed him. Actually *touched* him! Without radiation gloves! How had the man known Qarlo was not booby-trapped with radiates? He could have died in an instant.

Where was he? What war was this he was engaged in? Were these Ruskie-Chink or his own Tri-Continenters? He did not know, and there was no sign of an explanation.

Then he thought of something more important. If he had been captured, then they must want to question him. There was a way to combat *that*, too. He felt around in the hollow tooth toward the back of his mouth. His tongue touched each tooth till it hit the right lower bicuspid. It was empty. The poison glob was gone, he realized in dismay. *It must have dropped out when the blue-coat clubbed me*, he thought.

He realized he was at *their* mercy; who *they* might be was another thing to worry about. And with the glob gone, he had no way to stop their extracting information. It was bad. Very bad, according to the warning conditioning he had received. They could use Probers, or dyoxl-scopalite, or hyp-no-scourge, or any one of a hundred different methods, any one of which would reveal to them the strength of numbers in his company, the battery placements, the gun ranges, the identity and thought wave band of every officer...in fact, a good deal. More than he thought he knew.

He had become a very important prisoner of War. He *had* to hold out, he realized!

Why?

The thought popped up, and was gone. All it left in its wake was the intense feeling: I despise War, all war and *the* War! Then, even that was gone, and he was alone with the situation once more, to try and decide what had happened to him...what secret weapon had been used to capture him...and if these unintelligible barbarians with the projectile weapons *could*, indeed, extract his knowledge from him.

I swear they won't get anything out of me but my name, rank, and serial number, he thought desperately.

He mumbled those particulars aloud, as reassurance: "Mar-names Qarlo Clobregnny, pryt, sixfifwunohtootoonyn."

The drunks looked up from their table and their shakes, at the sound of his voice. The man with the rosedrop nose rubbed a dirty hand across fleshy chin folds, repeated his philosophy of the strange man in the locked cell.

"Screwloose!"

He might have remained in jail indefinitely, considered a madman or a mad rifleman. But the desk sergeant who had booked him, after the soldier had received medical attention, grew curious about the strangely shaped weapon.

As he put the things into security, he tested the Brandelmeier— hardly realizing what knob or stud controlled its power, never realizing what it could do—and melted away one wall of the safe room. Three inch plate steel, and it melted bluely, fused solidly.

He called the Captain, and the Captain called the F.B.I. and the F.B.I. called Internal Security, and Internal Security said, "Preposterous!" and checked back. When the Brandelmeier had been thoroughly tested—as much as *could* be tested, since the rifle had no seams, no apparent power source, and fantastic range— they were willing to believe. They had the soldier removed from his cell, transported along with the pouch, and a philologist named Soames, to the I.S. general headquarters in Washington, D.C. The Brandel-meier came by jet courier, and the soldier was flown in by helicopter, under sedation. The philologist named Soames, whose hair was long and rusty, whose face was that of a starving artist, whose temperament was that of a saint, came in by specially chartered plane from Columbia University. The pouch was sent by sealed Brinks truck to the airport, where it was delivered under heaviest guard to a mail plane. They all arrived in Washington within ten minutes of one another, and without seeing anything of the surrounding countryside, were whisked away to the subsurface levels of the I.S. Buildings.

When Qarlo came back to consciousness, he found himself again in a cell, this time quite unlike the first. No bars, but just as solid to hold him in, with padded walls. Qarlo paced around the cell a few times, seeking breaks in the walls, and found what was obviously a door, in one corner. But he could not work his fingers between the pads, to try and open it.

He sat down on the padded floor, and rubbed the bristled top of his head in wonder. Was he *never* to find out what had happened to himself? And *when* was he going to shake this strange feeling that he was being watched?

Overhead, through a pane of one-way glass that looked like a ventilator grille, the soldier was being watched.

Lyle Sims and his secretary knelt before the window in the floor, along with the philologist named Soames. Where Soames was shaggy, ill-kept, hungry-looking and placid...Lyle Sims was lean, collegiate-seeming, brusque and brisk. He had been special advisor to an unnamed branch office of Internal Security, for five years, dealing with every strange or offbeat problem too outré for regulation inquiry. Those years had hardened him in an odd way; he was quick to recognize authenticity, even quicker to recognize fakery.

As he watched, his trained instincts took over completely, and he knew in a moment of spying, that the man in the cell below was out of the ordinary. Not so in any fashion that could be labeled—"drunkard," "foreigner," "psychotic"—but so markedly different, so *other* he was taken aback.

"Six feet three inches," he recited to the girl kneeling beside him. She made the notation on her pad, and he went on calling out characteristics of the soldier below. "Brown hair, clipped so short you can see the scalp. Brown...no, black eyes. Scars. Above the left eye, running down to center of left cheek; bridge of nose; three parallel scars on the right side of chin; tiny one over right eyebrow; last one I can see, runs from back of left ear, into hairline.

"He seems to be wearing an all-over, skintight suit something like, oh, I suppose it's like a pair of what do you call those pajamas kids wear...the kind with the back door, the kind that enclose the feet?"

The girl inserted softly, "You mean snuggies?"

The man nodded, slightly embarrassed for no good reason, continued, "Mmm. Yes, that's right. Like those. The suit encloses his feet, seems to be joined to the cape, and comes up to his neck. Seems to be some sort of metallic cloth.

"Something else...may mean nothing at all, or on the other hand..." he pursed his lips for a moment, then described his observation carefully. "His head seems to be oddly shaped. The forehead is larger than most, seems to be pressing forward in front, as though he had been smacked hard and it was swelling. That seems to be everything."

Sims settled back on his haunches, fished in his side pocket, and came up with a small pipe, which he cold-puffed in thought for a second. He rose slowly, still staring down through the floor window. He murmured something to himself, and when Soames asked what he had said, the special advisor repeated, "I think we've got something almost too hot to handle."

Soames clucked knowingly, and gestured toward the window. "Have you been able to make out anything he's said yet?"

Sims shook his head. "No. That's why you're here. It seems he's saying the same thing, over and over, but it's completely unintelligible. Doesn't seem to be any recognizable language, or any dialect we've been able to pin down."

"I'd like to take a try at him," Soames said, smiling gently. It was the man's nature that challenge brought satisfaction; solutions brought unrest, eagerness for a new, more rugged problem.

Sims nodded agreement, but there was a tense, strained film over his eyes, in the set of his mouth. "Take it easy with him, Soames. I have a strong hunch this is something completely new, something we haven't even begun to understand."

Soames smiled again, this time indulgently. "Come, come, Mr. Sims. After all...he *is* only an alien of some sort...all we have to do is find out what country he's from."

"Have you heard him talk yet?"

Soames shook his head.

"Then don't be too quick to think he's just a foreigner. The word *alien* may be more correct than you think—only not in the *way* you think."

A confused look spread across Soames's face. He gave a slight shrug, as though he could not fathom what Lyle Sims meant... and was not particularly interested. He patted Sims reassuringly, which brought an expression of annoyance to the advisor's face, and he clamped down on the pipestem harder.

They walked downstairs together; the secretary left them, to type her notes, and Sims let the philologist into the padded room, cautioning him to deal gently with the man. "Don't forget," Sims warned, "we're not sure *where* he comes from, and sudden movements may make him jumpy. There's a guard overhead, and there'll be a man with me behind this door, but you never know."

Soames looked startled. "You sound as though he's an aborigine or something. With a suit like that, he *must* be very intelligent. You suspect something, don't you?"

Sims made a neutral motion with his hands. "What I suspect is too nebulous to worry about now. Just take it easy...and above all, figure out what he's saying, where he's from."

Sims had decided long before, that it would be wisest to keep the power of the Brandelmeier to himself. But he was fairly certain it was not the work of a foreign power. The trial run on the test range had left him gasping, confused.

He opened the door, and Soames passed through, uneasily.

Sims caught a glimpse of the expression on the stranger's face as the philologist entered. It was even more uneasy than Soames's had been.

It looked to be a long wait.

Soames was white as paste. His face was drawn, and the complacent attitude he had shown since his arrival in Washington was shattered. He sat across from Sims, and asked him in a quavering voice for a cigarette. Sims fished around in his desk, came up with a crumpled pack and idly slid them across to Soames. The philologist took one, put it in his mouth, and then, as though it had been totally forgotten in the space of a second, he removed it, held it while he spoke.

His tones were amazed. "Do you know what you've got up there in that cell?"

Sims said nothing, knowing what was to come would not startle him too much; he had expected something fantastic.

"That man...do you know where he...that soldier—and by God, Sims, that's what he *is*—comes from, from—now you're going to think I'm insane to believe it, but somehow I'm convinced—he comes from the future!"

Sims tightened his lips. Despite himself, he *was* shocked. He knew it was true. It *had* to be true, it was the only explanation that fit all the facts.

"What can you tell me?" he asked the philologist.

"Well, at first I tried solving the communications problem by asking him simple questions...pointing to myself and saying 'Soames,' pointing to him and looking quizzical, but all he'd keep saying was a string of gibberish. I tried for hours to equate his tones and phrases with all the dialects and sub-dialects of every language I'd every known, but it was no use. He slurred too much. And then I finally figured it out. He had to write it out—which I couldn't understand, of course, but it gave me a clue—and then I kept having him repeat it. Do you know what he's speaking?"

Sims shook his head.

The linguist spoke softly. "He's speaking English. It's that simple. Just English.

"But an English that was been corrupted and run together, and so slurred, it's incomprehensible. It must be the future trend of the language. Sort of an extrapolation of gutter English, just contracted to a fantastic extreme. At any rate, I got it out of him."

Sims leaned forward, held his dead pipe tightly. "What?"

Soames read it off a sheet of paper:

"My name is Qarlo Clobregnny. Private. Six-five-one-oh-two-two-nine."

Sims murmured in astonishment. "My God...name, rank and—"

Soames finished for him, "—and serial number. Yes, that's all he'd give me for over three hours. Then I asked him a few innocuous questions, like where did he come from, and what was his impression of where he was now."

The philologist waved a hand vaguely. "By that time, I had an idea what I was dealing with, though not where he had come from. But when he began telling me about the War, the War he was fighting when he showed up here, I knew immediately he was either from some other world—which is fantastic—or, or... well, I just didn't know!"

Sims nodded his head in understanding. "From *when* do you think he comes?"

Soames shrugged. "Can't tell. He says the year he is in— doesn't seem to realize he's in the past—is K79. He doesn't know when the other style of dating went out. As far as he knows, it's been 'K' for a long time, though he's heard stories about things that happened during a time they dated 'GV'. Meaningless, but I'd wager it's more thousands of years than we can imagine."

Sims ran a hand nervously through his hair. This problem was, indeed, larger than he'd thought.

"Look, Professor Soames, I want you to stay with him, and teach him current English. See if you can work some more information out of him, and let him know we mean him no hard times.

"Though Lord knows," the special advisor added with a tremor, "*he* can give us a harder time than we can give him. What knowledge he must have!"

Soames nodded in agreement, "Is it all right if I catch a few hours sleep? I was with him almost ten hours straight, and I'm sure *he* needs it as badly as I do."

Sims nodded also, in agreement, and the philologist went off to a sleeping room. But when Sims looked down through the window, twenty minutes later, the soldier was still awake, still looking about nervously. It seemed he did *not* need sleep.

Sims was terribly worried, and the coded telegram he had received from the President, in answer to his own, was not at all reassuring. The problem was in his hands, and it was an increasingly worrisome problem.

Perhaps a deadly problem.

He went to another sleeping room, to follow Soames's example. It looked like sleep was going to be scarce.

Problem:

A man from the future. An ordinary man, without any special talents, without any great store of intelligence. The equivalent of "the man in the street." A man who owns a fantastic little machine that turns sand into solid matter, harder than steel— but who hasn't the vaguest notion of how it works, or how to analyze it. A man whose knowledge of past history is as vague and formless as any modern man's. A soldier. With no other talent than fighting. What is to be done with such a man?

Solution:

Unknown.

Lyle Sims pushed the coffee cup away. If he ever had to look at another cup of the disgusting stuff, he was sure he would vomit. Three sleepless days and nights, running on nothing but dexedrine and hot black coffee, had put his nerves more on edge than usual. He snapped at the clerks and secretaries, he paced endlessly, and he had ruined the stems of five pipes. He felt muggy and his stomach was queasy. Yet there was no solution.

It was impossible to say, "All right, we've got a man from the future. So what? Turn him loose and let him make a life for himself in our time, since he can't return to his own."

It was impossible to do that for several reasons: (1) what if he *couldn't* adjust? He was then a potential menace, of *incalculable* potential. (2) What if an enemy power—and God knows there were enough powers around anxious to get a secret weapon as valuable as Qarlo—grabbed him, and *did* somehow manage to work out the concepts behind the rifle, the firmer, the mono-atomic anti-gravity device in the pouch? What then? (3) A man used to war, knowing only war, would eventually *seek* or foment war.

There were dozens of others, they were only beginning to realize. No, something had to be done with him.

Imprison him?

For what? The man had done no real harm. He had not intentionally caused the death of the man on the subway platform. He had been frightened by the train. He had been attacked by the executives—one of whom had a broken neck, but was alive. No, he was just "a stranger and afraid, in a world I never made," as Housman had put it so terrifyingly clearly.

Kill him?

For the same reasons, unjust and brutal...not to mention wasteful.

Find a place for him in society?

Doing what?

Sims raged in his mind, mulled it over and tried every angle. It was an insoluble problem. A simple dogface, with no other life than that of a professional soldier, what good was he?

All Qarlo knew was war.

The question abruptly answered itself: If he knows no other life than that of a soldier...why, make him a soldier. (But...who was to say that with his knowledge of futuristic tactics and weapons, he might not turn into another Hitler, or Genghis Khan?) No, making him a soldier would only heighten the problem. There could be no piece of mind were he in a position where he might organize.

As a tactician then?

It might work at that.

Sims slumped behind his desk, pressed down the key of his intercom, spoke to the secretary, "Get me General Mainwaring, General Polk and the Secretary of Defense."

He clicked the key back. It just might work at that. If Qarlo could be persuaded to detail fighting plans, now that he realized where he was, and that the men who held him were not his enemies, and allies of Ruskie-Chink (and what a field of speculation *that* pair of words opened!).

It just might work...

...but Sims doubted it.

Mainwaring stayed on to report when Polk and the Secretary of Defense went back to their regular duties. He was a big man, with softness written across his face and body, and a pompous white moustache. He shook his head sadly, as though the Rosetta Stone had been stolen from him just before an all-important experiment.

"Sorry, Sims, but the man is useless to us. Brilliant grasp of military tactics, so long as it involves what he calls 'eighty thread beams' and telepathic contacts.

"Do you know those wars up there are fought as much mentally as they are physically? Never heard of a tank or a mortar, but the stories he tells of brain-burning and spore-death would make you sick. It isn't pretty the way they fight.

"I thank God I'm not going to be around to see it; I *thought* our wars were filthy and unpleasant. They've got us licked all down the line for brutality and mass death. And the strange thing is, this Qarlo fellow *despises* it! For a while there—felt foolish as hell—but for a while there, when he was explaining it, I almost wanted to chuck my career, go out and start beating the drum for disarmament."

The General summed up, and it was apparent Qarlo was useless as a tactician. He had been brought up with one way of waging war, and it would take a lifetime for him to adjust enough to be of any tactical use.

But it didn't really matter, for Sims was certain the general had given him the answer to the problem, inadvertently.

He would have to clear it with Security, and the President, of course. And it would take a great deal of publicity to make the people realize this man actually *was* the real thing, an inhabitant of the future. But if it worked out, Qarlo Clobregnny, the soldier and nothing *but* the soldier, could be the most valuable man Time had ever spawned.

He set to work on it, wondering foolishly if he wasn't too much the idealist.

Ten soldiers crouched in the frozen mud. Their firmers had been jammed, had turned the sand and dirt of their holes only to icelike conditions. The cold was seeping up through their suits, and the jammed firmers were emitting hard radiation. One of the men screamed as the radiation took hold in his gut, and he felt the organs watering away. He leaped up, vomiting blood and phlegm—and was caught across the face by a robot-tracked triple beam. The front of his face disappeared, and the nearly decapitated corpse flopped back into the firmhole, atop a comrade.

That soldier shoved the body aside carelessly, thinking of his four children, lost to him forever in a Ruskie-Chink raid on Garmatopolis, sent to the bogs to work. His mind conjured up the sight of the three girls and the little boy with such long, long eyelashes—each dragging through the stinking bog, a mineral bag tied to their neck, collecting fuel rocks for the enemy. He began to cry softly. The sound and mental image of crying was picked up by a Ruskie-Chink telepath somewhere across the lines, and even before the man could catch himself, blank his mind, the telepath was on him.

The soldier raised up from the firmhole bottom, clutching with crooked hands at his head. He began to tear at his features wildly, screaming high and piercing, as the enemy telepath burned away his brain. In a moment his eyes were empty, staring shells, and the man flopped down beside his comrade, who had begun to deteriorate.

A thirty-eight thread whined its beam overhead, and the eight remaining men saw a munitions wheel go up with a deafening roar. Hot shrapnel zoomed across the field, and a thin, brittle, knife-edged bit of plasteel arced over the edge of the firmhole, and buried itself in one soldier's head. The piece went in crookedly, through his left earlobe, and came out skewering his tongue, half-extended from his open mouth. From the side it looked as though he were wearing some sort of earring. He died in spasms, and it took an awfully long while. Finally, the twitching and gulping got so bad, one of his comrades used the butt of a Brandelmeier across the dying man's nose. It splintered the nose, sent bone chips into the brain, killing the man instantly.

Then the attack call came!

In each of their heads, the telepathic cry came to advance, and they were up out of the firmhole, all seven of them, reciting their daily prayer, and knowing it would do no good. They advanced across the slushy ground, and overhead they could hear the buzz of leech bombs, coming down on the enemy's thread emplacements.

All around them in the deep-set night the varicolored explosions popped and sugged, expanding in all directions like fireworks, then dimming the scene again the blackness.

One of the soldiers caught a beam across the belly, and he was thrown sidewise for ten feet, to land in a soggy heap, his stomach split open, the organs glowing and pulsing wetly from the charge of the threader. A head popped out of a firmhole before them, and three of the remaining six fired simultaneously. The enemy was a booby—rigged to backtrack their kill urge, rigged to a telepathic hookup—and even as the body exploded under their combined firepower, each of the men caught fire. Flames leaped from their mouths, from their pores, from the instantly charred spaces where their eyes had been. A pyrotic-telepath had been at work.

The remaining three split and cut away, realizing they might be thinking, might be giving themselves away. That was the horror of being just a dogface, not a special telepath behind the lines. Out here there was nothing but death.

A doggie-mine slithered across the ground, entwined itself in the legs of one soldier, and blew the legs out from under him. He lay there clutching the shredded stumps, feeling the blood soaking into the mud, and then unconsciousness seeped into his brain. He died shortly thereafter.

Of the two left, one leaped a barbwall, and blasted out a thirty-eight thread emplacement of twelve men, at the cost of the top of his head. He was left alive, and curiously, as though the war had stopped, he felt the top of himself, and his fingers pressed lightly against convoluted, slick matter for a second before he dropped to the ground.

His braincase was open, glowed strangely in the night, but no one saw it.

The last soldier dove under a beam that zzzzzzzed through the night, and landed on his elbows. He rolled with the tumble, felt the edge of a leech-bomb crater, and dove in head-first. The beam split up his passage, and he escaped charring by an inch. He lay in the hole, feeling the cold of the battle-field seeping around him, and drew his cloak closer.

The soldier was Qarlo...

He finished talking, and sat down on the platform...

The audience was silent...

Sims shrugged into his coat, fished around in the pocket for the cold pipe. The dottle had fallen out of the bowl, and he felt the dark grains at the bottom of the pocket. The audience was filing out slowly, hardly anyone speaking, but each staring at others around him. As though they were suddenly realizing what had happened to them, as though they were looking for a solution.

Sims passed such a solution. The petitions were there, tacked up alongside the big sign—duplicate of the ones up all over the city. He caught the heavy black type on them as he passed through the auditorium's vestibule:

SIGN THIS PETITION! PREVENT WHAT YOU HAVE HEARD TONIGHT!

People were flocking around the petitions, but Sims knew it was only a token gesture at this point: the legislature had gone through that morning. No more war...under any conditions. And intelligence reported the long playing records, the piped broadcasts, the p.a. trucks, had all done their jobs. Similar legislation was going through all over the world.

It looked as though Qarlo had done it, single-handed.

Sims stopped to refill his pipe, and stared up at the big black-lined poster near the door.

HEAR QARLO, THE SOLDIER FROM THE FUTURE! SEE THE MAN FROM TOMORROW, AND HEAR HIS STORIES OF THE WONDERFUL WORLD OF THE FUTURE! FREE! NO OBLIGATIONS! HURRY!

The advertising had been effective, and it was a fine campaign.

Qarlo had been more valuable just telling about his Wars, about how men died in that day in the future, than he could ever have been as a strategist.

It took a real soldier, who hated war, to talk of it, to show people that it was ugly, and unglamorous. And there was a certain sense of foul defeat, of hopelessness, in knowing the future was the way Qarlo described it. It made you want to stop the flow of Time, say, "No. The future will *not* be like this! We will abolish war!"

Certainly enough steps in the right direction had been taken. The legislature was there, and those who had held back, who had tried to keep animosity alive, were being disposed of every day.

Qarlo had done his work well.

There was just one thing bothering special advisor Lyle Sims. The soldier had come back in time, so he was here. That much they knew for certain.

But a nagging worry ate at Sims's mind, made him say prayers he had thought himself incapable of inventing. Made him fight to get Qarlo heard by everyone...

Could the future be changed?

Or was it inevitable?

Would the world Qarlo left inevitably appear?

Would all their work be for nothing?

It couldn't be! It dare not be!

He walked back inside, got in line to sign the petitions again, though it was his fiftieth time.

SOLDIER

FADE IN: (TEASER)
1 THE WORLD (STOCK)
2 STYLIZED BATTLEFIELD—ESTABLISHING—LONG HIGH SHOT—NIGHT
A nightmare landscape seen in chioroscuro—shadows and light. Illuminated from moment to moment by a spiderwork tracery of light beams across the black sky. Nothing moves on this battlefield, though the sounds of warfare—the sizzling of the beams, the distant crackle of explosions—comes through dimly. Camera comes down toward a dark figure hunched over in a shallow foxhole as:
NARRATOR (V.O.): *Night comes too soon on the battle-field. For some men it comes permanently, their eyes never open to the light of day. But for this man, fighting this war, there is never total darkness; and the spidery beams of light in the sky are the descendants of the modern laser beam. Heat rays that sear through tungsten-steel and flesh as though they were cheesecloth.*
CAMERA STOPS ON CLOSEUP of the soldier. He wears an odd helmet equipped with antenna and night-vision glasses and padded earpieces that deaden sound. We see his heavy cape that he has pulled around himself as protection against the cold. The metal harness over his chest from which hangs a wicked-looking, strangely-constructed rifle. He pulls a cigarette from a metal tin and, holding it like a kitchen match, he scratches the end of the cigarette on the side of the pack. It ignites as camera moves into extreme closeup and we see his face clearly, the pattern of radiation burns that mars one side of his handsomely brutal face. He smokes, waiting, as: NARRATOR (V.O.) (continuing):

And this soldier must go against those weapons. His name is Qarlo, (pronounced) Kwahr-lo) and he is a foot-soldier, the ultimate infantryman. Trained from birth by the state. He has never known love, or closeness, or warmth...he is geared for only one purpose: to kill The Enemy.

During narration camera moves around Qarlo, showing us his almost bovine calm, as he waits. Abruptly, there is the sound of a tinny voice on filter and an electrical buzzing, both in his helmet. Qarlo's free hand presses to the ear piece as the voice repeats in his ear.

HELMET VOICE (FILTER) (urgent): *Attack! Kill!! Attack! Kill! Attack! Kill...*

The cigarette drops from Qarlo's mouth, unnoticed, as his eyes seem to re-focus.

NARRATOR (V.O.):...*and the Enemy waits for him.*

   3 CLOSE SHOT—THE ENEMY IN IDENTICAL FOXHOLE

   4 CLOSE SHOT—QARLO

He leaps out of the foxhole, rifle at the ready, and sprints forward, charging into the dark.

   5 THE BATTLEFIELD

Empty save for Qarlo running full-out from the right-hand side of the frame toward center of the frame; suddenly, the enemy running at top speed from the left-hand side of the frame toward center. Two broken-field attackers charging dead-on for each other, destined to meet at some central point in the middle of the frame, illuminated by the heat rays that now seem to have increased in number.

   6 MED. LONG SHOT—QARLO AND ENEMY AGAINST
   BLACK PROFILE

As they near each other, still separated by empty space, each man lifts his rifle to fire. As we angle on the men, two thick laser beams spear down directly out of the sky, one from either side, and zero down, directly on Qarlo and his enemy. They are instantly bathed in a coruscating aurora of flickering light that sizzles and pops. There is an insane electrical, like a thousand arc lights burning out all at once.

   7 CLOSEUP—QARLO

Arms flung up as though being crucified, still gripping the

strange rifle in one hand, he screams soundlessly, writhing, twisting, tormented, in the flickering eerie light-bath.

8 CLOSEUP—THE ENEMY

As the same happens to him, he contorts, huddles, tries to wring himself free from the insane forces that grip him.

9 TWO SHOT—QARLO AND THE ENEMY

The two men twisting, they suddenly vanish! They snap out of existence like two balloons popping. They are gone. The battlefield is empty and dark once more, and we abruptly

SHARP CUT THRU

10 SPECIAL PROCESS SHOTS

of reversed images against a grey background, flickering indistinct, warped, indicating dimensions and times being traversed, strange polarities and effects spinning eternity for us, a weird melange of special effects with no pattern.

DISSOLVE:

NOTES FOR REFERENCE TO THE PRECEDING
ACTION

1 THE WORLD. (STOCK)

2 STYLIZED BATTLEFIELD. (A weird silhouette) To be used for long shots and closeups.

2 (ALTERNATE) LONG SHOT BATTLEFIELD (STOCK) (If this is found, we may only build what is necessary for close action.)

3 A. FOXHOLE #1—QARLO

   B. FOXHOLE #2—THE ENEMY (Use same fox-hole for both men. Shoot #1 right to left. Shoot #2 left to right.)

   C. Section to cover enough of stylized battlefield for running shot of Qarlo and the Enemy in and out of light and shadow. (Use for both men: #1 right to left, #2 left to right.)

   D. Center section of battlefield where men come together. Laser beam hits them, they freeze. They vanish.

4 CLOSE SHOTS of both men against black velvet for space and time falling.

11 EXT. BUSINESS INTERSECTION OF CITY STREET—DAY

CAMERA ANGLE establishes one of the corners. On the sidewalk near the curb an old man is selling newspapers. O.s., we hear the sporadic blasts of a pneumatic drill in the street. Around the corner, a short distance from the newspaper man (but not in view of him), a police car is parked at the curb. One policeman is using a police call box in the street; the other policeman is seated in the car. There are several passers-by.

12 MED. SHOT—NEWSSTAND AND OLD MAN

Just as the newspaper man is using his knife to cut open a bundle of papers, Qarlo suddenly winks into existence at a point in front of the building about five feet behind the old man. He is, at this point, unseen by either the newspaper man or any of the pedestrians.

13 CLOSE SHOT—QARLO

looks about him, strangely disoriented, and wild-eyed at the sudden change of scene. We hold on this unusual setting for a moment and then

FADE OUT.

ACT ONE

14 EXT. THE STREET CORNER—LONG SHOT
We open the scene, as we closed it in the Teaser.

15 CLOSE SHOT—QARLO
seemingly abused by the strange noises, presses both hands to the ears of his helmet. During this close shot, as well as through all others on Qarlo, all the sounds we hear are muffled and subdued.

16 TWO SHOT—QARLO AND THE NEWS MAN
Now the sounds are normal again as the old news man slowly turns to face Qarlo, knife in hand. Qarlo quickly raises his rifle at him. Now the old man, who has turned around unwittingly, widens is eyes in surprise and terror as he clutches his heart. His face twists and he falls unconscious at Qarlo's feet.

17 FULLER SHOT
A WOMAN who has seen the incident screams. The startled passers-by turn quickly to see the weird soldier, and the unconscious man at his feet.
WOMAN (hysterically): *He killed him! He killed him!*
There is screaming and confusion and Qarlo menaces the group with his rifle. They scurry for cover, and he backs up toward the corner. Attracted by the screams and the commotion around the corner, the policeman in the car joins the other cop and they quickly advance on Qarlo who is backing toward them.
As they jump Qarlo, he turns quickly in a smooth, cat-like movement, and smashes the first one across the jaw with the butt of his rifle. The cop is thrown backward across the sidewalk in a disjointed heap. Qarlo disposes of the other cop in similar fashion. The screams of the crowd mount. Panic! Qarlo raises his

rifle at the second cop, who, lying prone near his police car, has drawn his revolver, but now quickly takes cover as the soldier fires the beam in the direction of the police car.

18 EXT. STREET—FULL SHOT—POLICE CAR—QARLO'S POV

The beam hits the car, and in a sizzling flash of light, the car puffs out of existence.

19 CLOSE SHOT—QARLO ON THE CORNER

With a wide-eyed panic of his own, based in confusion at his surroundings, as well as what has happened, Qarlo stands in trembling anxiety. (Once again, the sounds about him are muffled—including the pneumatic drill which continues on from this point.)

20 FULL SHOT—THE CORNER—QARLO

A newspaper truck drives quickly past the corner, and the man flings a heavy bundle of newspapers toward the newsstand. The bundle strikes Qarlo in the back, throwing him forward and down. As he falls, his helmet is knocked off.

21 CLOSEUP—QARLO (WHERE HE HAS FALLEN)

We see he has a small audio receiver in one ear. But now, with his helmet gone, the sounds all around him, and particularly the pneumatic drill, blasts in together with all the city noises, screaming insanely. The noise should be as high as possible to record.

As Qarlo's mouth opens in a soundless scream, he raises to one knee, his hands clapped to his ears to shut out the noise. His face is twisted in pain, and it is obvious the noise is destroying his ability to move. The rifle swings unnoticed on its harness.

22 MED. SHOT—THE TWO COPS

As they see Qarlo on one knee, they charge, camera going with them. As they stop in a two shot, one cop brings his billy down in the direction of Qarlo, but out of the frame. We hear the impact and a groan.

QUICK CUT:

23 FROM COP'S ANGLE

The soldier crumples to the sidewalk, unconscious. Camera pulls back as the people move in to look at the strange man unconscious on the sidewalk. The cop bends to slip cuffs on the soldier.

24 HIGH SHOT—QARLO

90° ANGLE DOWN on Qarlo's face. Camera comes down for extreme closeup of his unconscious face, as dimly, from the audio receiver in his ear we continue to hear the whispering metallic command, over and over:

HELMET VOICE (FILTER) (monotonous) *Kill! Kill! Kill! Kill! Kill!*...

CAMERA HOLDS on Qarlo's face, the mental command as we

DISSOLVE:

25 EXT. COUNTRYSIDE—THE HILL—CLOSE SHOT—THE ENEMY—NIGHT

Occasional lightning and thunder. Camera pulls back to reveal he is bathed in a coruscating glow of eerie light. Only *half* of him is visible. As though a cheese-cutter had neatly sliced him off at the waist, emptiness below and around him. He has been pulled only *halfway* through the time-warp. He clutches his weapon and struggles futilely with the invisible trap that has closed around him, locking him in stasis between the worlds.

NARRATOR (V.O.): *But time is fluid. The waters of forever close— and passage may not be completed. The present and the future are for a moment united. And the Enemy half-today, half-tomorrow, is locked between...*

During narration the Enemy flails around helplessly. For a moment he is silent, and in that silence the insistent, mechanical voice is heard in his helmet.

HELMET VOICE (FILTER): *Attack! Attack! Attack! Attack*!

Then, in insane fury at his helplessness, the Enemy begins to bellow almost like a rabid animal; a deep-toned, frightening shrieking torn form inside. Abruptly, there is a new sound— 'beep' 'beep' 'beep'—that causes him to look down at small electrical impulse machine strapped to his wrist. It is blinking and making the beeps. As he stares at it, o.s. we hear the wail of a police siren that seems to blend in with the sound of the beeps.

26 EXT. COUNTRYSIDE—LONG SHOT—HIGHWAY AND HILL—NIGHT

Two headlight beams scythe out of the darkness. As the car appears coming down highway toward camera.

27 INT. CAR BACK SEAT—CLOSE SHOT—NIGHT

Three men are seated in back. In the center is Qarlo who is securely bound and trussed up with heavy cloth strap around his neck. He is flanked on either side by two husky uniformed policemen. One of them has Qarlo's rifle in his lap. Qarlo starts to struggle violently attempting to get his rifle. The other men put more tension on his bonds to hold him down.

28 EXT. THE HILL—CLOSE SHOT—THE ENEMY

desperately trying to free himself and bring his rifle to bear as we hear the insistent, mechanical voice in his helmet. HELMET VOICE (FILTER): *Attack! Attack! Attack! Attack!*

29 EXT. HIGHWAY—LONG SHOT—THE CAR

as it goes down the highway and disappears into the blackness the beep beep fading with it.

DISSOLVE:

30 EXT. IRON GATE LEADING TO PRISON-TYPE
    ENCLOSED YARD—DAY

On the gate we can see the legend:

G. I. D. C.
PSYCHIATRIC SECURITY SECTION
AUTHORIZED GOV'T PERSONNEL ONLY

A uniformed guard stands at the gate. Through the gates we can see the rear entrance, or ambulance landing of a building. Standing in front of the gate is Tanner, a government agent. He is nervously waiting for someone.

31 ANOTHER ANGLE

A car drives up and stops a short distance from the gate. Kagan alights and approaches Tanner. Kagan is a short, intense man who looks as though he's been sleeping in his clothes. But there is a silent power in his features, a perceptivity and even a kindness. Tanner is the antithesis: tall, dapper, restrained, in every sense of the word "cool". Kagan extends his hand.

KAGAN: *Mr. Tanner?*

Tanner acknowledges.

KAGAN (continuing): *I'm Tom Kagan, the philologist. I was sent here by the local office of the Bureau.*

TANNER (confused): *Philologist?*

KAGAN (smiles tolerantly): *Right. Language expert. I read your* report. *The man seems to be speaking some sort of strange dialect. They decided I was the one to unravel it.*

Tanner shakes his head in shocked annoyance.

TANNER: *You've got to be kidding.* (beat) *Right? You're putting me on.*

KAGAN: *What's that supposed to mean?*

TANNER: *I'll tell you what that's supposed to mean, friend. Any minute now something will be arriving that is guaranteed to stand your hair on end. It took six beefy men to get him into the two strait jackets he's wearing...and they send down a...a philologist!*

KAGAN (lightly): *I know a little karate...*

TANNER (not amused): *Oh, say, Kagan, you are a real knee-slapper.*

They are interrupted by the sound of an arriving ambulance. As Kagan and Tanner move aside, the ambulance pulls to a stop in front of the gate. The guard opens the gate, the ambulance drives through followed by Kagan and Tanner on foot.

32 EXT. AMBULANCE LANDING

Ambulance pulls in and stops. The driver goes to the back and opens the doors. Two MP's wearing white helmets and armbands, pistol belts supporting unsnapped holsters, jump out.

As Kagan and Tanner enter and look on, the MP's roll out a stretcher with the mummy-wrapped-in-two-strait-jackets. (Qarlo strapped to the stretcher.) He is shaking with restrained fury, his teeth bared. Kagan stares dumbly as the stretcher rolls away, then turns to Tanner, realizing now what Tanner meant.

TANNER (concerned, yet amused): *I guess I didn't make my report strong enough.*

KAGAN (awed): *No...I...don't think...you...did.*

DISSOLVE:

33 INT. OBSERVATION CHAMBER — ESTABLISHING—NIGHT

CAMERA LOOKING STRAIGHT DOWN through a square glass window set in the floor of the observation room. We are looking down from a high ceiling into a padded cell. Below us, Qarlo paces back and forth like a caged animal. There is the sound of a high whining noise as a freight elevator starts.

Qarlo claps both hands to his head, falls against a wall, thrashes about. He comes off the wall, plunges across the room, slamming his fists against the unfeeling wall-pads. Camera pulls back to:

34 ANOTHER SHOT—OBSERVATION CHAMBER

It is almost totally dark, with only the illuminated square of the one-way observation window in the floor throwing a radiance up from below, casting light on the faces of Kagan and Tanner, staring down at the soldier. Their faces have an eerie underlit effect and they don't look at each other as they talk softly, but continue to stare down at what we know is the padded cell and Qarlo.

KAGAN: *What was that noise?*

TANNER: *Freight elevator.*

KAGAN: *Have them shut it off.*

TANNER: *What for?*

KAGAN: *Sharp sounds drive him wild. Apparently his hearing is on a more sensitive threshold than ours. That helmet you showed me—there were sound baffles built in, to deaden outside noise.*

TANNER: *So we'll give him back the helmet.*

KAGAN: *I wouldn't, if I were you.*

TANNER: *What harm can it do?*

KAGAN: *That's the point. I don't know.*

TANNER: *I think you're scared, Kagan.*

KAGAN: *That's the name of the game.*

TANNER: *So that calm exterior is just a pose. I'm glad to know there's somebody else in this boat with me.*

KAGAN: *Mmm. Up the creek, minus paddles.*

TANNER (offering): *Want a piece of gum?*

Kagan nods, takes it, unwraps it, and folding it, begins to chew it.

KAGAN: *Those scars...radiation burns, I'd say. But I can't be certain, it's outside my field.*

TANNER (agreeing): *Radiation all right. Johns Hopkins had him for five days. But it's outside their field, too. Whatever caused those burns we haven't seen anything like it around here.*

KAGAN: *He's shouting something! Hit that switch!*

Tanner reaches over, flicks a switch on the wall. From a grille beside the switch comes the hollow sound of Qarlo yelling.

(Note: the following is written phonetically for the benefit of the players.)

QARLO'S VOICE (O.S.) (FILTER): *M'nemzz Kwahr-loe Klo-breg-knee, pryte, sihz-fi-wun-oh-too-too-nyne, dammm-eeoooo!*

KAGAN: *Cut it.*

Tanner hits the switch, the voice stops.

KAGAN (continuing): *Same speech over and over. It's all he ever says.*

TANNER: *So what's it mean? What language is it?*

KAGAN: *I'm warning you, Tanner, ask a nitwit question, I'm going to give you a nitwit answer.*

TANNER: *Get smart with me, boy, and I take back your choon gum.*

KAGAN: *I'm not clowning, Tanner, I hear that line of gibberish in my sleep. There's something familiar about it, but I can't place the dialect.*

TANNER: *Have you been able to make anything from the tapes?*

KAGAN (shakes head): *Random sounds mostly. Anger, frenzy, a few scattered word-groups I can't decipher. Taking tapes of his mumblings locked in a padded cell aren't going to help me. I've got to go down in there with him.*

TANNER (shocked): *Oh, now wait just a second, friend. Have you lost your mind? That isn't some ordinary psycho down there...he's the most dangerous piece of equipment I've ever seen. He'll take you and tear along the dotted line!*

    35 CLOSEUP—KAGAN AND TANNER

    As Kagan looks across at Tanner for the first time.

KAGAN (seriously): *Tanner, you're not a scientist. That man down there is something we've never seen before. He's from somewhere or somewhen outside our knowledge. He's a walking challenge.*

TANNER: *He's a walking* bomb, *you mean!*

KAGAN: *Six of one, half a dozen of another.*

TANNER: *It's entirely possible we've put the wrong man in that padded cll.*

KAGAN: *Do I get the permission?*

TANNER: *Not a chance.*

KAGAN: *Can I try to persuade you? Logically?*

TANNER: *You can try till you grow webbed feet, Kagan. You'll never convince me.*

CAMERA HOLDS a long beat as Tanner sits smugly staring at the vaguely smiling little Kagan.

CUT TO:

36 CLOSEUP ON DOOR TO PADDED CELL

as the latch is thrown, and a guard opens the cell. Camera pulls back to show Tanner and a guard with drawn pistol, standing behind Kagan as the door opens and camera shoots through open door to the int. padded cell with Qarlo tensed against the far wall, framed by the doorway, ready to spring. Kagan moves into the room, stops, stares at Qarlo.

37 INT. PADDED CELL—TWO SHOT—KAGAN AND
    QARLO

as they face each other. Behind Kagan, through the open door, we see the Guard leveling his pistol. Tanner tensed. The man from the present and the man from the future stare at each other across an abyss of time and each other's natures. Qarlo looks as though he might leap at any moment. Then, slowly, Kagan reaches for a pack of cigarettes. Qarlo tenses. Kagan pulls out a cigarette, puts one in his mouth. Qarlo's eyes widen. He bites his lip. He recognizes tobacco! Kagan sees the recognition, offers the pack, shaking the cigarettes up for Qarlo to see. For a long beat Qarlo stares at him, then cautiously reaches out to the full length of his arm.

38 INTERCUT—THEIR HANDS

across the open space between the offered pack and the hard, brutal-looking reaching hand of the soldier. There is long hesitation, then the hand grabs the pack!

SHARP CUT TO:

39 ANOTHER ANGLE—THE SCENE

as Qarlo jumps back, the pack in his hand. Kagan watches as the soldier pulls a cigarette from the pack deftly. He tries to strike it on the side of the pack as we saw him do in the first scene. It crumbles into paper and bits. He looks surprised, then angry. He bares his teeth, snarling at Kagan for tormenting him with a smoke. Kagan dimly realizes what is going on. He pulls out a lighter, lights his own cigarette, draws deeply, exhales smoke.

Qarlo watches. Kagan moves toward him with the flickering flame.
Qarlo tenses. Kagan stops, extending the flame. Qarlo hesitantly
moves forward, eyes always on Kagan. He puts another cigarette
in his mouth and, still watching, gets a light. Then he moves
smoothly back to the wall, drawing deeply.

40 MED. SHOT—ON KAGAN

as he makes his next move. He walks slowly to the side wall
and sits down on the padded floor. He moves very slowly, very
studiedly, so as not to alarm the soldier. Kagan smokes for a
moment, studying Qarlo. Then he makes a fist, the thumb
pointing back at himself. He taps himself lightly on the chest
with the thumb-tip. He names himself.

KAGAN: *Kagan. Kagan.*

Qarlo stares at him. Kagan points to the soldier, makes a helpless
hands-open gesture, then points to himself again.

KAGAN (continuing): *Kagan? Hmmm? Kagan?*

Qarlo stares. He understands. We *know*, by his expression, that
he understands. But he isn't giving an inch. This is not—we
should realize at this point—a dumb brute, but a thinking entity.
A man with a mind. But what the nature of that locked mind
may be, we do *not* know. Kagan tries again.

KAGAN (taps himself): *Kagan. Come on, man, confound it,* Kaye-
gannn! *Kagan!*

He points to Qarlo, who smirks softly. Then the soldier speaks.
It is all run together, and totally unintelligible. But what he says
is:

QARLO: *M'nemzz Kwahr-loe Klo-breg-knee, pryte, sihz-fyfe-wun-
oh-too-too-nyne...*

CAMERA HOLDS A BEAT on Qarlo, then pans rapidly to Kagan,
who smiles, draws on his cigarette, and settles back against the
wall in a relaxed position. He has broken through.

KAGAN (softly, prayerlike): *You can say that again, brother...*

41 INT. OBSERVATION ROOM—DAY

The room is lit now, and a portable protective railing surrounds
the observation window in the floor. Kagan, Tanner and a
secretary taking notes on a courtroom stenographic transcriber.
She sits as Kagan paces, a cigarette hanging from his mouth,

ashes falling on his jacket-front. Tanner sits at the other side, listening, as Kagan dictates to the girl.

KAGAN (dictating): *Brown hair, clipped so short you can see the scalp. Brown...no, black eyes. Six feet, three inches. Radiation scars, right cheek. Smaller scars, above the eyes. Three parallel scars, left temple, running down cheek almost to chin; very faint, not like right cheek burns.* (beat) *Something else. It may mean nothing, but his forehead seems higher than normal, with a peculiar bulging, as though he'd been smacked with something hard, and the forehead's swelling.* (beat) *That's all, Karen.*

The girl stops typing, gathers her little machine, and leaves quickly. Kagan has continued pacing, and Tanner has sat through the entire scene without a word. It is apparent he is trying to be patient, though bugged.

TANNER: *Well?*

KAGAN: *Well* what?

TANNER: *Seven days and you ask me "well what?"*

KAGAN (smiles): *He's a soldier.*

TANNER (throws up his hands): *Any other late bulletins? I spent three years in the Rangers, Kagan, I* know *a soldier when I see one.*

KAGAN: *No, I mean he's* really *a soldier. There's but nothing about him not a soldier. The ultimate, perfect infantryman. I don't think he knows anything else.*

TANNER: *And what makes you think that?*

KAGAN: *That gibberish he's been spouting.*

TANNER: *Which is...?*

KAGAN (lightly): *English.*

TANNER (annoyed): *English? Come on, Kagan, I'm not the most fluent speaker in the world, but I know English when I hear it. The guy is obviously a foreigner of some kind.*

KAGAN: *Wrong word. Not foreigner. Try alien.*

TANNER (incredulously): *Alien? From another planet?*

KAGAN (shakes head): *No, from this planet.*

TANNER: *The Department wants facts, Kagan, not wild conjectures. Who is he, and what country is he from?*

KAGAN: *I'm not sure yet.*

TANNER: *Not sure? How the devil long does it take, man?*

KAGAN: *It takes time. Lots of time. I have to break down his speech syllable by syllable. It seems to be a corrupted form of American English, degenerated the way Canterbury English became the Cockney dialect.*

TANNER: *Lovely, but what do I tell them upstairs?*

Kagan spins on him, furiously; he is tired and involved.

KAGAN: *Tell them not to press me! Tell them I'm just starting to break through. Tell them he has to trust me implicitly. One slip and it may lose us the game!*

Tanner, snapped back by this sudden irrational tirade, realizes Kagan has been pushing himself to the edge. Kagan slumps down into the chair. Tanner uses a softer tone.

TANNER: *Hey...take it easy, Tom...*

KAGAN (wearily): *I'm just a little bushed, is all. It's like holding onto fog. One moment I think I've got it, and the next it's gone. He's by no means stupid...that's a strange, peculiar item we've got down there, but not a stupid one.*

TANNER: *You think you can hack it, Tom?*

KAGAN (nods): *Let me handle it my way, and I think I can get through to him. Trusting me is the key.*

TANNER (nods resignedly): *Okay, I'll do the best I can to run interference for you. But I just wish you could give me something to placate The Men Upstairs.*

KAGAN (nods agreement): *All right. I'll give you something.* (beat) *You want to know what he keeps saying, over and over, without any change? He's saying, "My name is Qarlo Clobregnny, private, six-five-one-oh-two-two-nine." His name, rank, and serial number.*

CAMERA HOLDS on Tanner's startled face as we

DISSOLVE TO:

42 EXT. COUNTRYSIDE—LIGHTNING AND THUNDER—
         CLOSE SHOT—ENEMY—NIGHT

Now, although he continues to flail, we can see that as a result of the lightning his body instead of being cut off at the waist is now cut off at the knees.

FADE OUT.

ACT TWO

43 INT. PADDED CELL—CLOSEUP ON PICTURE BOOK—
    DAY
It is of the Giant Golden Book variety, patently for a child. A
hand is pointing to a picture of a dog, a very large picture of a
dog. And Kagan is speaking.
KAGAN (V.O.) (repeating): *Dog. D-O-G. Dog, it's a dog, Qarlo, a
dog. You know it, you* must *know it, a* dog!
CAMERA PULLS BACK to show us Kagan with the book on
his lap, tapping the dog picture over and over, as Qarlo sits on
his haunches near him, smoking. It is obvious Qarlo is merely
tolerating what Kagan is doing. He smiles, just an edge of a smile.
Kagan is infuriated.
KAGAN (continuing): *Dog! Stop playing dumb*! DOG!
Qarlo claps his hands to his ears as Kagan shouts. His teeth bare.
He tears the cigarette from his mouth and grabs the book. He
holds it up, smashes his finger into the picture.
QARLO: *Dogizzadog! Dog! Dogdogdogdogdog…*!
He tears the book in half, flings the pieces against the wall, stares
defiantly at Kagan. Then he shrugs bitterly, smiles as though it
were spitting, and walks to the other side of the room, where he
slides down to a sitting position.
KAGAN (wearily): *I give up.*
Qarlo snickers. Kagan looks up, angry. Qarlo sneers. And then as
camera holds on Kagan he realizes: Qarlo understands! He has
reached him.
    44 PERSPECTIVE SHOT
FROM QARLO FAR ACROSS THE ROOM TO KAGAN with their
faces very distinct, every expression catalogued.

KAGAN: *You know, don't you? You understand everything I'm saying and doing, don't you? Not in my words, or yours, but you know! And you won't give me an inch will you? Will you, damn it!*

Qarlo says nothing.

KAGAN (continuing): *Where you come from, who you are, you'll tell me; yes, you will; soon enough. But not till I tell you where you are, who I am—right?*

Qarlo snickers deprecatingly. His face tells it all.

KAGAN (continuing): *How could they have thought you were a dumb brute. You're quicker than I'd be in your place, soldier. Qarlo. Private. 6-5-1-0-2-2-9.*

QARLO: *Dogdogdogdogdogdogdogdog...!*

KAGAN: *A-B-C-D-E-1-2-3-4-5-6-!*

QARLO: *DogaKaganaDogaKaganaDog...dammit!*

CAMERA COMES IN SLOWLY on Qarlo's face as he spits out the words rapidly one after another, like a machine gun spitting bullets, bambambambambambam as we

DISSOLVE:

45 INT. BALLISTICS LAB ENTRANCE DOOR—DAY

Door opens and Kagan enters. He looks o.s. and sees Tanner. Camera goes with him as he crosses to Tanner who is examining Qarlo's rifle along with a report in his hand. In the b.g. a ballistics expert is examining a piece of metal under a microscope.

KAGAN: *They told me you were here checking his rifle again. I've got to talk to you.*

TANNER (stunned): *Kagan, this weapon is incredible! There's no power source, none at all. It's inexhaustible. I could fire it steadily for a month and its power wouldn't decrease by a kilowatt.*

KAGAN: *Tanner...*

Tanner crosses and removes the piece of melted metal from under the microscope. Shows it to Kagan.

TANNER: *This is what's left of a 4 foot square, 3 foot thick solid steel bulkhead.*

KAGAN: *My God!*

TANNER (cuts him off): *Do you know we took this thing apart, disassembled every piece, and it has only three moving parts.* (1/2 beat) *And they tried leaving out half a dozen pieces, and it still worked! And we don't know how, not the faintest idea! (then) By the way, what's so important?*

KAGAN (sharply): *I broke through this morning. I think we talked.*

TANNER: *You* think *you talked?*

KAGAN (softly): *He's from the future, Paul. Eighteen hundred years in Earth's future.*

Tanner stares at him incredulously. Camera holds for several long beats as Tanner reorganizes his thinking. He shakes himself physically, draws deep breath.

TANNER: *But...how...*

KAGAN: *He doesn't really know. I don't think anyone could know, because it was a freak accident. In his future they fight their wars with beams of force—and he was caught between two of them. And the next thing he knew...* (he snaps his fingers)

TANNER (picks it up): *...he was here, in the present.*

KAGAN: *Correction: in the past. His* past, *our* present.

TANNER: *He told you all this?*

KAGAN (shakes head): *Only fragments of it. I had to piece it together and draw my own conclusions from most of it. He was about to attack someone he keeps calling The Enemy...with capital letters...*

TANNER: *You two are becoming very chummy. Coffee klatsches, yet*

KAGAN: *It's only rudimentary conversation. I think he's been able to decipher what I've been saying all along. It must sound to him like a phonograph record of English as spoken by—say—Chaucer, played at the wrong speed, a slower speed, would sound to us.*

TANNER: *Then it is English he's speaking.*

KAGAN: *Not really. Not entirely. It's what I thought, gutter English, vastly speeded-up, and filled with slang from his time.*

TANNER: *Eighteen hundred years...*

KAGAN: *...in the future. Exactly.*

TANNER: *How did you get that out of him?*

KAGAN: *I wasn't certain he was even from this planet, so I—*

SHARP CUT TO:

46 INT. PADDED CELL—EXTREME CLOSEUP ON STAR MAP—DAY

spread on floor. Camera pulls back to show Qarlo and Kagan looking at the map.

KAGAN: *This is our galaxy. These stars here. This is our sun, light, up there...and here: one, two, three. Third from the sun...Earth...*

Qarlo follows his fingers as they point out nebulae, white dots on the blue star map, the larger blowup of the Solar System. Kagan talks, but mostly to himself, knowing Qarlo cannot understand him:

KAGAN (tapping Earth): *Here. Here. Earth...*(makes wide arm movement in air) *Us. This dot. The Earth. Now...*(he taps Qarlo) *Which one is yours. Which star. Which planet. Qarlo...which...?*

Qarlo shakes his head as though Kagan was a dullard. He wipes his hand across the star map, finally settles on the same point Kagan had touched. The Earth.

KAGAN (wearily): *No, man, that's the* Earth! *Which planet is yours...?*

Qarlo taps the paper again. Same spot. Kagan registers a dawning realization. He pulls a large tablet of writing paper from his briefcase lying on the floor nearby, and with a ballpoint pen quickly sketches the Solar System, circling Earth heavily. He gives the pen to Qarlo.

47 CLOSEUP—QARLO

as he looks at the pen. He turns it over and over, examining it as though it were the rarest jewel he had ever seen. Then Kagan urges him, tearing off the top sheet, and indicating Qarlo should write. Qarlo quickly bends to the task, and though at first he uses the pen incorrectly, he masters it in a few moments and draws the same thing Kagan drew.

KAGAN: *Great! Imitation is the sincerest form of flattery, but it doesn't help us much—*

Qarlo cuts him off with a rapid wave of his hand. He pulls the star map to him, indictaes the Milky Way, the galaxy in which Earth spins around its sun.

KAGAN (continuing): *Right. Our solar system. Our galaxy. Okay. Now what?*

Qarlo begins sketching, faster and faster, making dots in concentric patterns. Kagan studies them. Finally Qarlo stops. He taps the Milky Way on the star map, then his own drawing. Kagan picks up Qarlo's drawing. He stares at it.

KAGAN: *It's our galaxy. The same as the star map, the same as—*

CAMERA COMES IN FOR EXTREME CLOSEUP as Kagan's eyes widen. His mouth opens in astonishment as we

SHARP CUT TO:

48 INT. BALLISTICS LAB

MATCHING SHOT AS SCENE 45 when we cut away. We have been in a *flashback* as we can see from the fact that Tanner and Kagan are in the same exact positions as when we left them in Scene 45.

KAGAN: *Except it wasn't our galaxy. At least not the way it is today.* (beat) *I took that drawing to a friend of mine at the Naval Observatory. He thought it was an amusing sketch. But it took him four hours to plot it correctly.*

TANNER: *Well? What was it?*

KAGAN (flat): *The position the stars of our galaxy will be in...in eighteen hundred years.*

Tanner's eyes widen. He wipes his mouth which is suddenly dry. He pulls out a pack of gum. Anti-climactically:

TANNER: *Have a piece of gum...*

CAMERA HOLDS on them as Kagan takes the gum, and they stare at each other across a drawing abyss of fear and anxiety.

DISSOLVE TO:

49 INT. PEDDED CELL—FULL SHOT—NIGHT

MOVIE SCREEN set up at one end of the dark cell. Kagan is running the projector, Qarlo watching various scenes on the screen, (stock). The first scene: a mother affectionately holding child.

KAGAN: *Love. Love. Love.*

The scene flashes: war; a shot of incredible violence.

KAGAN (continuing): *Hate. Hate. Hate.*

New scene: man and woman walking through forest, kissing.

KAGAN (continuing): *Love. Love. Love.*

As the scene of war flashes, Qarlo slides up the wall, watching with fascinated face. As the scenes of love flash, he looks confused, does not understand.

New scene: an attacker, teeth bared, sword raised, large in the frame, bearing down on them.

Qarlo suddenly leaps forward, pushes the projector on its side, knocking the reel off. The projector continues to run as Qarlo rushes to the screen. As he rips it to shreds, literally snaps the steel legs of the instrument, the flickering light continues on him. He spins on Kagan, stops and, pulsing like a furnace about to explode, clenches his fists.

QARLO (furious): *Why'dja'yoo peep me thiz?*

His speech is still slurred, run together, and dotted with slang from his own time, but we can now understand what he says without translation. Kagan tries to placate him. He turns on a lamp and turns off the projector.

KAGAN: *I want you to know. I want you to understand.*

QARLO (aims sharp finger): I *catch.* You! *You're'da drumbum. Send me home'a'ways.* Now! *Doncha know thereza war-ron?*

Kagan comes toward Qarlo. The soldier backs up. He is obviously restraining himself from tearing Kagan in half.

KAGAN (helplessly): *I can't send you home, Qarlo. I don't know how; no one knows how. Your home doesn't exist yet.*

QARLO: *Lovehate, lovehate, fret it.*

KAGAN: *I can't forget it.*

QARLO: *Fret it. Thinkspeek'll pull me.*

KAGAN: *I don't understand that. I'm sorry.*

Qarlo snarls. He shakes his head. He taps his head several times, trying to get his meaning across to Kagan.

QARLO: *Thinkspeek! Thinkspeek! C.O. See-Oh! See-Oh! Ah, fret it!*

He turns away, leans against the wall, and suddenly—but quietly—pounds his fist into the wall pads. His fury is a controlled thing, but the passion is there. Kagan moves in to touch him on the shoulder, a *compassionate* gesture. Qarlo whirls and with one catlike movement literally lifts Kagan off the floor, pins him against the wall, his feet dangling. The fires that have burned low in Qarlo suddenly blaze forth. He is the kill-machine.

    50 CLOSEUP—TWO SHOT—QARLO AND KAGAN

THEIR FACES close together as Qarlo hisses into Kagan's face.

    QARLO: *Donnever...touch...me...!*

He is banging Kagan against the wall mercilessly, repeating "don't ever touch me" over and over and over The sound of the door slamming open.

51 WIDE ANGLE—THE SCENE

as two MPs rush in, grapple with Qarlo; Kagan drops, clutching his neck; the MPs are tossed this way and that, finally club Qarlo into unconsciousness. They help Kagan up. He stumbles to Qarlo, looks at his wound. He shakes his head sadly as we

DISSOLVE TO:

52 INT. DISPENSARY—CLOSEUP—NIGHT

on a bare chest being taped up. As camera angle widens we see Kagan being attended by a doctor, who is neatly taping up his ribs in wide, white swaths of tape. Tanner sits nearby, one foot on a small stool, watching.

TANNER: *Well, how does it feel to be dribbled like a basketball?*

KAGAN: *It was my fault.*

TANNER: *Oh, cut it out, Kagan.*

KAGAN: *It was my fault! It was literally the first time in his life anyone had ever touched him!*

TANNER: *You just can't admit it when you fail, can you? Well get it straight, Tom, that soldier is only a half a step up from a wild animal, and he has to be treated that way. Caged!*

KAGAN: *Listen, Tanner...ouch!*

DOCTOR: *It'll be worse than "ouch" if you don't stop squirming.*

TANNER: *Five weeks, and what've you got to show? Nothing but a set of staved-in ribs and one beautiful headache from having your skull bounced off a wall.*

KAGAN: *And I've got him speaking our language.*

TANNER: *Not so's I noticed. Every third word's gibberish.*

KAGAN: *Not gibberish...common usage from his own, time. And have you stopped to think how valuable even those clues are to our future?*

DOCTOR: *That's it. Do us both a favor and try not to let him use you for a ping-pong ball. I have to requisition tape, and that's a nuisance.*

Doctor gathers his things and exits. Kagan starts to put on his shirt with Tanner's help.

TANNER: *Tom, we can't let you go back in there with him. He can't be controlled, he can't be predicted...he's—*

KAGAN: *He's a man!*

TANNER: *He's not a man, he's something else. Just look in his eyes, Tom, at the hate in them; you can see he was born to be a killer!*

KAGAN: *That's the point. He was born to be a killer; and trained to be a killer; and if he hadn't found his way into our time, he'd die a killer. But he doesn't hate, Paul! He doesn't understand hate...or love...or compassion.*

TANNER: *And you think you can teach him what they mean?*

KAGAN: *Not in that cell...*

TANNER (suspiciously): *Kagan...*

KAGAN: *I want you to release him.*

Tanner looks stupefied.

KAGAN (continuing): *I mean it. I want to take him home with me.*

TANNER: Home with you! *Oh, now come* on!

Kagan grabs Tanner's arm. He speaks with intensity. He *has* to convince him.

KAGAN: *He hasn't* done *anything to keep him penned up like a criminal. That old man only fainted, and Qarlo was simply defending himself in a strange situation when he fired at the police car.*

TANNER: *Don't you think we've considered that? It's not just a fine legal point, Tom. It's his freedom, I know that, they know it at the Bureau. But we can't turn him loose, ready to go off at any moment.*

KAGAN: *So let me try and teach him what it means to be a functioning human being. He can adapt; he's quick; he can fit in.*

TANNER: *Tom, it's lunacy.*

KAGAN: *But I can try.*

TANNER: *Forget it, it's too risky.*

KAGAN: *But I can try!*

TANNER: *I'm trying to tell you, Tom, it's not* my *decision to make. The Bureau has kept this thing top secret only by working full time. Right now there are half a dozen newspapermen whose mouths are shut only because they know what would happen if they leaked something like this.*

KAGAN: *Fine. Then no one would know he was at my home. We're in the country, few neighbors around...*

TANNER (blurts): *Tom, they want him in prison—*

Kagan stares at him, dumfounded.

KAGAN (stunned): *Prison...?*

TANNER (a little ashamed): *I didn't want to say anything. The Bureau's been getting static. A Top Secret like this is too hot to leave lying around. They want him boxed in permanently.*

KAGAN: *You can't do it, Paul.*

TANNER: *What else can I do?*

KAGAN: *Give him to me...(beat) Just a month. One month more, Paul. That's all I ask. I think he'll progress to a point where they'll reconsider. Just one month.*

TANNER: *I'd have to argue it out with the Men Upstairs. They'd never go along with it.*

KAGAN: *One miserable month!*

TANNER: *A week.*

KAGAN: *Not enough time...I need a month. Make it three weeks...*

TANNER: *Two weeks, can you do it in two weeks?*

KAGAN (relieved): *All right, two weeks...*

TANNER: *What about your family? How are they going to like the idea of a potential killer in the same house with them?*

KAGAN: *I've already talked to them about it.*

TANNER: *And . . ?*

KAGAN: *Abby's not sure. But both the kids are fascinated.*

TANNER: *I think that soldier's playing you for a sucker, Tom. I don't think he's as wide-eyed to learn as you make out.*

KAGAN: *He's confused. He needs to* know.

TANNER: *You're wrong, I* know *you're wrong. He's a crafty, dangerous animal. And he's got you working for him. Don't forget... even in the future, a captured prisoner of war's first obligation is to escape.*

Tanner spreads his hands helplessly. He shakes his head.

TANNER (continuing): *You're making an old man of me, Kagan.*

KAGAN: *But you'll do it.*

TANNER: *I'll* talk *to the Chief. That's all I guarantee. But after I*

*do, you'll probably be having conferences with me in the cell next
to Qarlo's.*
Kagan fumbles in his pocket, pulls out a pack, extends it.
KAGAN: *Have a piece of gum...*
Tanner smiles helplessly. Kagan could get around a plaster saint.
They start toward the door as we
DISSOLVE TO:
53 EXT. ENCLOSED YARD—FULL SHOT—DAY
Qarlo and Kagan. (This is the same set where Qarlo arrived in
ambulance.) As they enter scene from inside the building Qarlo
and Kagan stand close to each other. There now seems to be
something of a bond between them. Qarlo winces at the bright
day. Kagan's car is located where the ambulance was.
KAGAN: *On the other side of that gate is the world, Qarlo.*
QARLO: *Springin' out.*
KAGAN: *Yes, you're going home with me.*
QARLO: *Home? Define it.*
KAGAN: *A place to live, a house, a place where you can rest, where
no one locks you in.*
QARLO: *Barracks. C.O.?*
KAGAN: *No, there's no C.O. No Commanding Officer, no other
troops, no war, nothing but freedom. Do you know what I mean?
I've told you about freedom.*
QARLO: *Where I come from, everyone lives alone.*
KAGAN: *Alone?*
QARLO: *No one comes up to each other...*(indicates Kagan and
himself)*...like this. We don't mouthtalk.*
KAGAN: *Then how do you communicate?*
QARLO (taps head): *In here. Thinkspeek. When the C.O. wants us,
he orders us. In here.*
KAGAN: *You'll be close to people now, Qarlo. My wife, my son and
daughter. And me.*
QARLO: *I don't grasp. I'll have to see.*
KAGAN: *Yes. You'll have to see.* (beat) *We'd better go now.*
They walk to the car. Kagan opens rear door and pulls out a
trench coat and hat. He offers them to Qarlo.
KAGAN: *You'll have to wear these.*
QARLO: *Why?*

KAGAN: Because no one knows about you. They want to keep you secret, do you understand that?

QARLO: *I peep.*

He takes the clothes, puts them on. They stare at each other a moment, then Kagan opens the door for Qarlo; Kagan seems frightened suddenly.

KAGAN: *Qarlo...would you hurt me. The way you did when I touched you?*

QARLO: *You aren't The Enemy.*

KAGAN: *But...could I be an enemy?*

QARLO (it says it all): *You aren't The Enemy.*

Kagan nods. He indicates for Qarlo to get in. He does cautiously. Kagan goes to the driver's side, gets in and the car drives off as the gates are opened for them.

RAPID LAP DISSOLVE:

54 EXT. COUNTRYSIDE—DAY

The hillside and the white light that encases the Enemy. We see him as before, trapped halfway between tomorrow and today. Lightning flashes in the sky and thunder rolls heavily as camera moves back from the white.

55 EXT. COUNTRYSIDE—ANOTHER SHOT

On the Enemy as a sudden bolt of lightning arcs down out of the sky, and crackles around him. It touches his metal uniform, there is a blinding flash of light and when we can see again, the Enemy is free, completely seen now, for he has been pulled completely through by the lightning. Camera comes in rapidly on his killer's face, a frightening face. His eyes widen in pleasure, and he laughs at the sky, turning his face up. We hear a steady electrical impulse in his helmet, and he touches one dial on a small machine strapped to his left forearm. The sound grows louder, a spaced, metronomic beat beat beat that matches the voice we hear faintly in his helmet.

HELMET VOICE (O.S. FILTER): *Find your Enemy! Find your Enemy! Kill him...kill him...kill—*

As the call grows louder and matches the beat beat beat of the electrical impulse from the machine on his arm, he turns and sets out to find Qarlo.

FADE OUT.

ACT THREE

79 INT. KAGAN LIVING ROOM—CLOSEUP BLACK CAT
   F.G.—DAY

With room in perspective angle: we are up-looking from the cat bulking huge in f.g. to the action taking place at the far end of the room in b.g. At the open door stand Kagan and Qarlo. The soldier fills the doorway, and despite the fact that the people at that end of the room seem small in comparison to the cat, it is obvious Qarlo towers over the group. Greeting Kagan and Qarlo at the door is Abby Kagan, Tom's wife, a handsome woman who is a trifle too sophisticated and warm to be considered the Momma type. With her are Toni Kagan, an extremely-attractive 20-year-old girl with long hair and a fine figure, and Loren Kagan, 13 years old and very wide-eyed. They stand in a semi-circle, awkwardly, as Kagan allows Qarlo to enter the room before him.

KAGAN: *Qarlo, this is my wife, Abby; our daughter, Toni, and the little one is Loren. He's—*

Qarol has not been listening. He ignores the people, stalks between them and comes to camera, kneeling down to look directly at the cat and camera. He talks to the animal. The cat tenses. Qarlo speaks in future tongue.

QARLO: *See-Oh! Kwahr-loe Klo-breg-knee, pryte, sihz-fi-wun-oh-too-too-nyne. Reporting.*

The cat stares. Qarlo looks as though he is expecting the animal to answer. It bolts and runs away. Qarlo stares directly into camera and we see his face, which has been hard, crumble. He is lost. He has expected something to happen, and it hasn't, and he is mystified by this new world once more. He starts to rise as the Kagans come toward him from across the room.

80 GROUP SHOT—ON QARLO

as he rises, and the family comes up to him. All but Kagan himself are looking at Qarlo strangely. Kagan is confused, but there is curiosity and a desire to understand in his face.

KAGAN: *Cat. remember? The book? What did you want from the cat, Qarlo?*

QARLO (bitterly): *Nothing's same.*

KAGAN: *Cats are different where you came from?*

QARLO: *Different. C.O. prowler thinkspeek.*

KAGAN: *I don't understand that, Qarlo. The Commanding Officer, the C.O., uses cats?*

QARLO: *On patrol, troopers, cats tied together by think-speek; cats do prowl, spot the Enemy, troopers jump.*

The family is attentive, but their eyes widen at the strangeness of what Qarlo is saying. Kagan explains to them.

KAGAN: *I think what he means is that somehow, by some technique we don't even suspect, wars in the future are fought by men and animals…the cats used to do reconnaisance work, and by telepathy, they relay their messages.*

LOREN (excited): *And…and he thought he could get in touch with his Commanding Officer by talking through Macbeth!*

KAGAN: *It makes sense. What a fine patrol prowler a silent cat would make* (beat, to Qarlo): *It's not like that here, Qarlo. Macbeth is just a cat.*

QARLO (wearily): *Nothing'z here are like war zone.*

ABBY: *But we'll do our best to see that things are pleasant for you here, Qarlo.*

Abby moves to Kagan's side, puts her arm around his waist. Qarlo instinctively makes a movement toward her. She shrinks back as Kagan stops Qarlo.

KAGAN: *No, Qarlo. It's all right.*

QARLO: *Why does she touch you? There is Enemy and not Enemy… which is she?*

KAGAN: *Wife. Family unit, female C.O. Mother. Like your mother.*

Qarlo stares at him oddly.

QARLO: *Mother? My mother?*

TONI: *You have a mother, don't you?*

Qarlo looks superior for a moment, then recites:

QARLO: *Clobregnny. Creche Hatchery 559. I am the State, the State is All.*

They look at him uncomprehendingly. All but Kagan, who goes white, and who looks as though he may be sick.

KAGAN: *Loren, take Qarlo up to his room.*

Loren looks bugged, but turns and smiling indicates Qarlo should follow him.

They climb the stairs to the upper floor as camera holds past Kagan, Toni and Abby to their passage. Kagan turns to his women when Qarlo is gone.

81 THREE SHOT—ON KAGAN

as he wipes a hand across his forehead. There is infinite sadness in his face.

KAGAN: *Now I understand why he didn't respond to a film I showed him of a mother and child. He has no mother, he never knew a mother.* (beat) *A creche is a day nursery, a foundling hospital. He's a product of artificial birth…he has no real parents…he was born and raised in a hatchery, like an egg.*

TONI: *And that, about "the State"…?*

KAGAN: *The State: his mother, his father, his everything.*

ABBY: *How pathetic.*

KAGAN: *He knew about the position of the stars, because a foot-soldier always knows how to navigate by the stars…but he never knew the most elemental kind of love…*

ABBY: *Tom, can we help him…he seems so…so, lost, so confused. And from what you've said, he's capable of—of—anything.*

KAGAN: *We can help him.*

ABBY: *But are you sure, Tom. Loren and Toni—*

KAGAN (intensely): *We've got to help him, Abby. And not just for him, either.*

He turns and walks toward the stairs as camera holds on the faces of his wife and daughter, following with their eyes. They don't understand, but they think they should.

DISSOLVE TO:

82 INT. KAGAN DINING ROOM—NIGHT

Qarlo sits next to Kagan, who is at the head of the table. Loren sits across from Qarlo, and Toni next to Loren. The young boy obviously is enthralled by the soldier.

LOREN: *Hey, Qarlo, in the future they got baseball and football and the World Series, huh?*

KAGAN: *I don't think Qarlo under—*

QARLO: *Don't you know there's a war on?*

He has said it almost by rote, as though it were an explanation of *every*thing.

LOREN: *Yeah, I know. But I mean, when you* ain't *fighting.*

KAGAN: *Aren't fighting.*

LOREN: Aren't *fighting. Huh, Qarlo?*

QARLO: *Why do you peep me drumdum questions?*

LOREN: *Peep? Drumdum? Huh?*

KAGAN: *"Peep" is a slang word for ask, or show, or anything that informs him.* Drumdum *means just what it sounds like...I think your word is "square" or "dopey."*

LOREN: *Hey! That's wild! Peep and drumdum. I gotta use that.*

KAGAN (smiles amusedly at Loren, turns to Qarlo): *Isn't there a time when you aren't at war, Qarlo? It isn't drumdum of me...I just don't grasp...I want to know.*

As Qarlo speaks, Abby comes in from the kitchen, with a tureen of something steaming. She stands listening for a long moment, worry on her face.

QARLO: *When I had not as many time as him—*(points to Loren—*My Drillmaster gave me my first weapon. I had twelve by the time I killed my first Enemy.* (beat) *The War has been fighting from before my hatch-time. One hundred eighty.*

TONI: *Years? The war has been on for one hundred and eighty years?*

Qarlo nods. They are thunderstruck. Abby brings the tureen, sets it down in front of Kagan, next to Qarlo. Before Kagan can ladle out the soup from the tureen into the soup bowls stacked beside him, Qarlo seizes the bowl and shoves away from the table. He smoothly walks around the table, and into the living room. The sound of him going upstairs lingers in the room as they stare open-mouthed.

TONI (ruefully): *I've heard of lousy manners, but that's a bit much.*

KAGAN: *I forgot. In his time, it's considered obscene to eat in front of anyone else. Not so strange, really; there are primitive tribes that have the same custom. And when you think about it, watching some people eat is rather sickening.*

ABBY: *That's grand, just grand. But what do we do for soup?*

KAGAN: *I'll talk to him. We can pass on the soup tonight, and I'll have a long talk with him about table manners...but I suspect he'll think we're terrible boors.*

They stare at Kagan wide-eyed. He grins, enjoying the reversal of social protocol.

DISSOLVE TO:

83 LIVING ROOM—CLOSEUP—LATER THAT NIGHT

on an alarm clock. Camera pulls back to tight two shot of Qarlo and Kagan sitting across from each other at a small table, the clock on the table between them. Voices o.s. first.

KAGAN'S VOICE (o.s.): *Do you know what this is?*

QARLO'S VOICE (o.s.) *I saw a thing like it, once.*

KAGAN'S VOICE (o.s.): *We call it a clock. It tells us where we should be from hour to hour. Do you know "hour," Qarlo?*

QARLO: *Sure! Whaddyathink, I'm drumdum? Attack hour, sleeptime, feedtime...hours.*

KAGAN: *Yes, that's right. But you don't have clocks?*

QARLO: *Don't grasp why I need "clock." When it's time to jump, the C.O. tells me...*(taps head)*...in here.*

KAGAN: *Does the C.O. regulate everything you do?*

QARLO: *Hey, Kagan. I've peeped my warzone to you, but tell me, peep me, your—*

He makes vague hand-movements, indicating the world at large. Kagan grasps his meaning.

KAGAN: *My world? You want to know about my world?* Qarlo nods. Kagan looks troubled.

KAGAN: *I don't know what I can tell you...*

QARLO: *Peep me the little one, the one you call "son."*

KAGAN: *Loren?*

Qarlo nods silently.

KAGAN: *He's thirteen years old. He goes to school—you grasp the "school?"—good. He goes to school, where he learns about this world. Perhaps you can go to Loren's school, some time, and they'll peep you about this world completely* (idly hits fist on table): *Confound it, I shouldn't be doing this alone...I need a good philosopher, a semanticist, a mathematician, a sociologist...*

QARLO: *I don't grasp.*

KAGAN: *Nothing, just thinking out loud.*

QARLO: *My time, think out loud, C.O. investigates. Drumdum thoughts are monitored; all thoughts are monitored, on Thinkspeek.*

KAGAN: *There are people in this world who want to police thoughts, too, Qarlo.*

QARLO: *No monitoring here, none?*

KAGAN: *No. None. You can think anything you want, and it belongs only to you. Private. You grasp "private?"*

QARLO: *No.*

KAGAN: *All your own. No one else can have it, or use it, if you say no.*

QARLO: *Execpt the C.O.*

KAGAN: *No, not even the C.O. Just you.*

QARLO: *That's treason. State owns everything. I am the State, the State is me. Your "private" is a treason thing.*

KAGAN (sadly, nods): *There are some in this world who think just like you, Qarlo...*

Camera holds on the two men as we

DISSOLVE TO:

84 INT. KAGAN HALLWAY AND BATHROOM—NIGHT

Toni, in bathrobe, stands with toothbrush in hand, by the half-open door of the bathroom, talking to Abby, Camera med. close on them as they talk softly.

TONI: *Mother, you're getting hysterical. Daddy would never have brought him home if he thought we were in danger.*

ABBY: *Your father was* born *type-cast as the trusting scientist. All he knows is that—that creature may give him clues to the future.*

TONI: *Oh, I don't know. He's not Tony Curtis, but in a way he has a certain charm...*

ABBY: *Charm?!!*

TONI (another suggestion): *Sex appeal?*

ABBY (trapped): *I'm beginning to wonder who has what to fear from* whom!

TONI (lightly): *I'm just a jazz-mad baby, livin' a life of sin.*
Abby throws up her hands in exasperation, turns and goes into another doorway, obviously a bedroom. Toni grins, and opens the bathroom door. Camera shoots past her as she thrusts open the door suddenly and Qarlo spins around, his arms upthrust as though to strike her with a vicious karate chop. She gasps, falls back against the wall.

85 INT. BATHROOM—ON QARLO TO TONI

The water in the sink is running, and his face is wet, as is the floor and the front of his metal suit. His hands drop water as he speaks.

QARLO: *Get out!*

She doesn't get out. Her fear drains away and is replaced by temper and surprising verve.

TONI: *I'll do no such thing. I live here, too, you know.*

QARLO: *Sleeptime is for aloners.*

TONI: *I feel the same way about it, friend, but I still have to brush my teeth, and right now you're blocking the water.* (beat) *Say, what're you doing?*

QARLO: *Drinking.*

TONI: *Haven't you ever heard of a glass?*

Qarlo stares at her uncomprehendingly. Obviously he hasn't.

TONI. (continuing): *Forget it.*

They stare at each other silently for a moment. The girl is obviously appraising him, and Qarlo, for his part, is intested, but suspicious. *Very* suspicious.

TONI (continuing): *Anything I can help you with?*

QARLO: *Help me?*

TONI: *Yes, do you have a towel, a wash cloth…a partridge in a pear tree?*

QARLO (suspiciously): *What do you want from me?*

TONI: *What do I want from you? Oh, brother, how it saddens me to know men haven't changed a bit, even eighteen hundred years from now.*

Qarlo backs away from her. He becomes wary.

QARLO: *You're a one more danger to me than Kagan. What do you want from me?*

TONI: *Don't you trust anyone? Can't you even see we're trying* to help you? Didn't you ever want to get near someone, talk to someone?

QARLO: *That isn't possible. We can't close to each other, anyone can't. Thinkspeek comes best, not to touch.*

TONI: *You don't know what you're missing, friend.* (then, soberly) *What a lousy, lonely life you must lead.*

QARLO: *That's my world. It's fine.*

TONI: *Mm-hmm. Just fine. And I guess if you're blind from birth you don't miss the color red.*

QARLO. *I don't grasp.*

TONI: *Forget it.*

QARLO: *Fret it.*

TONI: *I'll do that little thing.*

He stares at her a moment, passes her and goes out. She stands tipped onto one hip, tapping her toothbrush against her palm. She shakes her head wearily.

CAMERA COMES IN on Toni. Closeup.

TONI: *You'll never make it, Tiger. I hope...but I don't think so.*

CAMERA HOLDS on Toni as we

CUT TO:

86 INT. LOREN'S BEDROOM—CLOSEUP LOREN—NIGHT

as his eyes widen and he looks about to shout something loud and nasty. Camera pulls back to wide angle as he speaks.

LOREN: *Hey, what's this?*

WIDE ANGLE OF ROOM shows all the furniture jumbled and piled in one corner. There is a desk and several chairs and a toy box and all manner of other kid's things on the bed, leaving a wide empty space in the middle of the room. The walls are pennant-covered, teen-style. Qarlo is lying in the middle of the floor, and as Loren comes in through the door, and speaks, Qarlo rises up, a heavy brass bookend ready to smash.

LOREN (anxiously): *Hey, hold it, stop, wait a minute!*

QARLO: *Sleeptime's for aloners.*

LOREN: *I just came in to get a comic book. They got me bunkin' in with Toni, I didn't mean to disturb you.*

QARLO: *Get out!*

LOREN: *Sure, sure...*(interested) *Hey, how come you're sleepin' on the floor? And all the stuff piled outta the way?*

QARLO: *Clear the perimeter. No Enemy gets past. Troopers can jump.*

LOREN: *Hey, that's cool. You sleep on the floor in the future?*

QARLO: *Sleeptime is anywhere. When a trooper hasta jump...he jumps!*

LOREN: That *figures. Geez, you must have a great time, just soldier'n all the time. But don't worry, Qarlo, there ain't —aren't— isn't any Enemy here. You're in the past now, remember?*

He smiles, grabs a comic book from a stack, and leaves, shutting the door behind him. Qarlo sinks back down, with the bookend in his hand, as camera comes in for closeup.

QARLO: *No. No Enemy here. Another time...a past time. No Enemy.*

His face seems to relax. He shoves the bookend away, and lies down. His eyes close as we

SHARP CUT TO:

87 EXA. STREET—NIGHT

(Same set as was used for Qarlo's appearance) The street is very nearly deserted. One pedestrian walks through. When he is gone, the Enemy is seen stalking in a darkened alley (or areaway). He starts to enter the street as a policeman saunters by. He quickly draws back until the cop is gone. Now, he enters. We hear the beep beep from the electrical impulse machine on his arm. He listens to it carefully, obviously sensing the direction it is leading him. Meanwhile:

HELMET VOICE (o.s.) *Find your enemy! Find your enemy!*

Grimly, he drifts off into the shadows and disappears.

FADE OUT:

88 INT. KAGAN LIVING ROOM—CLOSEUP KAGAN—DAY

using a tape recorder, speaking into a microphone. He is reading from notes. A phone sits near at hand on the desk. Through an archway we can see Loren and Qarlo throwing darts at a dartboard, and we can catch o.s. remarks, ad lib from the boy (e.g.: "Hey, you got a good eye, Qarlo! Bulls-eye! That's your ninth one in a row! Gee, it's great havin' you here." etc.) Kagan looks up from time to time, and smiles.

KAGAN: *I have asked the subject about his world, our future. His knowledge is incredibly limited. He knows war and soldiering, but little else. Comparison: if an Australian bushman were thrown into the future, his image of the world today would be one of barbarism. The situation is comparable with the subject Qarlo.* (beat) *The words love and hate still seem to have no meaning for him. However, subject provided a clue to his conception of honesty by laughing when a man on television returned some food dropped by another actor. Subject's remark was: "Drumdum. He gave away free food."*

PHONE RINGS. Kagan picks it up.

KAGAN: *Hello?* (beat) *Paul! How are you? I was just preparing the weekly for you.* (beat) *They what?*

    89 INTERCUT—PAUL TANNER

He sits behind a desk, receiver in hand.

TANNER: *They've made a dispensation in Qarlo's case, Tom. Two weeks are up. They feel he's made as much progress as can be expected...*(beat) *I know that's for you to decide...but the papers have gotten wind of the experiment, and there's a chance there'll be repercussions—and they've been talking about Civic Obligations and Danger to the Community...*(beat) *I know, I know! But they won't listen to that. All they know is he's a psychopathic killer by our standards, and he's on the loose.*

    90 SAME AS 88

KAGAN: *So what have they decided?*

TANNER'S VOICE (filter): *He'll be remanded to my custody, and be put under protective surveillance in a maximum security pri—*

KAGAN (cuts him off, furiously): *—prison! A bloody prison? The man hasn't* done *anything, Paul! He's merely bewildered, lost, out of joint with his Times. That's no crime, no sin...he didn't ask to be warped into the past.*

TANNER'S VOICE (filter): *I'm sorry, Tom. That's the way it is.*

KAGAN (defeated): *When?*

TANNER'S VOICE (filtered): *As soon as possible. Tonight; at the latest tomorrow. Can you get him ready?*

KAGAN: *Physically...or emotionally?*

TANNER'S VOICE (filter): *Tom, don't take it out on me, for crine out loud, I'm only—*

KAGAN (bitterly): *I know: you're only doing your job! That's rapidly becoming the slimiest alibi of our times.*

He slams the receiver down on the deskset, buries his head in his hands for a moment, then rises.

91 TRUCKING SHOT—WITH KAGAN

as he walks across living room to edge of archway, watching Qarlo and Loren shooting darts. Qarlo is expert with them, but he does the act with little comprehension of competition. He might as easily be emptying garbage or tying shoelaces.

LOREN: *Gee, you're good, Qarlo!*

QARLO: *Drumdum, throwing these.*

LOREN: *I thought you were having a good time. You're winning.*

QARLO: *Don't grasp "winning." War?*

LOREN: *No, not winning a war. It's like we were having a little war, you and me, and the one who throws the best, he wins the war.*

QARLO. *Drumdum.*

LOREN: *Yeah, maybe. I don't know.* (beat) *Gee, it's great havin' you here with us. It gets lonely out here sometimes, y'know, cause all the kids live nearer into town...*

Kagan smiles softly, turns and walks away. They have not seen him there. He walks back to tape recorder.

92 INT. KAGAN LIVING ROOM—ON KAGAN

Abby comes into the room. He turns to her. Camera into two shot.

KAGAN: *They've decided to put him away. Tonight or tomorrow.*

ABBY (mixed emotions): *I can't say I'm sorry, Tom. It's been terrifying.*

KAGAN: *Abby, cut it out. You're dramatizing again.*

ABBY: *You see what you want to see, only what you want to see. And not that Toni has been spending more and more time with him...that Loren is beginning to idolize him...that...*

KAGAN: *Isn't that what we wanted, for him to fit in, to adjust, to learn what caring means?*

Abby is getting worked up now. There is a note of hysteria in her voice.

ABBY: *But he doesn't care! He's just as he was when he came here. He's playing with us, Tom. Letting us think he understands, that he wants to make the best of it.*

KAGAN: *I think you're seeing shadows.*

ABBY: *From the future, Tom. Shadows from the future. That man is a killer...he was trained from birth for only one thing! To kill! Do you think two weeks with us is going to erase all that?*
KAGAN: *I hoped it would...*
ABBY: *I'm afraid, Tom. Afraid of him...and afraid of the future he comes from.*
Kagan turns to the window. His voice is filled with sadness as, back turned, he speaks to her—and himself.
KAGAN (distantly): *Dr. Jung (pronounced: Yoong) once said: "The only thing we have to fear on this planet—is man."*
CAMERA HOLDS on Kagan's back, and Abby staring at him with helplessness, and the sounds of Qarlo and Loren playing darts as we
SLOW DISSOLVE TO:
93 EXT. CITY STREET OR ALLEY—THE ENEMY—NIGHT
Extreme closeup on the electrical impulse machine. It beep beep beeps for a moment then begins to crackle as though being jammed by interference. In the distance we hear the sound of an airplane approaching—the roar of the motor gets louder and louders. Camera pulls away and rises rapidly to high spot of enemy standing in shadows of an alley. He spins around as though looking for source of airplane sound. Suddenly he stops and looks up.
94 EXT. SKY—STOCK—POV—NIGHT
A large plane, its night lights blinking, is flying low as though approaching an airfield.
95 EXT. ALLEY—CLOSE SHOT THE ENEMY
He spots the plane, raises his rifle in its direction and fires beam.
96 EXT. SKY—STOCK—NIGHT
Beam hits the aircraft and it sizzles out of the sky—gone—
97 BACK TO ENEMY
looking in the direction of the kill. He is satisfied as the beep beep on his impulse machine resumes. The voice from his helmet produces an evil smile on his strange face.
HELMET VOICE (o.s.): *Find your enemy! Find your enemy; Kill... Kill...Kill....*

He stalks out of darkened alley toward lighted street in search
of his prey.

DISSOLVE TO:

98 INT. KAGAN LIVING ROOM—NIGHT

Kagan and Qarlo sit talking.

KAGAN: *They've decided you can't stay here.*

QARLO: *Who? Who has decided?*

KAGAN: *Some men who make decisions for the rest of us, because
we let them.*

QARLO: *C.O.?*

KAGAN: *In a way, yes. They've decided you might hurt someone...
that you have to be...sent to a place.*

Qarlo's face suddenly goes cold and hard. This he understands.

QARLO: *Pee-owe-dubbel-yoo. I peeped that'd happen. I knew you
troops would jump.*

KAGAN (hastily): *Not a prisoner of war camp, Qarlo. Nothing like
that. It's a—a—*

QARLO (intensely): *Liar!*

KAGAN: *It wasn't my idea...I tried to keep them from doing it...
but these men, they—*

QARLO: *Qarlo Clobregnny. Private. Six five one oh two two nine.*

KAGAN: *Listen—*

QARLO (bitterly): *Where I come from, it's true, it's right. No two
ways. Us and them. The Enemy. We know who they are, they know
us. No two-ways troopers who jump sometimes one way, sometimes
the other.*

KAGAN: *It's better here, Qarlo, if you could only understand...if
you could only grasp...*

QARLO: *Grasp? Your words, your drumdum empty words, love,
hate, dog, mother...?*

KAGAN: *Yes, yes!*

QARLO: *No! I want my time, my world.*

KAGAN: *It's better here, now, Qarlo. We don't have the War...*

QARLO (sneers): *Better? In my world we don't grasp these love,
hate, all of them. We never know, so we don't want. Here, you peep
love...then take it away.*

KAGAN (dawning realization): *Qarlo...do you...feel sorry to be
going away from us—?*

QARLO: *I don't grasp your "sorry." In this time, like my time, there's Enemy, and not-Enemy. You aren't Enemy...*
KAGAN: *But you're not sure I'm a friend, is that it?*
QARLO: *Don't grasp "friend."*
KAGAN: *Not-Enemy.*
QARLO: *Yes. You aren't Not-Enemy. So I can stay here. But the others...the ones who put hands on me...*
KAGAN: *Qarlo, you can't let your other life ruin it for you here. You've got to live here...if they have to touch you...*
QARLO: (hard): *They won't.* (beat) *And you...two-way jumper. One way or the other.*
Qarlo turns, starts to stalk away. Macbeth, the cat, lies there. Camera shoots past Qarlo to cat as he pauses, and with a gentle, pathetic tone, he speaks a question, expecting no answer.
QARLO: *C.O....?*
No answer. He leaves the room. Camera moves in on the eyes of the silent cat as we

DISSOLVE TO:

99 INT. TANNER'S OFFICE—CLOSEUP TANNER'S BACK—
    DAY
He is sitting behind his desk, in a swivel chair, facing a large window looking out over the city. Suddenly he spins around, smashing palms flat on desk.
TANNER: *Now listen, Kagan, don't chew on my ear. I haven't any control over what they're doing.*
CAMERA PULLS BACK to show Kagan leaning over the desk, arms wide and tensed on the desktop. He is furious.
KAGAN: *But you didn't fight them...*
TANNER: *Fight them? Say, what's the matter with you, boy. I work for the government, for the Bureau; I'm not some free-lance hot-rock they call in like The Lone Ranger.*
KAGAN (contemptuously): *Company man.*
TANNER: *Oh, ha ha. Fancy phrases for all occasions. Instant mirth, merely add Kagan.* (beat) *I did fight them, if you'd like to know. I batted my head against the wall for almost two weeks while you sat out there playing ABC's with King Kong.*
KAGAN: *Paul...you've got to...*
TANNER: *Got, got, got. I don't got to do anything, but come pick*

up that big ugly piece of furniture, and take him where my bosses tell me to take him.

KAGAN: *I need more time. He's coming around. He's adapting to the family unit.*

TANNER: *Adapting how? Has he offered to wash the dishes or make the beds? What have you got out there, Kagan, the perfect scullery maid?*

KAGAN: *I've learned a million things about his world, Paul. You can't cut off a source of information like that. It'll never happen again.*

TANNER: *You can always talk to him in a cell.*

KAGAN: *Don't be ridiculous. Put him away, and he'll revert. He'll get surly, silent, we'll be worse than when we started.*

TANNER (wearily): *Oh, Kagan Kagan Kagan, what'm I gonna do with you? How do I make it clear that my hands are tied?*

KAGAN: *Listen...if you gave them some new things about the future I've learned, would that quiet them?*

TANNER: *I don't think so.*

KAGAN: *Perhaps another week...?*

TANNER: *I—I don't think so.*

Kagan pulls a spool of tape out of his pocket. He hands it to Tanner.

KAGAN: *Here, play this...*

Tanner opens a desk drawer, and a tape recorder lifts up. He drops on the spool, starts it playing. It is Kagan's voice.

(NOTE: this speech may be cut to any length sufficient.)

KAGAN'S VOICE: *Subject's world of the future. Divided into two warring camps, with children raised from birth on special war-islands devoted to nothing but training. When they reach early teens, they are sent into battle so brain-washed that the C.O.— the Commanding Officer—and his orders are the closest thing to God they know. (beat) There is no marriage, no family unit, no entertainment as we know it. The society is rigidly structured into classes, among which are The Factory Workers at the lowest level and what the subject calls The Purple, or Ruling Body, at the top. Qarlo has never seen one of The Purple. He talks about them as though they were mystic, almost holy, creatures. Apparently, so ingrained is the concept of "security," of keeping the Enemy from learning anything about battle plans or—in fact, anything at all about the state of war on Qarlo's side, that no one speaks to anyone else for fear of being tagged a spy. This has brought about a culture in which every man is literally and totally* alone. (beat) *Further than these facts, Qarlo is unable to go. Asked about other areas of the culture, he shakes his head or makes comments that indicate he has never been in contact with any area of his world outside training, battle and allied subjects. He has social "tunnel vision," trained to do a job and not consider the rest of the world in which he lives. He is, in every sense of the word, crippled.*

Tanner slaps the recorder off. He rubs his eyes as though he hasn't slept in weeks.

TANNER: *Okay. I'll try again. They're starting to wonder whose team I'm on, and when they start wondering that, the old bread line ain't far off.*

KAGAN: *Thanks, Paul.*

TANNER. *Don't thank me. If I'm out dancing for dimes on the Avenue, just toss me a few coins and pat my monkey on the head.* (beat) *Now get outta here so I can go lose my job.*

Kagan smiles, Tanner looks bemused, shakes his head.

DISSOLVE TO:

100 EXT. KAGAN HOUSE—ESTABLISHING HIGH SHOT—
    STOCK—NIGHT

A VERY HIGH SHOT looking down on the house. A dark, moonless night. Lightning splits up the sky every few seconds. Thunder rolls in the distance. A night for witches to think twice before mounting brooms. Camera comes down slowly as we

DISSOLVE THRU TO:

101 INT. KAGAN DINING ROOM—NIGHT

In the f.g. is the empty end of the dining table. At the far end, the head, sits Kagan himself, Toni to his right, Abby to his left, Loren next to Toni, nearest to us. Qarlo sits across from Loren. Macbeth, the cat, lies on the chair at the empty end of the table. It seems to be sleeping.

KAGAN (to Qarlo): *And so, that's how an automobile works, Qarlo. We call it internal combustion.*

QARLO. *Very not-work-well...uh,* unproductive. *Light beams* drive tanks, scout cars much more smoothlier, no "gas" and no noise.

LOREN: *Honest? You got cars that run on just light, like sunlight? Honest?*

TONI: *Do you have a car, Qarlo?*

QARLO: *For what? Troopers foot it.*

TONI: *Well, what do you take your girl out for a ride in?*

QARLO: *I don't grasp.*

ABBY: *Don't you have women in your time; ones that you can be with?*

QARLO: *I don't grasp. Troopers get service.*

ABBY (eyes widen): *You mean, you—?*

KAGAN (cuts in ruefully): *Uh, I think that's enough of that topic. But suffice it to say, I think this age has some distinct advantages over Qarlo's time.*

102 ON QARLO—CAT OBVIOUS ON CHAIR NEXT TO HIM
Toni and Qarlo reach for a basket of rolls at the same moment. Qarlo makes a sharp move to grab it, Toni senses it, but at that instant Qarlo draws back, lets her take it. Nothing is said about the interplay.

LOREN: *Whaddaya think, Qarlo, wanna stay here with us for always?*

KAGAN (quickly): *That may not be possible, Loren.*

LOREN: *Why not?*

KAGAN: *Well, there are others who—*

QARLO (interrupts): *I want to jump back. I want to find my war zone.*

LOREN: *What do you wanna go back for? I thought you liked it here, I thought we were friends?!*

QARLO: *Not-Enemy. You're Not-Enemy. But my way is best, my time is best for me...I want to go back...at sleeptime I think what Kagan calls "private" about it. I hurt for it.*

LOREN: *But why? Why do you wanna go to that place where everybody kills everybody?*

QARLO (can't explain): *My time is the best! For me! I need to jump. Find my unit, my C.O. Don't you know there's a war on, boy?*

LOREN (disillusioned): *I think you were lyin' to me...you aren't my friend...*

Qarlo's jaw muscles jump. There is silence. No one knows what to say. There is concern on Kagan's face.

KAGAN (softly): *He's a child. He doesn't know. He doesn't understand.*

LOREN: *I do too! He was just pretendin' to like it here...*

QARLO: *He grasps more than you, Kagan. He knows. He knows what I am.*

KAGAN: *It isn't true, Qarlo. You've seen it for yourself, in just the short time you've been here, you've changed tremendously...*

QARLO (firmly): *I am what I am. He knows, and I know. Why do you dream, Kagan? I know how to do one thing, be a trooper. I'll do it again...you know that's true.*

KAGAN (fervently): *Dear God, I hope not...if that's all we have to look forward to, then the future is lost!*

At that moment Macbeth yowllls and jumps up on the chair, hair stiffly erect on his back, eyes turned toward the blank wall of the dining room facing onto the street; the wall to which Qarlo sits. Qarlo leaps erect at once.

QARLO: *C.O.?*

The wall suddenly begins to blacken, as though great heat were being applied on it from the other side. Qarlo throws back his chair. The family jumps up, and Loren moves next to Qarlo.

103 ANOTHER SHOT—THE SCENE

as the wall suddenly vaporizes, a gigantic hole appearing as though by magic. And through the hole we see the dark, rainswept, lightning-filled night. Thunder rolls. As Abby and Toni scream, the Enemy leaps through the hole in the wall, his hideous face alert, his teeth bared, the rifle starting to tilt up. Loren is directly in front of the line of attack. Qarlo bodily hurls him to the side, moves a step toward the Enemy. We hear the soft beep beep beep of The Enemy's tracking machine and the helmet voice saying "Kill! Kill! Kill!"...as he advances a step.

As the Enemy begins to level the rifle, the cat, Macbeth, yowllls again, louder. The Enemy's glance is diverted. He looks at the cat. He seems about to speak to the cat, as...Qarlo launches himself at the Enemy. The Enemy brings up the rifle just as Qarlo plunges into him, clutching him tightly around the chest with both arms, so that the rifle is imprisoned between them. There is a sharp crackling zzzzzing sound, a flash of light as the rifle fires between them, and in the burst of light...they are gone.

The room is empty at that end. Just a dark burned smudge on the rug. The family stands wide-eyed in horror at the death of the two men, they can't move. But as camera comes in for closeup of the sooty smudge on the rug. Macbeth leaps down off the chair, and begins sniffing at the spot. Camera pulls back, up and up and up as narration over:

NARRATOR: *From the darkest of all pits, the soul of Man, come the darkest questions: in the end, did the soldier kill to protect those he had come to care for...or did he revert to his instincts.* (beat) *Questions from the dark pit. But no answers. For answers lie in the future. Is it a future in which men are machines born to kill, or is there time for us.* (beat) *Time. All the time in the world...but is that enough...?* CAMERA PULLS BACK UP AND UP as the family stands huddled silently together, as the cat sniffs the spot of death and we

FADE OUT

Harlan Ellison®

Harlan Ellison® was recently characterized by *The New York Times Book Review* as having "the spellbinding quality of a great nonstop talker, with a cultural warehouse for a mind." *The Los Angeles Times* suggested, "It's long past time for Harlan Ellison to be awarded the title: 20th century Lewis Carroll." And the *Washington Post Book World* said simply, "One of the great living American short story writers."

He has written or edited 76 books; more than 1,700 short stories, essay, articles, and newspaper columns; two dozen teleplays, for which he received the Writers Guild of America most outstanding teleplay award for solo work an unprecedented *four* times; and a dozen movies. Currently a member of the Writers Guild of America, he has twice served on the board of the WGAW. He won the Mystery Writers of America Edgar Allan Poe award twice, the Horror Writers Association Bram Stoker award six times (including the Lifetime Achievement Award in 1996), the Nebula award of the Science Fiction Writers of America three times, the Hugo (World Science Fiction Convention achievement award) 8-1/2 times, and received the Silver Pen for Journalism from P.E.N. Not to mention the World Fantasy Award; the British Fantasy Award; the American Mystery Award; plus two Audie Awards and a Grammy nomination for Spoken Word recordings.

He created great fantasies for the 1985 CBS revival of *The Twilight Zone* (including Danny Kaye's final performance) and *The Outer Limits*; travelled with The Rolling Stones; marched with Martin Luther King from Selma to Montgomery; created roles for Buster Keaton, Wally Cox, Gloria Swanson and nearly 100 other stars on *Burke's Law*; ran with a kid gang in Brooklyn's Red

Hook to get background for his first novel; covered race riots in Chicago's "back of the yards" with the late James Baldwin; sang with, and dined with, Maurice Chevalier; once stood off the son of a Detroit Mafia kingpin with a Remington XP-100 pistol-rifle while wearing nothing but a bath towel; sued Paramount and ABC-TV for plagiarism and won $337,000. His most recent legal victory, in protection of copyright against global Internet piracy of writers' work, in May of 2004—a 4-year-long litigation against AOL et al.—has resulted in revolutionizing protection of creative properties on the Web. (As promised, he has repaid hundreds of contributions [totaling $50,000] from the KICK Internet Piracy support fund.) But the bottom line, as voiced by *Booklist* in 2008, is this: "One thing for sure: the man can write."

And, as Tom Snyder said on the CBS *Late, Late Show*: "An amazing talent; meeting him is an incredible experience." He was a regular on ABC-TV's *Politically Incorrect* with Bill Maher.

In 1990, Ellison was honored by P.E.N. for his continuing commitment to artistic freedom and the battle against censorship, "In defense of the First Amendment."

Harlan Ellison's 1992 novelette "The Man Who Rowed Christopher Columbus Ashore" was selected from more than 6,000 short stories published in the U.S. for inclusion in the 1993 edition of *The Best American Short Stories*.

Mr. Ellison worked as a creative consultant and host for *2000ˣ*, a series of 26 one-hour dramatized radio adaptations of famous SF stories for The Hollywood Theater of the Ear; and for his work was presented with the prestigious Ray Bradbury Award for Drama Series. The series was broadcast on National Public Radio in 2000 and 2001. Ellison's classic story "'Repent, Harlequin!' Said the Ticktockman" was included as part of this significant series, starring Robin Williams and the author in the title roles.

On June 22, 2002, at the 4th World Skeptics Convention, Harlan Ellison was presented with the *Distinguished Skeptic Award* by The Committee for the Scientific Investigation of the Paranormal (CSICOP) "in recognition of his outstanding contributions to the defense of science and critical thinking."

To celebrate the golden anniversary of Harlan Ellison's half century of storytelling, Morpheus International, publishers of *The Essential Ellison: A 35-Year Retrospective*, commissioned the book's primary editor, award-winning Australian writer and critic Terry Dowling, to expand Ellison's three-and-a-half decade collection into a 50-year retrospective. Mr. Dowling went through fifteen years of new stories and essays to pick what he thought were the most representative to be included in this 1000+ page collection. Along with *The Essential Ellison: A 50-Year Retrospective* (Morpheus International), Mr. Ellison's first Young Adult collection, *Troublemakers* is currently available in bookstores.

Among his most recognized works, translated into more than 40 languages and selling in the millions of copies, are *Deathbird Stories, Strange Wine, Approaching Oblivion, I Have No Mouth, & I Must Scream, Web of the City, Angry Candy, Love Ain't Nothing But Sex Misspelled, Ellison Wonderland, Memos From Purgatory, All The Lies That Are My Life, Shatterday, Mind Fields, An Edge In My Voice, Slippage* and *Stalking the Nightmare*. As creative intelligence and editor of the all-time bestselling *Dangerous Visions* anthologies and *Medea: Harlan's World*, he has been awarded two Special Hugos and the prestigious academic Milford Award for Lifetime Acheivement in Editing. In 2006, Harlan Ellison was named the Grand Master of the Science Fiction/ Fantasy Writers of America.

In October 2002, Edgeworks Abbey and iBooks published the 35th Anniversary Edition of the highly acclaimed anthology *Dangerous Visions*.

In the November 2002 issue of *PC Gamer*, Ellison's hands-on creation of the CD-Rom game *I Have No Mouth, and I Must Scream*, based on the award-winning story of the same name, was voted "One of the 10 scariest PC games ever." ("I Have No Mouth, and I Must Scream" is one of the ten most reprinted stories in the English language.)

June 2003: A new Edition of *Vic & Blood*, published by iBooks in association with Edgeworks Abbey, collected for the first time both the complete graphic novel cycle *and* Ellison's stories including the 1969 novella favorite from which the legendary cult film *A Boy and His Dog* was made.

December 2003: Ellison edited a collection of Edwardian mystery-puzzle stories titled *Jacques Futrelle's "The Thinking Machine*, published by The Modern Library.

October 2004: A new edition of *Strange Wine*, published by iBooks in association with Edgeworks Abbey.

May 2006: Ellison and Oscar nominee Josh Olson (for his adaptation of *A History of Violence*) collaborated on a teleplay "The Discarded" (based on Ellison's short story of the same name) for the ABC television series *Masters of Science Fiction*.

November 2006: A new edition of *Spider Kiss*, published by M Press, in association with Edgeworks Abbey. The second book in the M Press /Edgeworks Abbey series, *Harlan Ellison's Watching*, was released in a new edition in 2008.

March 2007: Based on Ellison's work, *Harlan Ellison's Dream Corridor (Volume Two)* is released. Ellison introduces a dozen tales in this new collection, featuring adaptations of some of his greatest stories by some of the most respected names in comics, including Neal Adams, Gene Colan, Richard Corben, Paul Chadwick...and the very last work by the late, great *Superman* artist, Curt Swan.

April 2007: A special world premiere screening is held of *Dreams With Sharp Teeth*. For more than twenty-five years, documentarian Erik Nelson (*Grizzly Man*) has been interviewing Ellison and friends [including Josh Olson (*A History of Violence*), Neil Gaiman (*Anansi Boys*), Dan Simmons (*The Terror*), Peter David (*Fallen Angel*), Michael Cassutt (*Tango Midnight*), Ron Moore (*Battlestar Galactica*), and actor Robin Williams] to produce a feature-length look at the life and work of Harlan Ellison: *Dreams With Sharp Teeth*. In 2008, the documentary was featured at The South by Southwest Conference and Festival, The Edinburgh Film Festival, The Independent Festival in Boston and opened at both the prestigious Lincoln Center in New York and The NY Film Forum. In celebration of his 75th birthday, *Dreams With Sharp Teeth* premiered on the Sundance Film Channel and was released on DVD in May 2009.

Harlan Ellison lives with his wife, Susan, inside The Lost Aztec Temple of Mars, in Los Angeles.

YOUR ATTENTION, PLEASE!

Breinigsville, PA USA
05 January 2011
252721BV00001B/104/P